"How do I look now?" Claire asked, nervously tugging at the low-cut bodice of her gown, pulling it higher. "I feel naked."

Olivia laughed, brushed Claire's hands away and urged the bodice back down. "You look beautiful. And remember, you're not Claire Orwell—you're the brazen Duchess of Beaumont."

"That's true. I'm sure the duchess has no qualms about displaying her décolletage."

"None whatsoever." Olivia's smile became wicked when she said, "I've heard it whispered that since Charmaine Beaumont's husband—the pompous old duke—died five years ago, she has taken any number of handsome lovers. Are you planning to add a few to her list?"

"Only one," said Claire without hesitation, the image of the dark stranger she'd caught sight of this afternoon flashing into her mind. She stated the unguarded truth. "I would like—just once in my life—to have a grand passion. To know what it's like to make love with a man who can sweep me off my feet and dazzle me. I shall do the duchess proud. I assume Her Grace can choose any man she wants. So I fully intend to pick the most sought after man in Saratoga." She paused and added, "And then seduce him."

"Seduce him? How?" asked Olivia.

Claire smiled, catlike. "Why, by ignoring him, of course."

*Also by **Nan Ryan***

Duchess for a Day

NAN RYAN

MIRA
An international collection of bestselling authors

First published in Great Britain 2005.
MIRA Books, Eton House, 18-24 Paradise Road,
Richmond, Surrey, TW9 1SR

ISBN 0 7783 2141 X

63-1205

Printed and bound in Spain
by Litografia Rosés S.A., Barcelona

Duchess
for a Day

One

London, Wednesday June 26, 1895
Newgate Prison
6:00 p.m. British Summertime

At shortly after the hour, a stern-faced turnkey dropped a ladder down from his perch high atop the catwalk. He turned and handed a frightened Claire Orwell down that ladder and into the infamous prison's crowded Common Cell.

Claire's presence caused an immediate stir. The criminals snapped to attention. Bloodshot eyes popped open and clung to the blond, willowy young woman.

"Meet yer 'ospitable mates." The gruff turnkey gave a nasty grin as the curious crowded closer. "Street thieves. Pickpockets. Footpads. Shoplifters. And whores. You'll fit right in, eh?"

The turnkey kicked a sleeping derelict out of the way. The bony, sweat-soaked felon groaned, rolled over, belched loudly, then fell back to snoring. Sickened by the pungent scent of stale vomit emanating from the prostrate creature, Claire made a face of disgust.

The turnkey laughed again. "Not to fret. T'aint nothin' ye won't get used to, Queenie."

Claire felt her stomach roll.

"'ere, dearie, sit by me." This from a diseased-looking woman with brittle, dyed-black hair and grimy clothes.

The woman yanked her soiled skirts up around bruised thighs and batted her matted eyelashes. Claire shuddered as the others hooted and whistled, obviously enjoying the look of repugnance on her face.

A chill skipped up her spine. "I beg you, sir, allow me to speak to a barrister at once. You cannot imprison me before I've even been accused. A cell at police headquarters if you must, but don't leave me down here. I've done nothing wrong. I am innocent of any wrongdoing."

"Aye, that's what they all say," was his curt reply. He adjusted his black uniform coat with its two rows of brass buttons, shoved his billed cap forward on his broad forehead and, none too gently, propelled Claire forward. "A few nights down here, Miss Sticky Fingers, and you'll think twice 'fore ye go stealin' from yer betters again."

Claire said nothing more. It was no use. He wouldn't listen. No one would listen. She had spent the whole long day fruitlessly attempting to persuade the authorities that she had done nothing wrong. Now the terrible thought struck her that no one would know she was imprisoned here save the vengeful, titled knave who had lied to put her here.

Claire *had* to let someone know what had happened. Surely even prisoners were allowed to send messages, to have visitors, to retain counsel.

She firmly set her jaw as the turnkey, roughly gripping her upper arm, thrust her on through the motley horde of criminals lying about in clumps on the dirty dungeon floor. All were watching her every move, muttering, making lewd gestures and grinning slyly. Claire artfully dodged dirty hands reaching out to grab at her long, flowing skirts. She made eye contact with no one.

Newgate was everything she'd heard it was.

And more.

A filthy hellhole into which the very dregs of humanity had been cast and forgotten. A dank, putrid place filled with scum and riffraff and dangerous criminals of both sexes. A dungeon where the only light came from small, dirty windows high above the catwalk.

Shadows were deepening with the close of the day. Claire anxiously looked about for a place to sit apart from the other prisoners. There was no such place.

"Make yerself at 'ome," said the turnkey, finally releasing Claire's arm.

Claire frowned and exhaled heavily. Then she squared her slender shoulders. With single-minded determination, she made her slow, sure way toward the cell's western perimeter where fewer prisoners were gathered. The turnkey followed close on her heels.

Claire heard the big warder behind her say, "Move it, Green Tooth. We 'ave a new guest checkin' into our luxurious 'ohel. Scoot yer bony arse over and give the little lady some room to breathe."

Claire glanced down at the poor creature he had addressed. A stick-thin, graying, stringy-haired old crone who was badly in need of dental work and a fresh suit of clothing. The woman's thin face was wrinkled and dirty, her teeth rotted and blackened, but her eyes were bright and amazingly alert.

The old woman known to the criminal class as Green Tooth hurriedly moved out of the way. But she didn't take her eyes off the new female prisoner.

"What are you looking at, old woman?" Claire snapped, hoping to assert a firm authority and clearly demonstrate a lack of fear she didn't feel. "Stop staring! Keep away from me. I mean it."

The old harridan sank back into the shadows against the wall. But she continued to covertly stare at Claire.

Claire released a slow, shallow breath.

She turned about and sat down. She leaned against the wall, raised her knees, and wrapped her arms around them. She let her head fall back and rest against the rough brick. Warily, she looked around the teeming, reeking hellhole.

The prisoners were continuing to ogle and point and whisper. Claire felt goose bumps pop up on her arms and the fine hair rise at her nape. She was in a squalid pit surrounded by the dregs of humanity and darkness would soon fall.

She lifted her eyes to the catwalk above.

The burly turnkey who had escorted her down into the pit stood clutching the railing, looking down on the prisoners. A younger warder walked patrol around the catwalk.

Claire was relieved to see them there. They or their replacements would be on patrol throughout the evening, making certain there was no trouble. They wouldn't allow any real mischief to take place. She would be safe enough.

As darkness settled over the city of London the only light in the Common Cell of Newgate prison were the wall torches flickering on redbrick walls blackened by years of soot.

Claire didn't move as the others roused to eat the evening meal. While the ravenous prisoners tore at the stale bread and wolfed down the watery soup with loud slurping gusto, Claire made a face and closed her eyes. The smells and the sounds continued to assault her senses, but she didn't have to look at the human slime.

"Best 'ave a spot 'o yer soup," came Green Tooth's voice from out of the shadows.

Claire opened her eyes and her head snapped around. She glared at the dirty old woman. "I am not hungry. Stop bothering me."

Green Tooth lifted her own tin bowl and took a long final drink of the watery soup. She set the empty bowl down, wiped her mouth on a dirty sleeve, and informed Claire, "Need to keep yer strength up if you've any 'opes of stayin' alive down 'ere."

"I won't be staying long," Claire stated firmly. "I'm innocent and I—"

"'Course ye are," said the old crone, interrupting. "Ain't we all. Not a guilty soul in 'ere. Not a one."

"Yes, well, I *am* innocent and I'll be out of here by morning."

"Not bloody likely," said Green Tooth. "Innocent or no, it'll be weeks, p'rhaps months 'fore any court 'ears yer case."

"No, it will not," Claire said, dismissing her. "Now kindly stop bothering me."

Green Tooth said, "I'm tryin' to 'elp ye."

"I need no help," Claire said. "Not another word out of you, do you hear!"

Green Tooth fell silent, but she continued to carefully study Claire. She couldn't take her eyes off her. There was something hauntingly familiar about this young woman. That hair, the porcelain skin, those vivid violet eyes, the graceful curve of her throat. Surely a direct link to someone from the past. The name she couldn't quite bring to bear. She searched her memory.

Could she be? No, too young. But blood told… The daughter. She had to be the daughter.

Eyes closed, Claire sat on the hard stone floor and silently lectured herself. She couldn't let this hideous turn of events best her. She had to be strong and resourceful. She had to keep her wits about her and figure a way out of this terrible predicament. She was, she knew, in serious trouble.

Who would take her word over that of Lord Wardley Nardees?

No one.

She faced this outrageous charge on her own. All alone.

It wasn't the first time Claire had been alone. She was used to it. Had been used to it since losing both parents when she was a girl of eighteen. Shortly after their deaths she had accepted the proposal of an old family friend. Dear, stalwart, solicitous Keith Orwell. He would have gladly taken care of her for the rest of her life, but tragedy soon struck again.

Only four years after they'd wed, her kindhearted husband had died suddenly of apoplexy and she was widowed at age twenty-two. Orwell had left no money, so there'd been little time to grieve his passing. Claire had had to immediately find a way to support herself.

Well educated, she had promptly become governess to a fine family's two well-behaved boys. She'd spent five pleasant years in their employ ending with her young wards leaving for boarding school. She was then chosen to be governess to the wealthy Lord Wardley Nardees's three unruly children.

Claire shuddered now at the recollection of what had happened in the baron's huge mansion only last night.

She opened her eyes and again looked above. She felt a small degree of comfort in seeing the turnkey continuing to patrol on the catwalk. But as she watched, he suddenly stopped and moved directly to the rope ladder on which she had descended into the bowels of the Common Cell.

Her heart sank when he loudly announced to the prisoners below, "Raisin' the ladder, ye miserable scabs! Jest ye try and get out 'o the hole in the middle of the night!" He bent and swiftly drew the ladder up out of reach, rung by rung, and Claire saw her only connection with the world above taken away.

No sooner had the ladder been lifted than the turn-key moved around the catwalk extinguishing most of the wall torches. In minutes the Common Cell was cast into deep dark shadows.

She was to spend the long night in this pit at the mercy of dangerous criminals.

Nothing to worry about, she told herself. The turn-key was patrolling again. He would keep a close eye on the dungeon. She should try to relax and get some much needed rest. Tomorrow she would figure a way out of this travesty.

A quarter past midnight.

Claire was wide awake. Unfortunately the lone turnkey was not. He was no longer patrolling. He was snoring, dead to the world, somewhere out of sight above.

As the hour grew later the hellhole began stirring to life after hours of relative quiet. The new activity greatly unnerved Claire. She was not naive. She was fully aware that she had attracted the unwanted at-tention of the male denizens and the soulless whores. All had cast lascivious glances at her throughout the evening. All were dangerous. All were free to do as they pleased because the sleeping turnkey was not doing his job. She was helpless against them.

Claire's anxiety grew when a half dozen of the menacing villains began to gravitate steadily closer. She was paralyzed with fear when a big, strapping female squatted down before her, roughly grabbed Claire's left ankle and dragged her away from the wall.

"Come to me, beauty," said the woman, a leer on her chubby face.

Claire kicked wildly at her. "Stop!" she cried, her hips and shoulder blades bumping against the stone floor. "Leave me alone, let me be!"

The fat female smiled in mock surrender and, releasing Claire's ankle, rose to her feet. Claire scrambled to sit up. She held up her hands defensively as her heart pounded in her ears. She frantically looked around for an escape route. Even if she made it past the evil creatures now circling her, she couldn't get out of this snake pit.

"I'm first," announced a cadaverous man with open sores on his face and old scabs decorating his ropy forearms. Shoving the obese prostitute out of the way, he began unbuttoning his filthy trousers as he licked his droopy lower lip.

"The 'ell you are!" snapped a tall, thin woman with greasy corkscrew curls and a long nasty scar slashing down her filthy face. She easily shoved the thin man out of her way. Yanking her tattered skirts up past her knobby knees, she stated, "This one's mine."

She'd hardly gotten the words out before a big, muscular brute with a sweat-drenched bare chest and unshaven face stepped in, swung a quick right, and knocked the thin whore flat on her back.

"Stay away from me!" Claire warned as the reeking, half-naked man sank to his knees and reached for her.

Claire's heart stopped.

"You 'eard the lady," came a low feminine voice from out of the darkness.

Claire blinked as Green Tooth, roused from a fitful slumber by all the commotion, swiftly emerged from the shadows and pressed the tip of a long sharp piece of glass directly against the man's juggler vein. Firmly clutching the crude weapon by its handle fashioned of used twine, she said quietly, "Move back or get yer throat slit, gov."

The big man, his calloused hand already clutching at Claire's shirtwaist bodice, laughed off Green Tooth's threat. Bent on having the pale, clean beauty, he ripped Claire's bodice and she screamed.

"Now I will kill ye!" Green Tooth coolly promised. She jabbed the weapon's sharp tip into his glistening throat and drew blood.

He yelped in pain, released his hold on Claire's bodice, and rolled away, cursing. Green Tooth stepped directly in front of Claire, thrust the bloody glass weapon forward toward the others and said, "The same goes for the rest of ye. Touch one 'air on 'er 'ead and ye won't live to see daylight."

Two

No one doubted Green Tooth's threat.

They cursed her and vowed to get even and promised, come daylight, they'd tell the turnkey she had a weapon. Then they laughed and jeered and accused her of being a crazy old hag. But all of them slowly backed away.

For several long minutes the slight old crone continued to stay there unmoving, her stance denoting total authority and an absence of fear. Her thin arm extended, jaw set, she had the crude weapon gripped tightly in her hand and thrust forward.

She finally lowered the weapon and began to sink back into the shadows. Claire, clutching at her torn bodice, hurriedly rose to her feet and laid a hand on the old woman's arm.

"Thank you. You saved me! I'm very grateful to you. What would I have done if you hadn't intervened?"

Green Tooth brushed Claire's hand from her arm. "I knew ye'd be causin' trouble in 'ere," she said, shaking her gray head.

Without another word, she sat back down on the stone floor, frowning when Claire sank down close beside her.

"I never meant to cause any trouble," Claire defended herself. "I shouldn't be here. I don't belong down here."

"None of us do, lassie," said Green tooth tiredly. "I told you, we're all innocent 'ere."

"But you don't understand, my employer, Lord Nardees, grabbed me in the middle of the night and—"

"It's the same old story," Green Tooth interrupted, "'ve 'eard it all before."

"Yes, I know, but I—"

"I 'ave to get me rest," Green Tooth said, closing her eyes, shutting Claire out.

"Yes. Yes, of course," Claire said and fell silent.

Exhausted, nerves raw, afraid as she'd never been before in her life, Claire longed to unburden herself, to confide in someone who would listen and learn the truth.

But no one would believe her if she did.

She sat there in the darkness, berating herself for

accepting the position of governess to the powerful Lord Nardees's three spoiled children.

She had gone to Stonehaven in mid-June, only two short weeks ago.

Late last night, the portly Lord Nardees had pounded on her third floor door, awakening her from a deep slumber. She'd lunged up in bed, sleepy and confused. Before she could rise, the lord, dressed in white cotton attire that looked like a physician's protective gown, stalked hurriedly into her room and told her that she had to come with him at once. Supposing something untoward had happened to one of the children, she had thrown on a robe and anxiously rushed after him.

"What it is, milord?" she asked, alarmed, as together they dashed down the wide upstairs corridor.

"Shhh," he cautioned. "We must be quiet."

Claire said no more, but dutifully swept into the room when he opened the door at the end of the hallway. He hastily followed. Once inside she looked around.

No one was there. No sick child.

The room was empty. But it was well lighted, every lamp blazing. The only furniture was a physician's examining couch, which sat at the very center of the room. A white sheet was draped over it. Beside the couch, on a small utility table, was a white shaving mug and brush and a pair of scissors.

And, gleaming in the lamplight, lay a silver, fully opened straight-edged razor.

Instantly alarmed, Claire turned to give the lord a questioning look. She was horrified to find that he was now stark naked, the white uniform discarded and lying on the carpeted floor. Beneath his flabby overhanging belly, his male member was fully erect.

"Lord Nardees, how dare you!" she exclaimed in shock and outrage. "Cover yourself at once!"

She made a move toward the closed door. But the lord stood before it, blocking her way, his beady eyes gleaming and a drool of spittle slipping down from the left side of his mouth.

"My dear," he murmured, stepping close, "since the first moment I saw you, I've wanted you for my mistress."

And with that declaration, the naked nobleman had swiftly caught a stunned Claire up in his arms, pressed her against his big belly and tried to kiss her. Horrified and repulsed, she turned her face away and began to struggle to free herself.

"Let me go, damn you! Stop this at once!" she demanded, hitting his beefy arms and broad back with doubled up fists.

"Ah, yes, fight me a little while I rub myself against you, sweet beauty! I like my lovers to be fiery." The eager lord shoved Claire's robe off her right shoulder, yanked the yoke of her nightgown open down her chest and buried his wet, fleshy lips in the curve of her neck and shoulder.

"Let go of me, you miserable swine, or I shall scream so loudly your wife will come running."

Sucking eagerly on the tender flesh of her exposed throat, Lord Nardees ignored her threat. Claire was well aware that his homely, lazy wife was probably snoring soundly in their suite on the mansion's first floor and would not hear her screams. Claire continued to beat on the baron's bare back and tried to kick his shins. Vainly, she struggled to free herself from the excited, perspiring man.

Finally, having no other recourse, she turned her face inward and bit his jowls. Hard. Drawing blood. Shocked and in pain, he automatically raised his head and loosened his hold. Claire seized the opportunity and viciously kneed him in the groin. He released her and grabbing himself, sank to his knees, keening in agony there before the closed door.

Claire knew she had to get out of that room and out of that house. Finding strength she didn't know she possessed, she shoved him over onto his back, grabbed him behind the knees, and dragged him away from the door. She darted around him, opened the door and fled down the hall to her room. Heart pounding, she hurriedly dressed and began packing.

She wasn't sure what the thwarted lord would do next, but she had no intention of staying in his home long enough to find out. After only a few short minutes spent collecting her belongings, Claire was ready to make her escape.

But she was too late.

The door to her room was now locked and barred from the outside. Claire ground her teeth in frustration. The angry baron had already summoned his minions to confine her.

She dropped her valise and hurried to the tall leaded windows that faced the estate's rolling back gardens. She opened one of the windows and looked down. She had never realized how high off the ground this third floor room was. There was no balcony on which to step outside. No trellis on which to climb down. It was a sheer drop of forty feet to the ground below. If she jumped she would likely break a leg. Even if she didn't, guards patrolled the vast rear grounds at night. She'd never get past them.

She was trapped.

Throughout the long night Claire paced, worried and wondered what would happen to her.

Come the morning she found out.

While the entire staff watched and whispered, Claire was taken from the baron's house by two uniformed policemen. Lord Nardees had accused her of stealing some of his wife's valuable jewelry and had alerted the authorities.

At police headquarters Claire had vowed her innocence, but to no avail. Her repeated requests for counsel were refused. After the long tiring day of futilely demanding that a barrister be appointed for her, she was thrown into Newgate prison's Common Cell with a stern reminder that stealing from one of England's titled noblemen would surely get her several long years in prison.

Now in the prison's darkness, Claire swallowed hard and fought back the tears that clogged her tight throat. The terrible truth dawned that she might never get out of this dungeon.

Dawn was not far off when Green Tooth slowly turned her head, looked at the fair, blond young woman and saw that she was sleeping.

Finally.

Green Tooth glanced warily around at the rest of the prisoners to make sure all were asleep. Satisfied they were, she reached down and dug deep into her worn left shoe and pried from its sole a shiny gold coin. A coin she'd treasured for years.

She laid the coin in her lap and reached into the pocket of her filthy skirt. She withdrew a small pad of paper and a stubby lead pencil.

In minutes she was up and silently crossing the Common Cell. She waved a thin arm until she attracted the attention of the head turnkey who was back on his perch above. She motioned to him. He frowned, shook his head, but dropped the ladder over and came down it.

"Need a favor, gov," Green Tooth whispered and handed the guard a folded note and the gold coin.

The turnkey glanced at the note, bit the coin to check its authenticity, and nodded in affirmation.

Three

Alas, it wasn't weeks or months until Claire's arraignment. It was later that very same morning.

Nine sharp.

Thursday, the twenty-seventh of June, 1895.

Claire's case was first on the docket. If indicted—which seemed assured—she would be convicted and sentenced to twenty-five years in prison.

The honorable Percival Knowlton sat on the bench above in his colorful flowing judge's robes and curly white powdered wig. The prosecutor, Cecil Twiggs, a slight man with thinning, sandy hair and sallow complexion, was there to represent the Queen.

Claire stood beside him as Twiggs stated the charges. "Your honor, the defendant, Mrs. Claire Orwell, betrayed the trust and kindness of her employer, Lord Wardley Nardees. Mrs. Orwell was employed…"

The arraignment, a predetermined farce, had begun.

Once the charges had been fully read, the elderly judge sat back in his chair, reached up under his white wig and rubbed a spot on his temple.

He looked at Claire. "Who speaks for the defendant?"

Rising to her feet, Claire looked around, searching in vain for the aging hack barrister the crown had appointed as her counsel. She turned back to address the judge.

"No one, I fear, milord."

At that moment a large hand came to rest on her shoulder. She turned and looked up to see a giant of a man, resplendent in legal raiment bearing the Old Queen's own colors. The powdered wig only added to his towering height.

"I kindly beg to differ." The giant's voice was low and surprisingly soft. "I speak for the accused, your worship."

Cecil Twiggs paled and the slim prosecution brief slipped from his fingers. He bent and picked it up, his hand visibly shaking.

The judge sat upright, imperious in his tall-backed leather chair. He adjusted his spectacles, leaned forward and asked, "To what happy circumstance do we have the honor of the Queen's own Counsel gracing our humble criminal court? Welcome, Lord Northway."

Lord Northway thanked the judge and smiled at the

awed Claire. He was an impressive man in both stature and manner and well known for his keen legal mind.

Lord Northway's father, Henderson Northway, had been elevated by Queen Victoria forty-five years ago for the outstanding legal, diplomatic and political advice he had given as the Queen's Counsel on affairs both domestic and foreign. Most notable was his opinion that the Queen's highly opposed recognition of the Republic of Texas would, if done, be unchallenged.

The grateful Queen had rewarded him with a peerage.

Claire was as puzzled as the learned judge and the nervous prosecution that Lord Northway had come to her defense.

From his bench above, Judge Knowlton nodded toward Twiggs. "State the charge."

"Grand theft, milord." Twiggs opened the brief. "To be specific, jewelry belonging to Lord Nardees's wife, valued by these appraisals in the amount of three thousand pounds."

"Any witness besides the good baron?" asked the judge, a noticeable frown on his face.

Twiggs shook his head.

"What say you, Lord Northway? State your case."

"No case, milord, but a few questions for the crown, perhaps."

"We are honored to take questions of the Queen's Counsel." The judge waved a permissive hand.

"Thank you, milord." The tall barrister turned to Cecil Twiggs. "These appraisals you have before you in the amount of three thousand pounds?"

"Yes," Twiggs eagerly responded.

"How many separate appraisals and who made the appraisals?"

"There are six separate appraisals all made by Lloyd's of London, of course."

The quality and power of his voice demanding total attention, Lord Northway promptly pointed out that Claire Orwell's accuser had not filed any claims with Lloyd's of London.

"Your honor, Joseph Phillips, Esquire, of Lloyd's of London waits just outside. He will testify to the fact that no claims have been made by Lord Nardees. May I add that Lloyd's of London has insured the lord's belongings for thirty-five years." Lord Northway turned to Cecil Twiggs. "Over the last ten years, how many charges has Lord Nardees brought against his servants?"

Twiggs blanched, looking to the bench for help and direction.

"Answer," said the judge with a dismissive wave of his hand.

Twiggs spread the brief before him on the prosecution table. "Perhaps four accusations."

"Perhaps six," Lord Northway softly corrected.

"Possible," said Twiggs. "I have only—"

"Lord Northway, are you calling Lord Nardees a liar?" asked the judge. "That's your defense?"

"Not at all, your honor. I'm simply pointing out that perhaps a mistake has been made. Honorable people can disagree and—"

"Approach the bench," the judge interrupted.

Lord Northway again stated, "Nardees has filed no claims on past charges. Perhaps the items Lord Nardees thought were stolen have only been misplaced. And subsequently found." Lord Northway paused and drew himself up to his full, imposing height. "Are we to send this poor young woman—" he nodded to Claire "—who has no history of committing any crimes, to twenty-five years and ruin her life—or more accurately, end her life? She may not survive…" Again he paused, then said, "I respectably ask for all charges to be dismissed."

The judge looked intently at Lord Northway. "I will rule later today."

At 6:00 p.m. the judge told the prosecutor that he had dismissed the charges. He also considered the failure on the part of Lord Nardees to file insurance claims. He told the barristers he was going to deny a true bill and that Claire Orwell was to be set free. Claire and the barristers rose to their feet. The judge asked Lord Northway to stay. Claire turned to thank her gallant defender.

Lord Northway smiled warmly and said, "If you'll

wait just outside, I must speak with you before you go. I won't be long."

Claire nodded and walked out with the prosecutor.

"Tell me, old man," the judge beseeched when the two were alone, "what in the name of God brings you to defend this poor woman?"

Lord Northway smiled, reached into his weskit pocket and extracted a large gold hunter-case watch. He gave the stem a slight twist and the case opened, revealing a yellowing enameled miniature.

The judge gasped audibly.

"Yes," acknowledged Lord Northway, "an exact likeness of Claire Orwell."

"Painted years before Claire was born," the judge said.

Lord Northway nodded. "My father handed me this watch on his deathbed." He looked at the faded miniature. "She was the love of his life."

"I see," the judge sat back in his chair.

"Father instructed me to help her daughter, Claire, if ever she needed me."

"How did you hear about her being in trouble?"

"A timely missive from a miscreant in Newgate known as Green Tooth," said Lord Northway.

Claire looked up, smiled and rose from the bench in the corridor as Lord Northway approached. Still puzzled that he had come to her defense, she was even more puzzled when the stately lord handed her an envelope.

"My dear," he said in that rich baritone voice, "I've a bit of good news for you."

Claire listened and learned that she was being offered the opportunity to sail to America to open up the Saratoga Springs, New York, summer house of Britain's flamboyant Duchess of Beaumont. The young, blond widow was one of Britain's more colorful royals, a woman who cared not one whit what the gossips said about her.

Claire had read of the duchess's exploits and her photograph had often appeared in the *London Times*.

"Your duties," said Lord Northway, "if you choose to accept the position, will be to hire a small staff and have the Saratoga residence made ready for the arrival of the duchess herself. She'll be coming to the Springs in mid-August for the summer racing season.

"It is," said Northway, "entirely up to you. If you wish to accept this offer, all the necessary arrangements will be made for you."

"Yes, of course, I accept!" said Claire, excited. "I can think of nothing I'd like better than to…to…" She stopped speaking and frowned suddenly. She couldn't go. She couldn't leave the poor old woman known as Green Tooth behind. She owed the woman her life. She couldn't be ungrateful and turn her back on the poor creature.

Claire looked up at the tall, imposing man and said, "On one condition, milord."

"Which is?"

"I've a friend who must accompany me to America."

His eyebrows raised. "A male?"

"No, female."

"I see no difficulty. Your friend can serve in some capacity as part of the staff."

"Actually, it's not quite that simple," Claire said. She took a deep breath and informed him, "She's presently a prisoner in Newgate. But she's good-hearted. She saved me from a terrible physical attack and I will take responsibility for her."

"What's her crime?"

"I honestly don't know, but I would guess petty theft or some such minor charge. I beg you, Lord Northway, find a way to free the poor woman and allow me to take her with me."

Lord Northway reluctantly agreed to look into the charges and see what he could do. The astonished Green Tooth was freed that same afternoon.

The next morning Claire went directly to the bank and withdrew what meager funds she'd managed to save over the years. Then she requested entrance to her safe-deposit box. She took the box into a small private room, opened it and lifted from it a small velvet drawstring bag.

Claire loosened the tasseled drawstrings and

looked inside. She smiled, as she always did, when admiring the sparkling treasures inside. After only a few seconds, she reluctantly drew the strings tight once more.

Then she lifted her full skirts and pinned the velvet pouch in among the folds of her full petticoats. She dropped her skirts, patted the concealed treasure, and left the bank with a spring to her step.

With the money she'd withdrawn, Claire promptly sent the woman who had saved her life to the dentist and to have her hair cut and buy some new clothes. And Claire bought her frail friend a fine-looking hickory walking cane with a gleaming silver head.

Days later Claire Orwell and Olivia Sutton— Olivia Sutton looking nothing like the unkempt woman dubbed Green Tooth and Claire vowing she'd have Olivia speaking like a proper lady by the time they reached New York—happily set sail for America on a bright, clear June morning.

Four

Strong alpine sunlight streamed in through the open bedroom windows of an imposing three-story mansion perched on the cliffs high above the little mining city.

The sunshine had slowly marched across the spacious upstairs room until finally, at midmorning, it reached the bed. And the bed's occupants.

A man and a woman.

The man groaned when the penetrating light shone through his closed eyelids, disturbing him, annoying him. Without opening his eyes, he grabbed a feather pillow, stuck his dark head under it, muttered a curse and promptly fell back to sleep.

The woman slowly awakened, stretched and raised up onto an elbow. Shoving her tousled dark hair out of her eyes, she yawned sleepily, then began to smile like the cat that got the cream. She gazed at the ruggedly handsome man stretched out naked on his belly beside her.

The darkness of his lean, bare body was in striking contrast to the whiteness of the silky sheets. Admiring him, she let her lazy gaze travel downward from his wide, sculpted shoulders and over the long, deeply clefted back to his trim waist. Her eyes brightened when they reached his firm buttocks, the smooth flesh of the rounded cheeks as deeply tanned as his leanly muscled arms. The sight of those strong arms and powerful thighs made her heart flutter pleasantly.

Recalling last's night tempestuous loving, she sighed with pleasure, laid back down, and was soon asleep again.

Another hour passed before the man began to stir. Slowly he pulled his head out from under the pillow, lifted it and looked warily around. He saw the sleeping brunette beauty and made a face. He had forgotten she was here. He wished that she weren't. Wished now that he hadn't insisted she come home with him last night. Then again, he wasn't sure he had. It might have been her idea.

Hank Cassidy made a face.

He tried to remember exactly what had happened at last night's rowdy Fourth of July celebration. He vividly recalled the earlier part of the evening. The food and fireworks and the six-shooters discharging in the air. The music and the street dance and pretty little Patricia Ann Vance, the young woman he had escorted to the festivities.

Hank turned his head, looked again at the naked woman beside him. She wasn't Patricia Ann. Patricia Ann was petite and had auburn hair and fair skin. This woman was tall and voluptuous and her hair and skin were almost as dark as his own.

Hank felt his head began to mildly throb. Then it dawned on him. He had, at the good-natured dares of his boisterous buddies and over Patricia Ann's strong objections, made several visits to the make-shift outdoor bar for shots of rotgut whiskey. It was coming back to him now. He'd had one too many bourbons and Patricia Ann got huffy and warned as they danced, "Henry Columbus Cassidy, so help me if you have one more drink, I am leaving!"

"Well don't let us keep you," said a seductive long-legged beauty with dark hair, deftly stepping between him and the furious Patricia Ann to offer him a drink.

And herself.

Hank couldn't remember seeing Patricia Ann after that. He did remember drinking and dancing and laughing with this brazen beauty. And, he vaguely recalled, much later in the evening, the two of them moving their little party on up the hill to the privacy of his home. Articles of discarded clothing had left a telltale trail from the room's closed door to the bed.

He glanced again at the woman. In last night's haste to get undressed and into bed, she had missed one sheer stocking. It still enclosed her long left leg enticingly. A saucy black lace garter rested just above her knee.

Hank eased over onto his back and scratched his stubbled jaw in puzzlement. What the hell was her name? As he recalled she was visiting from California; he'd never seen her before last night. They had not been formally introduced, but surely she'd told him her name at some point in the evening. Nonetheless, he couldn't bring it to mind. Whoever she was, it was time she left.

He had a train to catch.

Hank drew a deep breath, reached out, touched the woman's shoulder and gave her a firm shake. "Darlin', time for us to wake up."

Her dark eyes slowly opened. She saw him and began to smile. "Good morning, Hank, my love."

"Mornin'…ah…honey." He turned away, sat up and threw his long legs over the edge of the mattress. "Get dressed and I'll have Brady drive you home."

"I don't want to go home," she said, hastily sitting

up and stripping off her lone stocking and black garter. Before Hank could rise to his feet, she scrambled across the mattress and looped the stocking around his waist from behind. Playfully biting his left ear, she murmured, "Have you forgotten what you promised last night, Hank?"

Hank screwed up his face. *What could he have possibly promised this woman whose name he did not know? Had he mentioned Saratoga to her? Surely not.* "No, of course I haven't forgotten."

"Then you'll take me with you to Saratoga Springs?" she shrieked happily, releasing the sheer stocking. It whispered down to Hank's lap and fell to the floor. She wrapped her arms around him and, lowering her face to press butterfly kisses to his tanned shoulder, said, "I can be ready in no time and—"

"Hold it, baby," Hank interrupted, freeing himself from her arms. He stood up, lowered his hands to modestly cup himself, then turned to face her. "Now we both had a little too much to drink last night and we had us some fun together and I like you a whole lot, really I do. But we'll have to continue this party when I return."

"No!" she firmly protested. "I want to go with you," she whined, desperate to make him want her so much he'd give in and take her to Saratoga.

He was everything she'd ever wanted—handsome

and charming and fun and virile and the thrilling lover of her wildest dreams. And he was, she had heard the minute she arrived in Virginia City, one of the richest men in America.

"Now listen…ah…I…" Hank shook his head. "All right, I admit it. I can't recall your name, you'll have to remind me."

"Paula. Paula Gentry," she said with a hurt look. "How could you possibly forget?"

"I humbly apologize, Miss Gentry. I'm not very good at names." He smiled disarmingly at her. "Now, please, get dressed and when I get back to Virginia City in a couple of months, you and I will—"

"A couple of months? No! I will not get dressed!" she declared. She sat back on her bare heels and crossed her arms over her chest. "Not if you won't take me with you."

"Be reasonable, Miss Gentry. We've only just met. And as I apparently mentioned last night, I leave for Saratoga Springs today, but it is strictly a business trip. I wouldn't have time to entertain you."

"I could entertain myself and in the evenings we could—"

"You are not going anywhere but home," Hank said. He dropped his hands to his sides and turned away.

Paula was up off the bed in a flash. She grabbed his arm and anxiously stepped in front of him. "Very well. If you must go, you must, but I'll see to it that you won't forget me while you're away." She spread hands on the steely muscles of his chest, then smiled devilishly as she rubbed warming circles around the flat brown nipples. At the same time she pressed her pelvis against his and began slowly gyrating her hips. "You want to make your train? Then you'd better take what I'm offering because I'm not letting you leave until you carry me back to the bed and make love to me."

Half annoyed, half aroused, Hank lifted a hand, slid long fingers into her lustrous dark hair, clasped a generous handful, tightened his grip and urged her head back. He was both irritated and intrigued as he lowered his head until his lips were an inch from hers.

He said, "I'm not carrying you back to bed, Miss Gentry. You want me, you'll take me standing right here or not at all."

"Oh, Hank," she sighed, breathlessly, "yes, yes, kiss me, darling."

"No time for kisses," he said, "ten minutes is all we have."

Paula shrieked with excitement when he put his hands around the backs of her thighs and easily lifted her from the floor. He locked long arms around her thighs and raised her higher. Her bare toes dug into his knees. She giggled with delight and braced her hands on his shoulders. With her pelvis now pressed against his hair-covered chest, she already appeared dizzy with desire.

She anxiously clasped his handsome head in her hands, pushed it back, looked into his sky-blue eyes, and began to wiggle and hunch her back, bending and sliding lower so that her breasts were at his face. She held her breath as she eagerly brushed her heavy left breast against his lips.

"Kiss it, Hank," she begged. "Please. Lick it a little and then—"

She ahhhed with pleasure when his mouth captured the nipple and he raked his teeth over it, then sucked greedily.

On fire, so aroused she could hardly keep from crying out, Paula Gentry learned that making love while standing in the middle of a room with the summer sunlight spilling in and the sounds of people talking and laughing on the street below was pleasurable beyond belief.

She wasn't sure if she was a contortionist or if he was or if they both were; all she knew was that this incredibly sexual man managed to get her legs wrapped around his waist and a hand between their pressing bodies to coax and tease her burning flesh until she was dripping wet while his heated mouth continued to dazzle her by feasting hungrily on her breasts.

Doubting he could penetrate her without his mouth releasing her aching nipple, she gave a shout of joy when, as if he'd read her mind, he did just that.

While he expertly lowered her down onto the surging tip of his hard, thrusting flesh, he bowed his back so that his lips continued to cling to her stiffened nipple, giving her what she desired.

It was rapture.

His pulsing erection was only just barely inside her, making her yearn for more, making her look eagerly forward to the incredible instant when he would force her down onto it and fill her completely. It was a splendid kind of torturous teasing, a preview of the pleasure to come. For a thrilling moment they stayed just like that until finally, unable to wait one more second, Paula at last urged his head up, put her lips to his ear and whispered, "You won't ever forget this moment, Hank, nor will I." And she slithered down onto him, until she was fully impaled upon him.

Hank moved his bare feet wider apart to brace himself, then stood there in the bright Nevada sunlight, hands filled with the twin cheeks of her bottom, controlling her, while he rhythmically thrust into her. Paula gave as good as she got, opening fully to him, sucking him in, squeezing him tightly, gripping his ribs with her knees.

Locked in lust as they were, they began to reel around the spacious room. She moaning, he groaning, they did a dance of desire that found them first tangled in the heavy drapery blowing in the open windows while deep masculine laughter rose from the street below. Seconds later they were half leaning against a heavy drum table. Then they found themselves balanced against the high back of an easy chair. Finally, they landed roughly up against the wall, Paula's bare backside pressed into the lush flocked wallpaper, Hank hammering her hard.

Ten minutes after he'd first lifted her from the floor, both exploded in wrenching orgasm.

Five

At straight-up noon the handsome, thirty-two-year-old Hank Cassidy stepped onto his private rail car—alone—for the journey across the country. The muscular, rough-around-the-edges, hardworking Westerner who had made tens of millions in the mines was better known as Nevada's young Silver King.

Hank looked the part of royalty on this sunny summer day. With his smoothly shaven face bronzed by the Nevada sun and wind and glowing with good health, his midnight hair slightly damp from his bath, Hank was impeccably dressed in buff-colored custom-tailored trousers and sky-blue linen shirt. He had the self-assured manner and sleek, self-satisfied appearance of a man who had been born to the purple.

Nothing could have been further from the truth.

Hank Cassidy came from modest means. He never

knew his mother. She died giving birth to him. When he was seventeen his quiet, frugal father, a lifelong miner who rarely talked or smiled, was killed in an explosion deep underground. To Hank's surprise, his undemonstrative father had managed to save a small sum of money and left it to his only son.

Hank had invested every cent of his meager inheritance in what everyone told him was a worthless hole in the mountain. He hadn't listened. He'd bought the long-boarded-up quarry from an old miner who was a pallbearer at his father's funeral.

Hank christened his mine the Black Cat and immediately went to work. He spent years laboring deep in the darkness, searching for buried veins, patiently coaxing the precious metal out of stubborn solid rock. The mine hardly yielded enough silver to pay his hands.

Hank didn't give up.

Four long years after his first day in the Black Cat, Hank and his employees hit the mother lode. Overnight, young Hank Cassidy was a millionaire. He bought more mines. He made more millions. He continued to work alongside his men, sweating and straining and toiling and, as he worked, filling the cavern with the sound of his rich laughter. He encouraged the miners to joke around and make play out of work as much as possible.

His men loved him.

Hank paid his workers far above the average wage and supported their widows when things went wrong below.

Soon every miner within hundreds of miles had heard of Hank Cassidy and all wanted to work for the young, likable Silver King.

Hank's mining empire grew and finally he came up out of the darkness into the daylight to enjoy his riches. He had a huge three-story mansion built on the bluffs above Virginia City. He purchased, sight unseen and fully staffed, a stately home on New York City's Fifth Avenue. He ordered a private rail car from the Pullman company. He commissioned the building of a yacht to be harbored in San Francisco with a full crew at the ready for whenever he felt like a cruise.

A generous man, he also lavished expensive gifts on his trusted employees. Especially on their delighted wives. Hank liked to say that they were the only wives to whom he would be giving presents. He had no plans to ever have one of his own.

No one doubted he meant it. Everyone who knew the handsome, footloose, cavalier Silver King agreed that marriage was not in Cassidy's cards, to the disappointment of many a young lady.

A lover of fast horses, Hank was leaving today for Saratoga Springs where he would spend the summer racing season. Prized Thoroughbreds from his Kentucky farm were being shipped to Saratoga to compete at the historic old track.

The blooded horses would be transported in special rail cars, escorted by Hank's loyal friend and winning horse trainer, Fox Connor.

Once Hank reached Saratoga, he would spend the warm, pleasant days watching his Thoroughbreds go up against some stiff competition. And the cool, mountain nights dining and dancing and taking strolls with the fairest of the Eastern beauties.

Life was good indeed for the Nevada Silver King.

Now as Hank settled comfortably in a big easy chair in the plush private rail car, he felt the vibration of the wheels beginning to turn on the tracks, heard the engine's whistle sound a loud warning blast.

Hank smiled, took a Cuban cigar from a nearby humidor and sniffed its fragrance, nodding his dark head in approval. He stuck the cigar in his mouth, clamping it firmly between his even white teeth, then lifted his feet up onto an ottoman. He reached for a match, struck it and lighted his expensive cigar. He dropped the smoking match into a crystal ashtray and took a long, slow pull.

Hank exhaled with pleasure, blowing the smoke out as he turned his head and glanced out the window. The train was slowly moving now, leaving the station where dozens of well-wishers had gathered to bid him goodbye. A half-dozen pretty women had surged forward to hug him and whisper, "You'll miss me, Hank. You'll be lonely way off over there in Saratoga." His answer to each had been noncommittal—a gentle squeeze, a nod of the head, and no promises.

Hank Cassidy knew he wouldn't be lonely.

The summertime population of the Springs swelled with all sorts of diverse and interesting people. Millionaires, gamblers, respectable family folk, politicians and famous actors and actresses could always be found at the upstate resort. Saratoga Springs was a favorite gathering spot for wealthy men and beautiful women. The cream of Eastern society would be in residence for the season.

Engraved invitations to the many private dinners and parties would be collecting in a silver bowl there in the foyer of his reserved hotel accommodations. The upper crust had warmly accepted him since his first visit to the Springs. Especially the ladies. And he had learned, on his very first visit to Saratoga, that some of those elegant, expensively gowned ladies were not ladies at all once those gowns came off.

Claire Orwell experienced a tingling excitement when the locomotive began to slow as the train chugged closer to the depot at Saratoga Springs, New York.

The weariness of the long ocean voyage and the anxiety of the switch from ship to train in bustling New York City had miraculously disappeared.

She was no longer exhausted, but instead filled with a great surge of energy. And, she felt optimistic and hopeful in a way she had not felt since she was a young girl with her whole life ahead of her.

Her sense of excitement escalated when the train screeched to a stop. "Olivia—" she gently shook her companion "—wake up. We're here! We're at Saratoga."

Olivia sat up, yawned, grabbed her silver-headed cane, then reached for the new hat she'd bought back in London. She clamped it on her head. "How do I look?"

Claire reached up and straightened the fashionable straw hat, pulling the brim forward a little, then carefully smoothing a wispy lock of gray hair back from Olivia's face. "Like an elegant, well-bred lady," Claire said with a conspiratorial smile.

Olivia's eyes sparkled.

Both women were smiling when they stepped down from the train onto the platform outside the passenger depot. A building befitting a resort favored by the fashionable set, the little depot was of red brick with elaborate iron trimmings.

Claire took a deep breath, grabbed Olivia's hand and hurried toward the depot door.

* * *

Hank Cassidy stepped down from his private rail car at the train's rear. He caught a fleeting glance of pale blond hair, gleaming golden in the sunlight. That golden head abruptly turned and Hank saw her face. He smiled foolishly, admiring her. He started to call out, stopped himself, but anxiously stepped down and started toward her.

But the platform was crowded with arriving passengers and friends and family who had come to welcome the travelers. He quickly lost sight of the golden-haired beauty.

Hank uttered an oath under his breath, feeling a sense of loss, then immediately laughed at himself for his foolishness. No need to hurry after her. Obviously, she would be staying at the Springs for the season. They were sure to cross paths at some point in time.

Claire, with Olivia in tow, was swept along with the crowd into the depot with its muted interior of black walnut. The two women fought their way through the crush of travelers and out the depot's side doors.

Directly in front of the station was an open square adorned with splashing fountains and trees. And parked near the redbrick depot were landaus and phaetons and barouches. Hotel porters shouted and an omnibus driver was calling for passengers desiring transportation.

Claire stepped forward, raised a gloved hand, and called out to a hack driver. Minutes later she and Olivia were driven directly to the long-shuttered estate of Britain's merry widow, the Duchess of Beaumont.

The impressive estate was secluded on a heavily timbered rise of land a quarter of a mile east of Saratoga. Claire and Olivia exchanged glances of awe when the carriage rolled up before the white stone mansion rising from the leafy forest and surrounded by landscaped gardens.

"I understand only a caretaker lives here full-time," Claire said, alighting from the carriage, gazing at the mansion's many windows, all of which had the shades securely drawn. "I imagine we have our work cut out for us."

"We can handle it," assured Olivia.

The hack driver left them standing outside the mansion, valises at their feet.

"Shall we go inside and find out what must be done?" asked Claire.

"After you," said Olivia and lifted her valise.

Midway up the front walk, both abruptly stopped when the aged caretaker came out of the mansion's front door. Thin, stooped, he looked as if a puff of wind would blow him down. And he was, they quickly learned, half blind and hard of hearing.

Blinking in the dappled sunlight and easing himself down the mansion's veranda steps, he grimaced as though every bone in his body was aching.

"You must be Walker," Claire said, smiling, and hurried to him, her hand thrust out.

The thirty-three-year-old Duchess of Beaumont had not been to Saratoga in years. And, like Claire, she was a tall, slender woman with pale golden hair. Squinting, the nearsighted caretaker saw Claire's light hair and mistook her for the duchess.

"Your Grace," he said and attempted a creaking bow.

"No, no, Walker. You see, the duchess has not yet—"

"Eh, Your Grace?" he said, cupping a hand to his ear. "Speak up, please."

Claire gave Olivia a helpless look. Olivia stepped forward. Raising her voice, she attempted to set the old man straight. "Walker, the Duchess of Beaumont will not be arriving until later in the month. This is Claire Orwell and I am Olivia Sutton. The duchess sent us on ahead to—"

Hearing only a word here and there of what Olivia was saying, the caretaker listened, frowning as if in pain, and before she had finished speaking, he interrupted.

"Come along, Your Grace, you must get in out of the harsh sunlight lest you blister."

Claire tried again, "No, Walker, you've misunderstood, I'm *not* the duchess. My friend, Olivia Sutton, and I have come to ready the house for…" She patiently explained that she and Olivia had been sent ahead to open and staff the house for the duchess's impending arrival.

When finally she concluded, Claire gave him an expectant look, hopeful that he had understood.

He smiled, nodded, and said, "How many years since you were here last, Your Grace? Five? Ten?"

Claire started to speak, but Olivia touched her arm and stopped her. "Let it go for now," she said, shrugging. "We'll clear it up later." To the old man she shouted, "Thank you, Walker. We can manage from here. You're dismissed. Go take a nap. A nice, long nap." She gave her cane to Claire, raised her hands, folded them against her cheek and closed her eyes for a second.

When she opened her eyes the old man turned to Claire, half bowed once again, and said, "If you need me, Your Grace, I'll be in my quarters out back."

Six

Once inside the mansion's shadowy drawing room, Olivia and Claire exchanged looks of dismay. They had been told that an in-town service had an ongoing contract to clean the house thoroughly at least once every two weeks. The service had apparently been derelict in their duties. Sheets blanketed the fine furniture, but the heavy drapery was covered with dust and the entire place smelled musty.

It was obvious that no one had been there for weeks, maybe months. Olivia took off her hat and tossed it on a sheet-draped chair. She and Claire immediately went about yanking the curtains apart and throwing open the windows to admit the fresh mountain air.

"Not to worry," Olivia assured Claire "We'll have this place sparkling clean within forty-eight hours."

Claire nodded and smiled. "And neither of us will so much as pick up a feather duster!"

"Let the servants handle it," said Olivia in her best impersonation of a high-toned lady of leisure.

They laughed merrily.

When they'd sobered a bit, they explored the mansion, each deciding they'd choose a bedroom. Olivia picked one on the ground floor near the back of the house. They then ventured upstairs. At the top of the curving staircase they opened a set of tall white double doors into a large, opulent suite. A cozy sitting room with a white marble fireplace and covered sofas was open to the raised bedroom, which was reached by climbing three wide white marble steps.

Directly off the bedroom, tall glass-paned doors led onto a balcony overlooking lush gardens.

"The duchess's suite," Claire stated the obvious, stepping out onto the balcony, charmed by the total privacy the well-planned garden and tall sheltering trees afforded.

Olivia stepped up beside her. "But the duchess is not here." She paused, waiting for Claire to respond. Claire remained silent. Olivia ventured, "The suite can be yours until she arrives."

"Dare I?" Claire asked, eyebrows raised.

"Why not? Who's to know?" Olivia turned away. "I'll bring up your valises. Make yourself at home."

"I believe I will," Claire said, yanking the covering dust cloth from an upholstered chair, and running her hand over the plush white velvet.

Once their valises had been deposited in their respective rooms, Claire immediately sent Olivia forth to handle the hiring of a small staff of servants, as instructed.

And she set out to explore the picturesque resort.

The carriage moved slowly down traffic-choked, elm-shaded Broadway. Hank Cassidy, seated comfortably in the leather-cushioned back seat, nodded to the laughing, well-dressed people in horse-drawn vehicles parading down the avenue.

It was an afternoon ritual in Saratoga enjoyed by the summer set. They relished showing off their fine equipages. Surreys with fringe around the tops. Basket phaetons with high-stepping, bob-tailed hackneys. Heavy victorias with glittering silver monogrammed harnesses, two men in scarlet livery on their boxes, ladies behind with lacy parasols, sitting in richly upholstered seats.

Ah, it was great to be back in Saratoga.

Hank turned his attention to the pedestrians strolling along the sidewalks in front of the hotels. He paid little attention to the gentlemen in their tailored summer finery. His gaze naturally focused on the ladies in hats with parasols to match their dresses. Colorful dresses with all manner of feminine frills; pleats and ruffles and lace and ribbons and swelling puffed sleeves.

Hank was smiling with pleasure when suddenly he blinked and sat up straighter. A slender young woman stepped out of P. Durkee and Sons Stationers and Books and into the sunlight. Her pale hair blazed like spun gold and her face was as white and flawless as fine porcelain.

It was her!

The woman from the train depot—and she was every bit as breathtakingly beautiful as he'd thought when first he'd spotted her.

"Stop the carriage!" Hank called to the driver and didn't wait for the man to obey.

He leaped down into the street and narrowly missed being hit by an oncoming four-in-hand. Cursing under his breath, looking anxiously for an opening in the traffic, Hank found himself wedged between the four-in-hand and a big landau filled with laughing people calling out to him.

By the time he managed to get around the landau to the safety of the sidewalk, the golden-haired goddess was gone. Disappointed, Hank looked up the street and down, then dashed into the stationers.

To the clerk behind the counter, he said, "A woman with gold hair was just in here. Do you know where she went? Who she was?"

The clerk shook his head. "She looked at the books, but purchased nothing and—"

"Any idea who she is?"

"No, sir, I'm sorry."

"So am I." Hank exhaled with frustration. "Which books? Were there any special ones that she—?"

"Why, yes, as a matter of fact, there was a book that seemed to catch her fancy," said the clerk, heading for a shelf near the back. He took down a handsome, leather-bound book, held it up, and announced, "This is it. *The Prisoner of Zenda* by Anthony Hope. It was published just last year and has sold quite well. The lady picked this book up, thumbed slowly though it, then placed it back on the shelf."

"I'll take it," said Hank. "Gift wrap it."

"Right away, sir," said the clerk. "I hope you find her."

"I will."

The wrapped book under his arm, Hank exited the store. He stood outside for a long moment, carefully scanning both sides of the street.

But she was gone.

He returned to the carriage, jumped inside and settled in for the short ride to his hotel.

The carriage soon reached the five-story United States Hotel with its soaring pillars and Victorian scrollwork and wide, sweeping veranda. On that veranda stood a thousand white wicker rocking chairs, more than half of them filled with hotel guests watching the parade of people on Broadway on this sunny July afternoon.

Hank didn't disembark in front of the hotel. His carriage drove on and once past the hotel, immediately turned into a side street. It then pulled over to the curb just outside the hotel's private cottages. The cottages were suites of coveted rooms at the back where the giant hotel was U-shaped. Private verandas looked out on landscaped gardens and big trees and well-tended flower beds.

Such accommodation suited his desire for privacy. Unlike the hotel proper where it was necessary to go through the guest-filled lobby and then into an elevator to reach a room, he could enter the cottage through the outside entrance at any hour of the day or night and be seen by no one.

Hank bounded out of the carriage, stopped and stood for a minute speaking to the driver. He turned and hurried up the steps, unlocked the cottage door, and went inside. The scent of fresh-cut flowers greeted him as he stepped into the marble-floored foyer. He smiled when he saw the many vellum envelopes resting in a silver bowl on a small walnut table. He dropped the book he'd bought onto the table and scooped up the envelopes. He turned and walked into the parlor with its black walnut furniture, lush carpets and thick Brussels lace curtains over the tall windows.

On an end table by a big easy chair, a bottle of fine champagne was cooling in an ice-filled silver bucket along with a note of welcome from the hotel staff. Two sparkling crystal flutes stood beside the bucket. While the driver and a hotel porter unloaded his luggage, carrying the many valises into the master suite, Hank popped the champagne's cork.

Foolishly wishing that the golden-haired angel was here to drink the bubbly with him, he filled both glasses and sank down into an easy chair to begin sifting through the invitations.

Some were for next week and beyond. Some for tomorrow night. Some for tonight. Hank tossed aside all but those requesting his presence for this evening. There were six. Three were for late-night gatherings. Three were for dinner. He considered the dinner invitations, shrugged wide shoulders, closed his eyes and chose one at random.

Horace and Lillian Titus.

Dinner at eight.

Claire was enchanted with Saratoga Springs.

The pristine mountain hamlet was like a fabled fairyland with its grand hotels, quaint shops, beautiful parks and mineral fountains and handsomely dressed visitors.

She strolled leisurely up Broadway passing the Grand Union Hotel, Congress Inn and the Clarendon, each unique and magnificent and unlike anything she had seen back in London. As she approached another impressive building, the huge brick-and-stone United States Hotel, she glanced down the narrow street bordering its side.

And so it was that she was looking directly at a carriage when a tall, lean man bounded out of the back seat. He stood for a second on the sidewalk, smiling and gesturing as he spoke to his driver. Claire's eyes widened and her lips parted.

Midnight hair glistening in the sunshine, broad shoulders appealingly straining the fine linen of his sky-blue shirt, buff-hued trousers draped just so on his slim hips and long legs, he was, without doubt, the most attractive man she had ever laid eyes on.

Unable to tear her gaze from the handsome stranger, Claire stood across the street and stared until he turned away, sprang agilely up a set of steps, unlocked a door and disappeared inside. Even then she continued to stay where she was, her rapt attention fixed on that door.

She wondered who he was and where he was from and if she would ever see him again. Her heart began to race. Of course she would see him again! He, like she, had come to Saratoga for the season. He was obviously a guest at the United States Hotel and she would very likely run into him there. All she had to do was go inside.

Beginning to smile with anticipation, Claire eagerly crossed the narrow street and hurried down the sidewalk until she reached the front of the hotel. She climbed the steps to the wide veranda where people were gathered to talk and laugh and enjoy refreshments served by uniformed waiters.

Claire crossed the veranda and went inside the vast, high-ceilinged lobby. Attempting to appear casual, she sauntered unhurriedly about, glancing at the milling guests, searching for the one who was sure to stand out from the crowd.

Nodding and smiling to people she'd never met, Claire would have, on any other occasion, noticed how incredibly friendly everyone seemed. But she was preoccupied. She was looking for the handsome, dark-haired man in the blue linen shirt.

After several fruitless minutes, Claire gave up the hunt. She was too late. He wouldn't be coming to the lobby. He had obviously already checked in at the desk moments earlier and collected his key. No need to stay longer.

She made her unhurried way through the crowded lobby and out the tall doors onto the veranda. She was descending the front steps when a middle-aged, well-dressed woman came hurrying up the steps toward her.

Reaching her, the woman smiled and said, "Oh, Your Grace, we heard you were coming to Saratoga this summer. How thrilling to have the Duchess of Beaumont here for the season!" When Claire gave the woman a questioning look, she said, "Don't you remember me? Lillian. Mrs. Lillian Titus. How wonderful to see you after all these years! My, my, you are lovelier than ever."

Taken aback, Claire, when she was finally able to get a word in, said, "No, no. I'm afraid you…you've made a…you see, I'm not…I…" Claire stopped speaking. She paused for only a second, then said, "Why, yes, it has been quite a long time."

"It must be at least seven or eight years," declared Lillian. "Now Horace and I are giving a dinner party this very evening. You simply must come. Everyone will be there. Our cottage at eight sharp. Say you'll join us, please, Your Grace."

Claire smiled. "I'd be honored."

Seven

Then and there the usually level-headed, rarely-take-a-chance Claire Orwell decided that for once in her life she would toss caution to the wind. Until just before Charmaine Beaumont arrived in Saratoga, *she* would be the Duchess of Beaumont! For a few golden days and nights, she would live the life of a wealthy, daring duchess amidst the Gilded Age glamour of Saratoga Springs.

Claire wasn't worried that she'd be out of her element. She knew how the wealthy lived, how they behaved. Her dear deceased mother, before she was married, had for a short time been lady-in-waiting to the Queen, her title Woman of the Bedchamber. Her mother had treasured the invaluable experience and had shared many fond recollections.

Claire could hold her own around this wealthy

crowd, could convince them that she was the duchess. And she intended to do just that.

Beginning this very evening she'd hobnob with America's rich and powerful. She would drink chilled champagne and laugh merrily and flirt with the well-heeled gentlemen and dance until dawn and have not a care in the world.

Her cheeks flushed, Claire hurried back to the secluded estate to tell Olivia of her scheme.

The older woman met Claire at the front door and began, "I made great progress in town, Claire. By tomorrow morning we'll have—"

Claire waved a silencing hand and interrupted, "Your news about the staff can wait, Olivia. Come out onto the veranda and sit down, please. I've something to tell you and it can't wait another minute."

Curious, Olivia stepped outside. She obediently took the rocking chair Claire indicated. When she was seated, Claire, continuing to stand, told of her planned deception. Surprised, but fully approving of such a lark, Olivia listened as Claire talked excitedly of her intentions.

"I honestly believe that we can fool them," Claire stated emphatically. "The duchess has not been to the Springs in seven or eight years. Many of the people who are here this summer have never even met her. The others have had plenty of time to forget exactly how she looks."

"And she is tall and slender like you and has pale blond hair," Olivia offered, nodding.

"Exactly. It should be relatively easy to convince everyone that I am indeed the Duchess of Beaumont. I ran into a middle-aged woman—a Mrs. Lillian Titus—at the United States Hotel this afternoon. She mistook me for the duchess and invited me to a dinner party at her home this evening. Said she'd send a carriage round to collect me. That's what gave me the idea for this fling of fancy."

"I've seen photographs of Charmaine Beaumont," Olivia said. "There's a resemblance perhaps, but you're much prettier than she."

Claire smiled. "You are prejudiced. Besides, if that is true—which I doubt—everyone will suppose that I got better looking as I fully matured. The duchess is thirty-three, an age when most women are at the top of their form, are they not?"

"You don't look thirty-three, child. More like twenty-three."

The twenty-seven-year-old Claire smiled again and said, "Well of course I look young. We noble ladies take good care of ourselves." She laughed then and, impulsively sinking to her knees before the seated Olivia, took the older woman's frail hands in hers, squeezed them affectionately, and said, "Oh, Olivia, I know what I'm planning to do is wrong, even unforgivable. But I just don't care. I've made up my mind. I am going to be happy! I'm going to have a gay time and enjoy every minute of every day. I'm going to have pretty clothes and do just as I please as if I were the real duchess."

"But how, Claire? We haven't the money to—"

"We will have," Claire again squeezed Olivia's hands, then released them and shot to her feet. She looked about to make sure Walker was nowhere in sight. Then she grinned impishly as she lifted her skirts and unpinned the purple velvet bag concealed in her petticoats. Sinking again to her knees, she poured out the bag's contents onto the veranda's smooth wooden floor.

Olivia rocked forward and her pale gray eyes widened. Flashing and glittering in the fading sunlight were several pieces of valuable jewelry. Claire lifted an exquisite emerald-and-diamond necklace and handed it to the stunned Olivia.

The necklace resting in her palm, Olivia asked, eyebrows raised, "Claire Orwell, the baron's…?"

"No, I did not steal the jewels. They were my mother's. I have no idea where they came from, who gave them to her. I do know that my father could never have afforded the jewels and that my mother never once wore any of these exquisite pieces in our presence. I didn't know she had them until she died. On her deathbed she whispered in my ear, directed me to the purple velvet bag. It was taped beneath her vanity. There was a sweet note to me inside saying she wanted me to have the jewels. I believe they are worth a tidy sum, don't you?"

"Yes, of course, but you can't be considering…"

"Ah, but I can. We will pawn the precious stones to finance our little adventure. There's only one piece that I will not let go." From the mound of flashing stones Claire carefully untangled a delicate golden chain. Suspended from the chain was a one-inch medallion cut from mother-of-pearl with a gold figure of a woman's profile embossed on the front. The woman was Claire's mother. Claire draped the chain around her neck and fastened it. Touching the medallion where it rested warmly between her breasts, she said, "There."

The older woman was familiar with the unique medallion. Knew something of its prominence. But she kept her mouth shut.

"This piece I will keep," Claire said. "The rest will provide us with some much-needed cash for our royal venture."

Olivia's eyes were now flashing like the jewels that were spread out before her. She said, "If you'll trust me with some of the proceeds the jewels will bring, I'll make our stash quickly grow."

Taking the diamond-and-emerald necklace from Olivia and gathering up the glittering treasures, Claire began to smile knowingly. "Aha, so you're a gambler?"

"And a good one, Your Grace."

Both women laughed.

A band was playing an afternoon concert in the gardens behind his cottage when Hank went into the hallway with its row of bells used for summoning the chambermaid, waiter and valet. He rang for the valet, instructed the man to unpack and left.

He didn't call for a carriage, but walked the short distance to the Saratoga racetrack. He was whistling merrily when he skirted the grandstands and went straight to the rows of stables behind.

The place was alive with activity. Owners, trainers and jockeys were gathered around the many stalls of the prized Thoroughbreds. Hank stopped to shake hands with some of the gentlemen. These men liked racing. They liked to win. They liked the competition. They particularly liked new owners to come to Saratoga and offer a challenge.

Hank was no exception.

"Why, if it isn't Hank Cassidy, the Silver King," said Logan B. Bristow, a real estate magnate from New Jersey and a proud Thoroughbred owner. The round-faced, short-of-stature Bristow laughed and teased, "You really think that gray nag of yours has a chance of beating my best three-year-old in the Travers Stakes?" He stepped forward and slapped Hank on the back.

"How you been, L.B.?" Hank smiled easily and shook Bristow's hand. Before the other man could reply, Hank said, "I sure hate to see you lose your money, but that's what's going to happen if you pin your hopes on that badly outclassed plow horse you're entering." He inclined his head toward the sleek sorrel stallion in the stall directly behind Bristow.

Bristow laughed loudly as Hank walked on through the alley between the stalls, shaking hands here, exchanging pleasantries there, having a look at the competition.

A slimly built, silver-haired man stepped out of a hay-filled stall near the end of the lane. Seeing Hank, he began to smile broadly.

Hank hurried forward.

He caught the older man up in a bear hug and warmly embraced him. The sixty-two-year-old Fox Connor was more to Hank than simply the most talented horse trainer in America. He was that all right, but he was also a trusted friend and confidant, the man who knew Hank better than anyone else.

Wise, loyal, never judgmental, Fox Connor had been with Hank since the day Hank had bought his first racehorse a decade ago. The two had come to regard each other as family. Fox Connor had no family of his own. He hadn't married and therefore had no children. Hank was like the son he'd never had. Fox took pride in Hank's triumphs, found joy in sharing the young man's life, looked forward eagerly to the day Hank married and had children who would hopefully call him Granddad.

"When did you get in?" Fox asked when Hank released him.

"An hour ago," Hank said. "How did they make the trip?" he asked, referring to the dozen valuable Thoroughbreds Fox had escorted up from Kentucky.

"Black Satin has a sore muscle, but he should be fine in a couple of days. Red Eye Gravy wouldn't eat any oats this morning, was listless, but he's already feeling better. Tempest, Eastern Dancer, and the rest seem to be in excellent shape. All had good workouts this morning."

"Silver Dollar's okay?" Hank inquired about the big silver-coated speedster he hoped would take the Travers Stakes.

"He was in fine form for this morning's exercise," Fox assured Hank. "Ran the mile in one-fifty."

Pleased, Hank stepped into the stall where Silver Dollar was stabled. The stallion nickered a greeting. Hank wrapped a long arm around the big Thoroughbred's sleek neck and patted him affectionately.

"You gonna win the Travers Stakes for me, pal of mine?" he asked and the Thoroughbred pricked his ears and shook its great head. Hank laughed and pressed his cheek to the beast's left jaw. "Yes, sir, you're going to make me proud. I know you are."

After carefully examining the horse, Hank exited the stall and motioned to a groom. He reached in his pocket, pulled out a bill, and handed it to the lad. "Let no one come near this silver stallion."

"Yes, sir."

Hank and Fox Connor left the stables together for the short walk back to town. At the hotel, Fox asked, "Any plans for this evening?"

Hank nodded. "A dinner party at Horace Titus's house. You?"

Fox grinned. "You know me, Hank. I'll dine at Canfield's then play a little roulette or faro."

"Might see you there later in the evening.

"I seriously doubt that. I would imagine there'll be any number of eligible ladies at the Tituses' dinner party." He gave Hank a knowing look.

Hank said nothing, but the thought occurred that his golden-haired angel might be among tonight's guests. Lillian Titus had a special talent for attracting the most glamorous and interesting people to her parties.

"See you tomorrow, Fox," Hank said and hurried toward the cottages.

Looking after him, Fox Connor chuckled, then turned and headed for the main hotel and his top floor suite.

At seven, Claire came down the stairs dressed for the dinner party. Olivia anxiously waited in the foyer.

"What do you think?" Claire asked, reaching the marble-floored foyer and turning slowly around.

Olivia gazed on Claire with a critical eye. Claire's golden hair was attractively swept atop her head and held in place with invisible pins. The blond tresses blazed in the light of the chandelier overhead. Her cheeks were flushed and her violet eyes glittered with excitement. Her lips were perfectly tinted with a modest touch of rouge. Face and hair were perfect.

But the dress.

The color was right—violet faille that was the exact same hue as Claire's beautiful eyes. But that was about the only good thing Olivia could say for it.

"Long sleeves in July? A throat-high yoke? A choking collar right up to your chin?" Olivia shook her head. "You look more a schoolmarm than a wealthy duchess."

Claire sighed heavily. "I know, but this is the best I can do until I go shopping. I have nothing suitable for evening wear."

"How long before you leave for the dinner party?"

"Mrs. Titus said they'd send a carriage round for me. Eight sharp."

Olivia glanced at the tall grandfather clock standing in the foyer. "Then I've got an hour. You're in luck, Duchess. I once worked in a gentlemen's tailor shop on Savile Row. I get a needle in me hand and I can alter just about anything. Take off the dress and I'll see what I can do."

She threw herself into her task.

Within the hour, a lovely, lively Claire stood waiting in a shimmering dress of deep lavender faille. The gorgeous gown now had stylish short puff sleeves that appealingly caressed Claire's ivory shoulders. Gone were the yoke and collar.

The hastily remodeled gown's bodice was cut so low and Claire's full breasts were pushed so high by a tight corset, the pale swell of her bosom was generously exposed.

"I believe I hear the carriage coming up the drive, Your Grace," Olivia announced with a smile.

"How do I look now?" Claire asked, nervously tugging at her low-cut bodice, pulling it higher. "I feel naked."

Olivia laughed, brushed Claire's hands away, and urged the bodice back down. "You look beautiful. And remember, you're not Claire Orwell, you're the brazen Duchess of Beaumont."

"That's true. I'm sure the duchess has no qualms about displaying her décolletage."

"None, whatsoever." Olivia's smile became wicked when she said, "I've heard it whispered that since Charmaine Beaumont's husband—the overweight, pompous old duke—died five years ago, she has taken any number of handsome lovers. Are you planning to add a few to her list?"

"Only one," said Claire without hesitation, the image of the dark stranger she'd caught sight of this afternoon flashing into her mind. She stated the unguarded truth, "I would like—just once in my life—to have a grand passion. To know what it's like to make love with a man who can sweep me off my feet and dazzle me. My late husband was a good, kind man, but ours was never a love match and there was no real ardor." Claire shrugged bare ivory shoulders, smiled slyly and declared, "I shall do the duchess proud. I assume Her Grace can choose any man she wants. So I fully intend to pick the most sought-after man in Saratoga." She paused and added, "And then seduce him."

"Seduce him? How?" asked Olivia.

Claire smiled catlike. "Why, by ignoring him, of course."

Eight

The most sought-after man in Saratoga was the good-looking, fun-loving Nevadan, Hank Cassidy. The wealthy young Silver King whose mines produced more than ten thousand dollars a day. A man so darkly handsome and blatantly male he awakened intense romantic longings in females from sixteen to sixty.

Hank's afternoon arrival at the resort had caused as much of a stir as that of the Duchess of Beaumont. News quickly spread that he was back and had checked into one of the coveted cottages at the United States Hotel. Within an hour of his arrival, it was whispered that he had accepted an invitation to Lillian Titus's dinner party. It was further whispered that the flamboyant duchess would be in attendance, as well.

Those who had not been invited to Lillian's gathering felt slighted. Competing hostesses were disappointed that Lillian had snagged both the Silver King and the Duchess of Beaumont.

Hank's intent was to put in a short, obligatory appearance at the dinner party where the stellar guest list would include the likes of Morgans and Vanderbilts and Rockerfellers. And, according to his talkative hotel valet, a beautiful widowed duchess.

He'd paid little attention to the gossip. Titles did not impress him. He wouldn't have cared if the Old Queen herself showed up at the Springs unless she brought along a string of racehorses. Let the other guests fawn over the visiting duchess, making fools of themselves.

Not him.

It was five minutes of eight when Hank, impeccably dressed in dark tuxedo, snowy white shirt and black tie, arrived at the Tituses' mansion with a promise to himself that he would stay for one short hour, no more. As soon as dinner was over, he would make his excuses and leave.

"My dear Hank," Lillian Titus gushed, gazing up at him as a young, impressionable girl might. "Horace and I are delighted that you could join us this evening."

"Thanks for having me, Mrs. Titus," Hank replied.

The plump, happy hostess wrapped a possessive arm around Hank's and maneuvered him about the drawing room, introducing him to those he didn't know, reuniting him with old acquaintances from summers past.

When finally she released her death grip on his arm, Hank exhaled with relief and milled about. He hardly noticed the longing looks he drew from the ladies. He was used to such frank appraisals. Unfortunately, he saw no one here with whom he'd like to get better acquainted. He hoped dinner would soon be announced.

It was coming up on 8:30. What were they waiting on?

A glass of port in his hand, Hank was standing across the large parlor, his back to the room, when the last guest finally arrived. He paid no attention to the buzz of excitement that swept through the crowd. He was talking to a fellow Thoroughbred owner when Lillian Titus stepped up and interrupted him in midsentence.

"Excuse me, Hank," Lillian said with a smile. "There's someone I'd like you to meet."

Hank slowly turned.

And found himself face-to-face with the elusive golden-haired woman he had not been able to get out of his mind. His heart skipped two beats. Then began pounding furiously. She was even lovelier than he had thought. Those luxurious golden locks were dressed appealingly atop her head. Her beautiful, un-blemished skin appeared to glow in the soft light.

Her eyes, an incredible violet hue and seductively shaded by long, thick lashes, were large and luminously expressive. Her half-petulant lips looked soft and sweet. He immediately wanted to kiss them along with her beautiful bare shoulders and elegant throat.

She was tall and willowy, at least five-eight or nine, with hips that were lush, feminine and gently rounded. Her violet-hued gown was so tight it thrust her rounded breasts blatantly upward. The pale swell of her bosom made his mouth water and his knees grow weak.

She stood there looking cool, unruffled, totally serene. Yet he would have bet every Thoroughbred he owned that she was fiery, tempestuous and passionate. Without so much as moving or saying a word, she exuded a healthy sexuality and wholesome sense of herself as a desirable woman.

Hank wanted her instantly.

"Hank, dear," Lillian Titus was saying, "may I present the Duchess of Beaumont. She just arrived this afternoon and will be with us through the season." She turned to Claire, "Your Grace, Mr. Hank Cassidy of Nevada."

Claire took one look at Hank and recognized him as the man she'd seen going into the hotel cottages this afternoon. She knew she had found the man she was going to seduce. The mere sight of him caused a fluttering sensation in her stomach and an aching tightness in her breasts.

He was tall, a couple of inches over six feet. He was also tanned, muscular and fit. His hair was coal black, thick and gleaming with blue highlights under the glow of the chandelier. She had the strongest urge to reach up and run her hands through those silky raven locks.

His face was beautiful, but strong. Hooded eyes of striking summer blue were focused on her and deep in their depths flashed unmistakable sensual fire and unspoken challenge. His nose was straight and proud. His mouth was wide, generous, with warm, sensual lips that likely knew the art of kissing.

He was staring at her and Claire caught the slight dilating of his eyes and the little smile that began to play around the corners of his mouth as if he knew something she didn't. It made her uneasy. It made her curious.

He wore an elegant tuxedo with satin lapels and cummerbund that fitted his tall, lean body perfectly. The whiteness of his pleated shirt was striking against the darkness of his skin. He held a glass of port in his right hand and she noted that his fingers were long and tapered, the nails clean and cut short. She found herself wondering how it would feel to have that tanned hand touching her. Caressing her face. Stroking her shoulders.

Without so much as moving a muscle, his raw sexual power was obvious, almost tangible. There was absolutely no doubt in Claire's mind that this was the man who could invoke a feverish passion in her.

Ah, yes here was her unsuspecting target. But she wouldn't let him know it.

Not yet.

Smiling down at her, Hank was already counting the minutes until they could take their leave and he could take her in his arms. He saw no obstacle in his path. Like everyone else, he had heard the stories of the uninhibited duchess's affairs. That she was a libertine suited him fine. He preferred women of experience. His only regret was that the two of them had to endure the boring dinner party when they could be back at her place or at the hotel cottages getting properly acquainted.

Hank took the soft hand the duchess offered and acknowledged her. She spoke his name and it sent tingles up his spine. But all too soon she freed her hand from his.

"You'll excuse us, Hank," said Lillian Titus. "The others are anxious to pay their respects to the duchess."

Hank nodded. But he was surprised and oddly disappointed that the duchess turned away without a parting glance. All at once he had the uneasy feeling that she was not particularly interested in him.

Taken aback, he watched as she swept regally around the room, smiling at guests as she was introduced, warmly greeting those she had known from summer seasons past.

Hank never took his eyes off the vision in violet. His body tensed. Teeth clamped down, he silently willed her to turn and look at him. To give him some subtle sign. To let him know that she was aware of him.

It never happened. Not once did she so much as glance back in his direction.

Nonplussed, Hank was relieved when finally a smartly uniformed butler stepped into the open double doors of the drawing room and announced, "Dinner is served."

Hank felt a hand on his arm. "You're the Silver King!" trilled a feminine voice and Hank reluctantly took his eyes off the duchess. A winsome redhead in a figure-hugging gown of emerald-green satin was smiling seductively at him. "You don't remember me, do you, Mr. Cassidy?"

"No, I'm sorry."

"Well, you should be," she teased and her eyes sparkled. "I'm Caroline Whit. We met three years ago. I was here with my husband, Rodney. Ring a bell? Rodney Whit from Vermont."

"Rodney Whit? Sure. Is he here this evening?"

"I hope not," she said with a laugh. "I divorced him last winter. And please don't say you're sorry.

I'm not." She leaned closer and whispered, "The only good thing I got from dear old Rodney was a love of racehorses. I understand they're your passion, as well."

"That's why I'm in Saratoga," he said.

"We have a lot in common, Hank. We'd better go in to dinner," she said. "I hope you're seated next to me."

Hank gave no reply, but graciously escorted Caroline Whit into the candlelit dining room where the long, linen-draped table was set for fifty guests.

"Caroline, you're at the far end of the table, to the right of my Horace," said Lillian Titus, stepping forward to direct Caroline to her seat. "Horace finds you so entertaining, he insisted you be seated close to him." Caroline Whit made an unsuccessful attempt to hide her disappointment.

"And you, Hank, I've placed you here next to the Duchess of Beaumont." Lillian leaned close and whispered, "I'm counting on you to charm Her Grace so that she'll enjoy herself this evening."

Hank smiled. Nobody wanted the duchess to enjoy herself this evening more than he did.

Claire *was* enjoying herself.

Everyone had greeted her and accepted her as the Duchess of Beaumont. There had been no looks of doubt or probing questions or whispers behind raised hands. She could hardly keep from laughing out loud. She had—for now—been successful in her duplicity. She hoped Olivia was as successful bucking the tables as she was playing the belle of the ball.

Claire had also succeeded in concealing her fierce attraction to the handsome Hank Cassidy.

When Hank took his seat next to her, she didn't turn and smile at him. Nor did she acknowledge his presence. Instead she pretended to be totally engrossed in conversation with the gentleman on her right, Parker Lawson of New York City. Lillian Titus had whispered in Claire's ear that the blondly handsome Lawson, an eligible bachelor, was one of the heirs to the late Jay Gould's vast fortune. Upon Gould's death in '92, Parker Lawson had become a very wealthy man.

But as she talked with him, Claire was vitally aware of Hank Cassidy. There was no doubt in her mind that this big, handsome Westerner knew how to please a lady. The prospect of making love to him made her wish that there was no need to wait. She wished that their heated, but impersonal affair could begin that very evening.

But she was too clever to let that happen. She could not let him know that she fully intended to entice him into her bed. Not yet. She would wait a week or two. And while she waited she would arouse his interest by feigning indifference.

* * *

Hank scowled when the duchess laughed merrily at something Lawson whispered to her. When finally Lawson was distracted by a lady seated on his right, Hank seized the opportunity.

"You'll be here for the entire season?" he asked.

"That is my intention, Mr. Cassidy," she said, then turned her attention to the bowl of vichyssoise before her.

"Call me Hank," he coaxed. "And what do I call you?"

"Your Grace," she said coolly.

She had set the tone and it did not change throughout the dinner. Hank broached every subject he thought might interest her. None did. He got clipped yes or no answers to any and all questions. And barely a nod of her golden head to any amusing story he shared. Nothing he said seemed to engage her. He tossed her many a signal. She swatted each one down without batting an eyelash.

Never had he tried so hard to charm a woman and failed so miserably. His ego was totally deflated. Damn her. He should dislike her for treating him badly. She was cold and rude and a terrible snob.

And he was captivated.

Claire knew her plan was working. And she was pleased.

She pretended, throughout dinner, to take little interest in him. In truth she clung to his every word, was amused by his entertaining tales, was warmed by his every smile and dreamed of the moment when he would come into her arms.

But she wouldn't let it happen tonight. It was too soon. She'd make him wait.

When the seventh and final course was finished and the guests were directed back into the drawing room, Claire didn't join them. Instead she bade her hosts good-night, explaining that she was still a trifle tired from the trip.

The carriage was promptly brought around. Parker Lawson, who'd been at her elbow from the minute they exited the dining room, suggested that he escort Claire back to her estate. She thanked him, but declined.

On Parker's arm she descended the mansion's front steps. He handed her up into the carriage and asked, "May I escort you to Congress Springs in the morning? Everyone will be there, you know."

"You're so kind, Parker. I've accepted an invitation to join a half-dozen of the ladies who are here this evening."

"Then I will see you there?"

"I'm sure you will. And now, good night."

"Good night, Your Grace," he said and reluctantly backed away. Claire glanced past Parker to the lighted mansion. She smiled with satisfaction.

Hank Cassidy stood on the veranda in the moonlight, his muscular shoulder leaning against a pillar.

He didn't look happy.

And that made the duchess very happy.

Nine

"Olivia, where are you? Come quickly! I've met him. I've met the man who will be my lover," Claire announced the minute she reached the estate and stepped into the foyer.

"Already?" Olivia, in robe and gown, promptly came out of her room leaning on her hickory cane. "How can you be sure? We just arrived today. You've only met a handful of the—"

"Does it matter?" Claire interrupted, her violet eyes aglow. "I have found him and need look no further. He was at the dinner party and every female present envied me because I was seated next to him."

Claire's exhilaration was infectious. Olivia felt suddenly giddy with excitement. "Come to my room and tell me all about him."

Arm in arm the two women went down the wide

center hallway and into Olivia's bedroom. They sat down on a sofa before the cold fireplace and Claire sighed happily.

"His name is Hank Cassidy," she began. "A big, suntanned Westerner from Nevada. He's handsome and charming and intelligent and eligible." Claire breathlessly described Hank, concluding by declaring that there was a natural arrogance about him; an easy assurance of male power that was tremendously appealing. "I tell you the man is utterly irresistible."

"I don't doubt it," said Olivia, then asked, "What does he do? What is his profession?"

"I have no idea," Claire said flippantly. "I never asked and he never said, but some of the guests called him the Silver King. Why should I care what he does? What difference does it make? I am not looking for a life mate. I only want a lover for a few thrilling nights." She sighed.

"True enough. But tell me, is this irresistible Hank Cassidy the kind of man with whom you can have an affair and then end it with no regrets?"

"I don't see why not," Claire said with a smile. "Perhaps the repressed, unsophisticated Claire Orwell couldn't. But no doubt the daring Duchess of Beaumont could." Claire shrugged slender shoulders. "I will behave as she would. Love him and leave him."

"And never look back, you naughty girl, you?"

"Never," Claire was quick to answer. She stood up. "Now unhook me, please. I must get some rest so I'll look my best in the morning."

Olivia rose, stepped around behind Claire and made short work of the tiny hooks and eyes going down her back. "What's on the agenda for tomorrow?"

"Out to Congress Park early in the morning to drink of the mineral waters," Claire said. "Then breakfast with a Mr. Parker Lawson from New York City. Not that I'm romantically interested in Lawson. No, no, not at all. But I'm hoping Hank Cassidy will hear that I've been seen with him." She smiled playfully, then continued, "Later I'm to have luncheon at the Grand Union with a half-dozen of the ladies I met this evening. Then back here in the afternoon to rest before attending a concert on the veranda of the United States Hotel at twilight."

"Sounds like your dance card is sufficiently full."

"You wouldn't believe how these wealthy Americans fawned over me. I'm confident not a soul in attendance doubted that I'm the Duchess of Beaumont. I received so many invitations to parties and soirees, I can't possibly attend all of them."

"What a lovely dilemma," said Olivia. "And I suppose this handsome Hank Cassidy will be at many of the gatherings?"

When Claire's dress was parted, Olivia unlaced

the tight-fitting corset and Claire gave a great sigh of relief. She turned about to find Olivia looking stern.

"I'm certain he's at the top of everyone's guest list," Claire said. "And you can just stop your frowning, I have no intention of losing my heart."

"And what of Hank Cassidy's heart? What if he should fall in love with you?"

"That," said Claire, "would be his misfortune." She laughed and added, "Dear, dear Olivia, please do not trouble yourself about either of us. Hank Cassidy is a big boy. I'm quite sure he can take care of himself. I've an idea that a brief summertime affair with no strings attached will be just as appealing to him as it is to me. And when the time is right, when I've got him right where I want him, I will be totally honest with him."

"Honest?" Olivia's eyebrows rose accusingly.

"Let me amend that statement. I'll never reveal my true identity, but I will be honest about wanting nothing more than an affair. Now, it's late and I'm tired. Good night." She moved toward the door.

"Sweet dreams," Olivia said. "By the way, like you, I made great progress today." Claire turned back to listen. "I have engaged a housekeeper, maid, cook and a distinguished-looking butler who will double as our driver. He's promised to lease a decent carriage which we'll keep here at the estate for the season. All of the newly hired staff will be here first thing in the morning and…and…oh, yes, Walker, has requested your permission to travel down to South Carolina to visit his granddaughter. Said she's his only family and he hasn't seen her in more than a decade. He reminded me that the last time you were here—some eight years ago—you quite generously insisted that he take a six-week holiday."

Claire smiled. "Tell Walker he's free to leave tomorrow and need not return until mid-August."

Olivia nodded. "Then it's settled. Within a week, this house should be in tip-top shape and running smoothly."

"You're a treasure," Claire said and meant it.

"Speaking of treasures, I will discreetly begin pawning your jewels tomorrow. Then, with your permission, I will take a portion of the cash and see if I can get lucky."

"You have my unlimited permission," Claire said.

Feeling wonderfully lighthearted, Claire climbed the stairs to the second floor. Once inside the master suite, she kicked off her shoes and danced around on the plush Aubusson carpet, humming happily. She took the pins from her hair and let the long locks spill down around her shoulders.

As she swayed, she pushed the loosened gown to the floor and stepped out of it. Her petticoats and the unlaced corset followed. She spun dizzily over to the bed, sat down on the edge of the mattress and removed her silk stockings, letting them float to the carpeted floor. Then she was up again and dancing around the room.

Her energy soon beginning to wane, she yawned, came back to the bed and stripped off the last of her underthings. She picked up the nightgown Olivia had laid out for her. She didn't put it on. Holding the gown against her body, she wondered, "Would the duchess sleep in a long, choking nightgown? Or would she sleep in the nude?"

Claire tossed the nightgown aside. She put out the bedside lamp and the room was cast into darkness. Naked, she climbed into bed. The silky sheets felt good against her sensitive flesh. She kicked the top sheet and coverlet to the foot of the bed. She stretched out on her back and purred like a lazy cat.

The double doors stood open to the balcony. A rising night breeze stirred the sheer curtains and wafted into the room to stroke Claire's bare body and awaken her senses. She took a deep breath and flung her arms above her head. The gentle gusts were pleasantly cool.

Claire hadn't realized, until now, that she felt feverish, as if she were running a temperature. She was not deceived. The source of her fever was not some malady she'd contacted; not an illness she was coming down with. It was the vivid recollection of

Hank Cassidy's beautiful, artistic fingers wrapped loosely around his stemmed wineglass at dinner, caressing it, exciting her.

Claire abruptly sat up and swung her legs over the mattress's edge. She pushed her long hair back off her face. Rising from the bed and grabbing up her robe, she slipped her arms into the sleeves, but didn't tie the sash at her waist. She crossed to the open double doors and stepped out onto the balcony, looking cautiously around to be sure no one could see her.

She moved across the balcony and placed her hands on the wide, waist-high railing. While the night wind tossed her hair around her head and billowed her unsashed robe out behind her and chilled her overwarm body, a thrilling image flashed into her mind. Hank Cassidy standing naked on this very balcony with her, taking her into his arms, making love to her here under the moon and stars.

She shivered deliciously.

It was not such a far-fetched idea. It was a very real possibility. It could happen. She could make it happen. But she had to wait. And she would.

Claire was a disciplined woman.

She had carefully laid out a time line to which she would strictly adhere. For no less than two full weeks, she would demonstrate casual indifference toward Hank Cassidy. At the same time she would make it a point to be where he was. And she would go out of her way to laugh happily and flirt outrageously and make Cassidy suspect that she was living up to her reputation as an uninhibited wanton.

Ten

Hank was up early.

Much earlier than usual.

Bare-chested, a towel draped around his broad shoulders, he stood before the mirror shaving with a sharp, straight-edged razor. When he had finished shaving and blotted away the last of the foamy lather, he bent and splashed several handfuls of cold water on his face. He lifted the clean towel and patted his closely shaven face dry.

He tossed the towel aside and walked into the bedroom to dress. The valet had laid out a freshly pressed suit of tan cotton poplin. A pale blue cotton shirt and dark brown neck piece completed the ensemble. Hank left the tie where it was. And he left a couple of the shirt's buttons undone.

When he was dressed, Hank left his cottage and

hurried toward Congress Park. He wasn't going there to drink of the waters. The waters tasted like burned matches and he couldn't understand how anyone would actually drink from the springs.

But they did.

Before breakfast each morning a colorful parade of well-dressed, happily chattering ladies promenaded to Congress Park. Gentleman gathered at the springs to watch the morning procession. It was a ritual, a social event not to be missed. Or so Hank had heard. He hadn't bothered to visit any of the many springs since his very first year at Saratoga.

But now as he neared the white-latticed pavilion built over the springs, anticipation sent the blood zinging through his veins. He was sure the Duchess of Beaumont would visit the springs on her first morning in Saratoga.

And he'd be there to greet her.

A beige silk parasol shading her fair face from the morning sun, Claire joined a group of ladies for the short stroll to Congress Park. Claire admitted, when accused, to never having visited the springs on any of her previous visits. She, on the other hand, had a strong desire to drink thirstily of the mineral waters.

"The Congress waters are the most favored of all," declared Lillian Titus, with great authority.

"Now, Lillian, dear," said the handsomely

dressed, middle-aged banking heiress, Pauline Quinn, "there are others the Duchess must visit, as well. Why there's High Rock and Empire and Excelsior and Triton and—"

"Yes, yes," Lillian impatiently cut Pauline off. "But Congress Springs is the place to be."

"Your Grace," offered Maxine Delaney, an age-wrinkled tiny little woman in a big-brimmed straw hat, "the waters have a wondrous healing effect on both body and soul."

The pretty divorcée, red-haired Caroline Whit, did not extol the benefit of the waters. She said nothing and Claire concluded that Caroline came to the springs to see and be seen. Claire's eyes narrowed minutely as she watched the ravishing redhead saunter leisurely along, her hips swaying, breasts freely bouncing beneath her high-necked dress of shimmering yellow silk. Claire gritted her teeth, recalling suddenly that at last night's gathering, Caroline had entered the dining room with none other than Hank Cassidy.

Soon Claire's little group reached the beautiful park, which was filled with pavilions, splashing fountains, the lake, benches, obelisks and a bandstand. The lush, tree-shaded park was crowded with people, all dressed to the nines.

Claire noticed that it was mainly ladies who gathered in the pavilion to drink of the healing mineral waters.

It appeared that the gentlemen had made the trek to the springs solely to watch the morning parade. A band began to play as Claire reached the white pavilion. She patiently waited her turn and when she stepped up to the springs, the smiling dipper boy ladled up a half-pint tumbler of mineral water and handed it to her.

Claire thanked him, turned, and strolled away from the others. She sat down on a bench in the shade, raised the tumbler to her lips and took a big healthy swill.

And fought the strong desire to spew it out of her mouth. It tasted awful. Worse than any medicine she'd ever taken. Trying very hard not to make a face, she looked anxiously around to make sure no one was watching her.

But someone was.

Not thirty yards away, Hank Cassidy, arms crossed over his chest, stood leaning negligently against a marble statue. He was looking straight at her.

And he was laughing.

While Claire struggled to swallow the foul-tasting water, Hank pushed away from the statue and headed in her direction. He reached her, plucked at the crease in his tan trousers, lifted a well-shod foot up onto the bench beside her and leaned a forearm on his trousered knee.

Giving her a I'm-about-to-wink-at-you look, he

said, "Go ahead, spit it out, Duchess. I won't tell anybody."

Claire swallowed anxiously, then swallowed again. "There's nothing to tell, Mr. Cassidy. I find the waters quite refreshing."

"Really? Then drink up and I'll get you another dipper full." He grinned devilishly then, lowered his foot to the ground, took the tumbler from her and tossed out the water.

"I wish you hadn't done that," Claire stated haughtily.

"No you don't."

Not waiting for an invitation, Hank sat down beside her. Claire was secretly delighted. She was sure he had come to the springs this morning in hopes of seeing her. She glanced at him and felt her breath immediately grow short. He was extraordinarily handsome with the kind of dark good looks that won women without any effort.

His hooded cerulean eyes were shaded with sinfully long black lashes and his beautiful lips were turned up into an appealingly boyish smile. His shirt collar was open and a couple of the buttons were undone revealing his smooth, tanned throat. Claire found it hard to take her eyes off him. She had to force herself to look away.

"Come to breakfast with me, Duchess," Hank said and his rich baritone voice was most persuasive. "A cup of strong black coffee will get the bad taste of the water out of your mouth."

"I think not, Mr. Cassidy," Claire said dismissively and rose.

Hank stood up. Before she could stop him, he had reached for and taken hold of her hand. When his fingers closed around hers, Claire's heart fluttered alarmingly.

But she remained outwardly composed. Hank laced his fingers through hers, squeezed gently, and said, "No breakfast? Fine. Then have dinner with me this evening."

Claire made a halfhearted attempt to free her hand. Hank allowed her to unlace their fingers, but he didn't let go of her hand. Instead his closed possessively over hers and Claire felt the warmth of his touch quickly spread through her entire body.

"I'm sorry, Mr. Cassidy," she said, "I have prior plans this evening."

Hank's hand loosened on hers but still did not release it. He slid lean fingers up to encircle her fragile wrist and placed the tip of his thumb on her pulse. And felt it race.

"Are you feeling well, Duchess?"

"I'm perfectly fine," she said, hoping her face wasn't flushed.

"Your face is flushed and your pulse is rapid. Perhaps you'd better let me see you home before you—"

"There you are," came a firm male voice, interrupting.

Hank and Claire looked up to see Parker Lawson fast approaching. Claire anxiously wrenched her hand free of Hank's and smiled warmly at the handsome Parker Lawson.

The men acknowledged each other, shook hands, then Parker turned his full attention on Claire. "Have you drunk of the waters, Your Grace?"

"Yes. Yes, I have," she said.

"She thought the water tasted real good," Hank said with a grin. "You might want to bring her another dipper full."

Ignoring Hank, Claire smiled at Parker. "I'm ready for breakfast if you are." She opened and raised her parasol.

"Yes, I'm famished," said Parker, taking Claire's arm. "Congress Inn serves a sumptuous spread. Shall we go there?" Claire nodded her approval. To Hank, Parker said, "I'd invite you to join us, Cassidy, but I'm sure you're on your way out to the track."

Not waiting for a reply, Lawson hurriedly ushered the duchess away. She left without a backward look. And, to Hank's chagrin, Lawson leaned close and whispered something to her. She playfully slapped at him and laughed merrily as if she'd never before heard anything quite so amusing.

Hank Cassidy muttered an oath under his breath.

Eleven

Saratoga Springs was a small, close-knit resort community. Summer guests were endlessly sociable. Most attended several pleasant activities each and every day. And then were present for glittering gatherings at night, encountering many of the same people with whom they'd spent the afternoon.

Or had been with the evening before.

It would have been next to impossible to avoid seeing someone who was spending the season at the Springs.

And so it was that there was not one single day— or night—that Hank Cassidy didn't run into the beautiful Duchess of Beaumont.

On each occasion, the gregarious duchess, who bantered and teased and laughed so readily with others, was—to Hank—consistently distant, barely acknowledging him. Baffling him. Bothering him. To the point that the sound of her frequent laughter had begun to annoy the hell out of him.

She never laughed with him no matter how hard he worked to entertain and amuse her. He'd had no trouble successfully charming other women with his special brand of flirtatious teasing. Most beauties easily fell under his spell.

But not her.

He was not accustomed to having women refuse invitations to dinner—and more—with him. With the exception of the frosty golden-haired duchess, every eligible lady in Saratoga—and a few who were not—jealously vied for his attention.

But Hank wasn't interested.

Perversely, he wanted only this gay, glamorous woman who seemed to take pleasure in rejecting him. It was a predicament that was totally foreign to him. And it was most unsettling to be strongly attracted to a beautiful woman who wanted no part of him.

The uncomfortable situation was made worse by the fact that he and the duchess were constantly at the same social functions. Be it afternoon band concert or evening dinner party or nighttime hop, the gadabout duchess never missed a good time.

She had managed, in the one short week she had been at the Springs, to thoroughly enchant everyone. Her striking blond beauty was not her only asset.

She was—with everyone but him—genial, good-natured, and adept at repartee. There was, he felt sure, no pretense about her, no Victorian humility or false modesty.

Not one ounce of hypocrisy.

It was taken for granted by the resort's well-informed gossips that the outgoing, flamboyant widow would very soon take a lover—or lovers—from the myriad dazzled gentlemen who were drawn to her as moths to the flame.

Hank Cassidy had his pride. He staunchly refused to play the drooling fool like all the others, but he did seize every opportunity their crossed paths afforded to try to attract her attention.

So far to no avail.

But he hadn't given up. Would not give up.

The duchess's brush-offs and rebuffs had only heightened his resolve to have her.

On a warm, sunny afternoon Claire stood before the glass counter in one of the stores at the Grand Union Hotel. A small, tastefully decorated, sinfully expensive shop that offered fancy goods. She was admiring a pair of imported French kid gloves when Hank Cassidy walked in and, uninvited, joined her.

"She'll take the gloves," he said to the clerk, "put them on my account."

"Do no such thing!" she quickly instructed the

clerk. She turned on Hank, her brow furrowed. "I do not accept gifts from strange gentlemen," she told him flatly.

"Take a good look at me, Duchess," Hank said and slowly turned about in a full circle. When he was again facing her, he asked, "See anything strange about me?"

I see the most compelling man I've ever met! A man in whose arms I can hardly wait to be. "I must agree with you on that. I see nothing out of the ordinary about you, Mr. Cassidy," Claire said with a slight smirk.

"Well, then how about letting this plain old ordinary fellow buy you a pair of gloves?"

"I do not need your charity," Claire scolded.

"What exactly do you need, Duchess?" he asked and his handsome face showed faint amusement. Claire felt her stomach do a turn. Hank took her elbow. "Let's go."

"Go? I'm not finished shopping."

"That can wait."

"So can you."

"No, I can't. Nor can you. If we delay, all the rockers will be taken. We must hurry." Hank gently propelled Claire out of the store, at the same time motioning to the clerk to wrap up the gloves.

"The rockers taken? Is there a reason I should care if—?"

"Yes, there is," he said, ushering her up Broadway, nodding and smiling to the people strolling past. "If you haven't spent a lazy afternoon rocking and enjoying fruit ices on the veranda of the United States Hotel, you don't know what you're missing."

Claire carefully concealed her eagerness to be in his company. Mildly aloof, she allowed him to escort her to the hotel. When they climbed the front steps to the vast veranda where hundreds of people were spending the summer afternoon, rockers immediately stilled, while conversations lowered and died away.

At once, all eyes were on the striking pair; the man, lean, hard, and handsome, the woman, delicate, beautiful, and feminine. The two most talked-about people in Saratoga; the Duchess of Beaumont and the Nevada Silver King.

"Your Grace," people called out from several directions. "There are chairs over here. Won't you join us?"

"Come this way, King, and bring your beautiful companion. Plenty of rockers here. Come. Come join us."

"Thank you, thank you so much," Hank smiled and acknowledged everyone, smoothly guiding Claire through the throngs of people, stepping around clusters of rockers and deftly shaking outstretched hands before hurriedly moving on. His hand at the small of Claire's back, Hank gently pressed her forward toward the end of the long, crowded veranda.

"Over there," he finally inclined his head, spotting a couple of empty wicker rockers slightly apart from the others on the shaded veranda. Claire nodded. They reached the chairs and Hank handed her down into one. She frowned at him when he pulled his rocker closer to hers. So close the wicker arms were touching. He folded his long frame down into the chair and slowly exhaled.

"Ah, is this the life?" he asked, beginning to rock slowly back and forth, his knees spread, long legs stretched out before him.

"Quite pleasant," she replied. She laid her hands on the chair's arms and blinked in surprise when Hank's hand casually covered hers.

"I can't stay," she quickly said.

"Sure you can," he replied. "What you need is a fruit ice to cool you off." He raised a long arm in the air and motioned. A white-jacketed waiter immediately appeared. "The lady would like a strawberry ice," Hank said and looked at Claire. "Wouldn't you?"

"I suppose so. What are you having?"

Hank lowered his heavily lidded gaze to her lips. "Perhaps just a lick off yours."

Claire inwardly shivered and looked away. "I really should be going."

But she didn't move. And when her fruit ice came,

she sat there savoring it and readily admitted that it was quite delicious. She was enjoying herself immensely despite the fact that she was on edge, girlishly nervous in his presence, while he seemed totally relaxed.

He made easy inconsequential conversation and Claire found herself smiling and hanging on to every word. She loved the timbre of his voice, the way his blue eyes sparkled when he spoke, the flash of his white teeth when he smiled.

Claire couldn't believe it when Hank yawned and closed his eyes. She stared at him, aghast. "If you're going to sleep, then I—"

"I'm not going anywhere, Duchess." Hank opened one eye and smiled at her. "I'm right where I want to be." He closed both eyes again.

Claire slowly released a breath. She should, she knew, get up and leave. But she didn't want to go. It was so nice here rocking in the shade on this warm summer afternoon beside this attractive man. She would never have told him, but she, too, was right where she wanted to be.

Claire cautiously turned her head and gazed admiringly at Hank. His handsome face in repose was like that of an innocent young boy. A wayward lock of gleaming raven hair fell casually over his high forehead. His mouth was relaxed, the sensual lips appearing to be soft, sweet, yet decidedly dangerous.

Claire slowly lowered her gaze to the broad chest which was gently rising and falling. His dove-gray linen suit jacket was thrown carelessly open. Beneath a shirt of fine white silk, the shadow of thick dark chest hair was a testament to his masculinity.

Claire felt her mouth grow dry.

Hank Cassidy was exactly what she was looking for in a summertime sexual playmate. Dark, seductive, a rogue if ever there was one. A rawly virile man who stirred the most shameful of longings in the bosoms of respectable woman, including her.

Claire wondered how he would look without his shirt. Without his clothes.

The prospect made the blood rush to her cheeks. She turned her attention to the lean, brown hand which was again warmly covering her own. His hand on hers looked like it belonged there. It felt right, felt good. Too good. She was weakening.

Time to go.

Silently, carefully she freed her hand from his. He didn't stir. Never moved. He was sleeping, for heaven's sake! Claire was more than a trifle insulted. Indignant, she left him there.

She was red-faced and angry by the time she reached the hotel's broad front steps. While she was still tingling from the mere touch of his hand on hers, he had not roused when she got up to leave.

Flustered, suddenly doubting her appeal, Claire

descended the hotel steps feeling as if everyone was staring and whispering that the fun-loving duchess might easily charm everyone else but she had so bored the handsome Silver King he had fallen sound asleep.

Twelve

"Apparently I have greatly overestimated my charms," Claire announced when she reached the estate and found Olivia out on the back veranda.

"Now I seriously doubt that," said Olivia, needle in hand, a sky-blue chiffon garment spread out on her lap. "Tell me what has happened—or *not* happened—that causes you to make such a foolish statement."

Claire sighed wearily and sank down onto a padded chaise longue. "I was in one of the shops at the Grand Union when Hank Cassidy walked in and…" She told, in detail, what had occurred, concluding with the distressing admission that Hank Cassidy had fallen asleep in his rocker. With a look of despair on her face, she said, "No question about it, Olivia, Cassidy was bored with me."

"I don't believe that for a minute. Perhaps the young

man was simply quite tired," offered Olivia. "Or maybe being with you made him feel so content he—"

"Content? I don't want him content!" Claire shot up off of the chaise and began to pace restlessly back and forth. "I want him intrigued. Impatient. Tormented. I want him to the point where he'll never sleep again."

"If anyone can do it, you can," assured Olivia with a throaty laugh. "Wait until he sees you in this." She lifted the blue chiffon gown she was altering. "With your fair coloring and golden hair, you'll be absolutely irresistible. If need be, I could have it ready for this evening if you'd like to wear it to dinner."

Claire took the beautiful gown and held it up before her. Smoothing a hand over the soft, frothy fabric, she smiled for the first time since leaving the sleeping Hank.

"Seeing me in this should wake him up, don't you think?"

"Guaranteed," said Olivia, nodding.

"The gown's not quite ready and neither am I," said Claire, her self-confidence quickly returning. She handed the garment back to Olivia and said, "Another week should do the trick." She pondered for a moment, then thinking out loud mused, "The Duchess arrives Saturday, August 10th. Today's date is Saturday July 20th. Which means I can delay the inevitable for another full week, during which time I will run hot and cold. Confuse him totally before I breathlessly surrender next Saturday night. And then I'll still have two entire weeks to spend with…" Her words trailed away. She smiled once more and declared, "Cassidy can continue to wonder and doubt himself for another seven days. And nights."

Olivia again nodded and told Claire, "Among the many invitations that came today, there's one from the William Kissam Vanderbilts. I understand William is the eldest son of the late Cornelius Vanderbilt, the rail tycoon who was one of the richest men in the world."

"I know," Claire murmured. "Since we arrived, I've heard a great deal about the Vanderbilts and Diamond Jim Brady and others. Saratoga definitely draws America's richest."

"Not just Americans," Olivia corrected. "I was in one of the small casinos last evening and overheard some owners talking about the Thoroughbred races. One complained to his companions that he had difficulty in obtaining stables. Seems several titled Englishmen are bringing over a string of fine Thoroughbreds for the final heats and…"

"Coming to Saratoga?" Claire anxiously interrupted. "No! Suppose they know the duchess, know her well? There's a great likelihood that one or all will be at the very least acquaintances of hers. They will expose me for the fraud I am! Did you hear any names?"

"No, but there's no need to worry," Olivia said calmly. "The gentlemen in question are not arriving until mid-August. Just about the time we'll be folding our tents and disappearing into the sunset."

"Thank heaven," Claire said, heaving a sigh of relief and relaxing immediately. Changing the subject, she said, "So…did we win any money today?"

"Call me Lucky," Olivia replied with a self-satisfied smile. "Almost three hundred dollars in less than four hours." They both laughed.

"Now about that invitation from the Vanderbilts," said Olivia. "They're hosting a festive gala at the United States Hotel ballroom Saturday next, a week from tonight."

"Perfect," said Claire. "Cassidy will be there, I'm sure, and I will—toward the end of the evening—make my move." She shivered at the pleasant prospect. "Please RSVP for the duchess."

Hank had been cautiously encouraged by the duchess's willingness to stay on the veranda with him, talk to him, smile at him. Looking at her took his breath away and touching her small, soft hand sent shivers throughout his body. He could have stayed there with her forever, rocking back and forth, relaxing, being lazy together.

He had not really fallen asleep in his rocker on the veranda of the United States Hotel.

His eyes had been closed, but he had been wide-awake. He'd known how the duchess had frankly examined him, believing he was asleep. He had felt her warm gaze moving over his face and down his body.

Just as he had planned.

It had taken great effort to lie totally still while she inspected him, but he'd managed. It had been harder still to stay where he was when she got up and left. But he had steeled himself, hoping that letting her think he had fallen asleep would throw her slightly off kilter. Make her doubt herself a little.

She'd never know it, but as soon as she'd gotten up out of her chair, he had opened his eyes just a fraction. From beneath sheltering lashes, he had watched, pleased, as she anxiously threaded her way through the filled rockers. Never moving a muscle, he had carefully observed her conduct and could hardly contain his delight.

She was insulted and upset. It was obvious from the expression on her beautiful face. This could mean only one thing. She *was* interested in him, despite her behavior to the contrary. And that degree of interest had elevated the moment she'd thought he had fallen asleep.

She would now question her appeal. Would assume that his surprising nonchalance revealed an indifference of the kind she had shown toward him.

Hank began to grin wryly.

He knew, instinctively, that he was a step closer to seducing the beautiful Duchess of Beaumont.

When next they met, she'd be doing back flips to get his attention or his name wasn't Henry Columbus Cassidy.

"Son of a bitch!" Hank swore when he returned to his cottage that very night after another long, disappointing evening. Ripping off his black neck piece, he tossed it on an overstuffed chair. "Damn her," he muttered as shrugged out of his tuxedo jacket. "Damn *me*," he grumbled, yanking the long tails of his pleated yoke-white shirt up out of his snug trousers.

When the shirt was open down his dark chest, Hank poured himself a stiff bourbon and downed it in one long swallow. He made a face, set the empty glass down and wiped his mouth on the back of his hand. He stepped out onto the balcony overlooking the hotel's lush gardens and inhaled deeply.

From a wooden box resting on a small metal table, he took a fine Cuban cigar. He bit off the tip, stuck the cigar between his teeth, struck a match, and lit it, cupping his hand against the night breeze that made the tiny flame dance and waver.

The cigar afire, he shook out the match and dropped down into a padded chair. He lifted his feet up onto the railing and leaned back on his spine. Taking a pull on the cigar, he held the smoke in for a moment, then blew it slowly out and exhaled heavily.

Soft feminine laughter floated up from somewhere in the vast gardens below and was immediately followed by the deep laughter of a man. Snatches of conversation drifted up as couples promenaded in the moonlight or sat on benches scattered about beneath the tall sheltering trees in the manicured gardens.

It was a night for romance.

It was pleasantly warm, with a hint of a breeze stirring the leaves on the trees and a big white moon sailing high overhead among the bright stars and high scattered clouds. From the expansive, well-tended gardens, the subtle scent of roses sweetened the night air.

Alone, Hank smoked in contemplative silence, his body tense. He was edgy, restless, frustrated. His yearning for a woman he could not have was becoming an obsession.

He had figured the Duchess of Beaumont all wrong.

Apparently she hadn't given a damn that he had fallen asleep on her this afternoon. He had arrogantly supposed that her ego would be bruised and her interest therefore piqued by his lack of interest. And she would therefore come buzzing around at tonight's wine supper at the Congress Inn.

Wrong.

She hadn't given him the time of day. Not a flicker of an eyelash or a flirtatious smile or any other signal that she was aware he was alive.

Hank released a deep sigh of frustration. His blood was up. He wanted the beautiful duchess with a passion that had become distracting and troublesome. He was baffled by her continued rejection. And disgusted with himself for caring. He was acting like a smitten schoolboy and it was high time he snapped out of it.

There were plenty of beautiful women at the Springs. Caroline Whit had made it clear she'd be happy to become his lover. As had the voluptuous brunette shipping heiress, Abby Hall. Rhode Island debutante, Dawn Fleming. Pretty Cynthia Warner. And Beryl Thomas. And Linda Jackson. And the list of willing beauties went on and on.

No need to spend another night alone.

Hank ground his even white teeth. He didn't want one of the others. He wanted the cold, cruel Charmaine Beaumont. He wondered where she was this very minute. And who she was with. And what they were doing. Unwanted visions of her in the eager arms of Parker Lawson rose in his mind's eye. Hank groaned in agony.

He knew he wouldn't be able to sleep if he went inside to bed. He was far too discontent. Too restless.

That damned duchess was spoiling his stay at the Springs. And he knew in his heart that worse torture was still to come.

He was right.

For the next full week the haughty Duchess of Beaumont made his life a hell on earth. He continued going to the track each morning to watch the workouts of his Thoroughbreds, but he was distracted, not totally focused as he'd been in years past.

Other than those mornings at the track, Charmaine Beaumont was everywhere Hank went. But she would have nothing to do with him. She looked right through him as if he didn't exist. Refused to give him a tumble.

"Damn her, anyhow," he complained now to his friend, Fox Connor, as he dressed on this warm summer Saturday evening for the Vanderbilts' gala. "I can't go anywhere without her being underfoot. Does she never tire? She'll be at tonight's big shindig, I know she will."

Fox took a drink of Kentucky bourbon, smiled and said, "No law saying you have to go, is there?"

Hank stopped tying his black silk tie, frowned, then laughed at himself and admitted, "No. The truth is I'm counting the minutes until I see her again. Which is ridiculous, since she goes out of her way to ignore me."

Fox drained his glass, set it aside, and rose to his

feet. "I can understand that. I feel the same way about seeing a roulette layout. Heart beats faster. Palms grow damp. Hope springs eternal. And, like your devilish duchess, Lady Luck constantly rejects me."

Thirteen

Claire was excited.

She felt like a young girl who knew she was soon to experience the wonder of a first kiss.

All afternoon she had swept in and out of the downstairs rooms, making sure the mansion was immaculate. Ready for the nighttime visit of one very special guest. When finally she was satisfied that the dark woodwork had been polished to a high gleam and the Aubusson rugs were spotless and the fine furniture and heavy drapery totally dust free, she issued the order to have six dozen long-stemmed ivory roses delivered to the estate at exactly midnight.

Claire did not ask if having flowers delivered at midnight was possible. She had quickly learned that any request from the Duchess of Beaumont became a command which was cheerfully carried out by those who had been so ordered.

"When the roses arrive," she explained to Jenkins, the butler, "three dozen are to be artfully arranged in vases here in the drawing room. The other half are to be placed upstairs in the master suite."

"Very good, Your Grace," said Jenkins. "Will that be all?"

"The champagne will be iced and ready?" Claire asked.

"At precisely 2:00 a.m., just as ordered."

"And no later than midnight all the servants will be in their quarters and sound asleep?"

"Saving me, Your Grace," he said without the slightest change of expression. "I will retire to my quarters shortly after two. The house will be dark, save for the low-burning chandelier in the foyer. The front door will be open."

"Thank you, Jenkins," she said. "Has my bath been drawn?"

"Indeed. It awaits you, steaming hot."

"Wonderful. If you can locate Olivia, please ask that she come up in half an hour."

"I shall convey your wishes," said Jenkins. He bowed and turned away.

Claire nodded, then moved around the drawing room one last time, humming happily. She straightened a sofa pillow here and smoothed a fold in the drapery there until finally she was pleased.

Smiling, she hurried out into the black-and-white marble-floored foyer, lifted her skirts and climbed the carpeted stairs to her suite. Once inside she closed the double doors behind her, leaned back against them and sighed.

It was nearing eight o'clock in Saratoga and the summer sun was beginning to set. The all white room was now bathed in a warm golden glow and Claire was so enamored of the sunset's soft sensual radiance, she left the lamps unlit.

Unhurriedly she crossed the carpeted room and moved toward the tall double doors thrown open to the balcony. She stood just inside the room, framed in the wide doorway.

Claire smiled wickedly, and began to remove her clothes.

The disrobing became like a secret pagan ritual, with the last rays of the spectacular summer sun streaming in to dazzle and dominate. And she was baring her flesh to this god of golden radiance. In seconds Claire stood totally naked before the powerful god of light and eagerly offered herself to him. She instantly felt the heat of his all encompassing kiss on her skin. It touched and tantalized every part of her bared body.

Claire gloried in the hedonistic exercise. The

dying sun was making love to her and she was enjoying every carnal moment of it. Her nipples tightened and tingled and she instinctively thrust her breasts forward, urging him not leave her, not take his seductive heat away.

Her flat belly contracted sharply and the muscles in her bare thighs bunched and jumped involuntarily. She moved her feet apart, threw her head back, and let her arms fall to her sides. Her hands were outstretched, palms open, as if to draw him to her.

She stayed there just as she was until the fickle sun god deserted her, dropping below the horizon, leaving the gathering twilight behind. And the naked Claire aroused and impatient for the dark lover who would soon take his place.

Claire turned away.

She walked into the shadowy bath where a white porcelain tub was filled and waiting. She lit a lone white candle and set the silver holder on the floor near the tub. She stood and twisted her long hair into an untidy knot atop her head and pinned it there. She climbed into the tub, stretched out, leaned back and sighed.

Claire sang as she lathered her slender limbs and thought of Hank Cassidy, the man whose kiss could surely bring her erotic dreams alive. If all went as planned, before this night was over the alluring man of the West that looked so good in his custom-cut clothes would be out of those clothes and in her bed.

Claire shivered deliciously, then immediately lectured herself. Was she building herself up for a fall? A terrible letdown? If indeed she managed—and it seemed a near certainty—to draw Hank Cassidy here to her luxurious lair and seduce him, would he disappoint? Would he be no more exciting a lover than her husband had been? Was ecstasy something totally different for a man than it was for a woman? Was there really such a thing as ecstasy for a woman? If so, would it ever be hers?

A knock startled Claire out of her thoughts.

"I'll help you dress," announced Olivia, entering the suite. "Why is it dark as pitch in here?" Her voice sounded suspicious, concerned. "Claire, are you all right?"

"I'm fine," Claire called out. "In the tub. Be out in a minute."

Olivia went about lighting the lamps. "Better hurry. You don't want to arrive at the gala so late Hank Cassidy will have come and gone."

Claire hadn't considered such a possibility. That would spoil everything. Frowning, she shot to her feet and grabbed a large white towel. Hastily drying off, she tossed the damp towel to the floor and yanked up another. She wrapped it around herself, tucked it in over her left breast, and rushed into the bedroom.

"Can you style my hair in five minutes?" she asked.

Olivia smiled. "Can you get into your ball gown in five minutes?"

Twenty minutes later a regal Claire skipped down the mansion's front steps to the waiting carriage. On the veranda, a proud Olivia smiled, waved and watched as the carriage rolled away.

Arms crossed, she continued to stand there even after the carriage had disappeared, leaving only a faint haze of dust hanging in the thin mountain air. Claire's excitement and anticipation had rubbed off on Olivia. It had made her remember what it was like to be young and vitally alive.

Olivia's smile soon faded and she sighed.

There were times—to this very day—that she could recall every detail of that warm June night so long ago when she'd met the only man she ever loved. What a summer that had been! What happiness she had known. What lovely dreams she'd had. Until…

Olivia shook herself from her painful reveries, turned and went back inside the silent house.

Every head turned when Claire, formally presented by her beaming host, W. K. Vanderbilt, entered the crowded ballroom of the United States Hotel at shortly after 9:00 p.m.

All but one.

Glancing out over the crowd, Claire instantly recognized Hank Cassidy by the set of his shoulders, the gleam of his midnight hair, and by the fact that he was taller than the other gentlemen. Hank's back was to her. He did not turn to stare or acknowledge her as the others did.

Claire experienced a quick stab of self-doubt.

"May I have the first dance?" asked Parker Lawson, and he didn't wait for an answer.

The other couples stopped dancing and watched as a pleased Lawson spun the duchess around the polished floor. Claire's hair gleamed golden beneath the blazing chandeliers and the skirts of her sky-blue chiffon gown swirled out around her shapely ankles. Smiling, Claire raised a hand in the air and beckoned the others to again take the floor.

Amidst laughter and applause the dance floor once more became crowded. Hank Cassidy finally turned around. But he remained on the perimeter of the ballroom, arms crossed, the hint of a scowl on his handsome face.

Eyes narrowed, Hank watched the duchess sway and turn and laugh. And when the orchestra paused between tunes, she graciously stepped into the arms of a middle-aged gentleman who had eagerly cut in on Lawson.

The duchess was, as usual, stunningly beautiful. Her ivory shoulders were bare and her tight-fitting bodice pushed her full breasts up in the most enticing way. Her pale hair was elaborately dressed atop her head, but a couple of wispy golden curls had escaped their restraints to lie appealingly on her nape.

Hank had a strong impulse to blow on those wayward locks until she shivered. What he really wanted to do was take the pins from her hair and watch it spill down around her back and shoulders.

"Your charms are apparently lost on the duchess." Hank turned to see that Caroline Whit had sidled up to him. "I've watched her closely these past two weeks and I'm afraid you've little chance of being chosen." She smiled impishly.

"Chosen?" Hank made a face.

"Why, yes. Surely you know that everyone in Saratoga is whispering that the Duchess of Beaumont has yet to choose a lover." Caroline gestured to the floor. "Parker is the odds-on favorite. I wouldn't be surprised if the eagerly awaited tryst takes place tonight." She gazed up at him. "Would you?"

"I'd say it's none of my business. Or yours."

"Ah, but it is," Caroline stated emphatically. "If the duchess chooses Lawson to be her lover, that leaves you for me." She wrapped her arm around his, pressed her breast against his biceps, and whispered, "How about it, Hank. I'll please you like she never could. I'll do anything you want. Everything. Let's leave. Go around to your cottage and—"

"Mrs. Whit, won't you do me the honor? Dance with me?" It was the tubby, swarthy, mustachioed Gordon Lancaster who was worth untold millions and in the market for a wife.

"She'd love to dance with you, Mr. Lancaster," Hank answered for Caroline, disengaging her arm and handing her forward.

Cursing Hank under her breath, Caroline danced away in the short arms of a smiling, puffing Gordon Lancaster.

Crossing his arms once more, Hank exhaled with relief and again found and focused on the vision in blue across the room. The duchess was no longer dancing. Her back to him, she was talking with a quartet of ladies.

While Claire stood talking to a small group of nodding, smiling ladies, she was conscious of Hank's eyes on her from across the room. She knew he was watching her, so she laughed and tossed her head and pretended to be totally absorbed in conversation.

All at once the ladies began to fall silent.

Claire knew that Hank was crossing the dance floor, coming toward her. But she pretended ignorance and continued talking. She was in midsentence when a warm hand gently cupped her elbow and the tall, imposing Hank Cassidy, said, "Let's dance, Duchess."

He nodded to the group of ladies and commandingly drew Claire away and out onto the floor.

"You did not wait for me to accept," she scolded, looking up at Hank. "Suppose I don't wish to dance with you, Mr. Cassidy?"

"Suppose I make you want to dance with me, Duchess," he said and wrapped a long arm around her narrow waist.

"Suppose that is impossible."

"Suppose I show you that it isn't," said Hank with a devilish smile.

"Suppose I—"

"Suppose you shut up and see what happens."

"Why, I—"

"Quiet," he cautioned. He folded their enjoined hands down onto his chest and pressed his smoothly shaven jaw against her temple.

Secretly pleased, Claire pretended displeasure, refused to lift her free hand up around his neck, but instead let it fall to her side. Hank was undeterred. Confident of his dancing skills and determined to show her how it felt to be in his arms, he boldly drew her closer and began turning her slowly, seductively about on the floor.

Enchanted, Claire was vaguely aware of the speculative stares and behind-hands whispers swirling around them. And then she was aware of nothing save Hank. She quickly learned that beneath his fine clothes was a lean, hard body with the strength and power to both frighten and excite.

She learned as well that he danced divinely. His physical grace and gliding pantherlike movements made it easy to follow his lead. Together they swayed and spun and dipped as if they were one body. It was incredibly thrilling.

Claire finally lifted her free arm, moved it up over his shoulder and around his neck. He wore his hair a trifle too long, appealingly so, the lustrous locks touching the stiff white collar of his shirt. Of their own volition, Claire's fingers eagerly tunneled through the silky black hair at his nape.

Hank lowered his head slightly, put his lips near her ear, and Claire was certain he was going to say something. He was going to ask her to leave the ball with him, to tell her he wanted her and no one else.

Hank said not a word but held her intimately close. Claire almost swooned with pleasure and excitement. The masterful manner in which his body pressed insistently against her own was surely a prelude to later physical action.

Breathless now, Claire could feel Hank's heart beating heavily against her breasts and his long, steely thighs brushing hers through their clothing. Captivated, she closed her eyes and sighed. And willingly gave herself up to this man under whose masterful physical control she felt herself blossoming like an exotic flower.

Claire blinked in surprise and disappointment when abruptly the music stopped and just as abruptly her partner released her.

"Thank you, Your Grace," Hank said, before turning and walking away.

Her heart still pounding from the erotic dance, Claire stared after him in stunned disbelief. While she was weak in the knees and faint, he was walking away from her as if nothing had happened between them.

Claire's brow furrowed. And she bit the inside of her lip when Hank stopped midway across the floor and took the red-haired Caroline Whit in his arms for the next dance.

Claire frantically searched for a dancing partner. A half-dozen hopefuls stepped forward. She accepted the first to ask. For the next hour Claire danced and laughed and flirted with any number of gentlemen.

At the same time she kept a close eye on Hank Cassidy.

Hank was outside on the hotel's deserted veranda smoking alone in the summer darkness.

It was just past 11:00 p.m. and the dance was in full swing.

He couldn't believe his eyes when the elegantly gowned duchess came out of the hotel, walked directly up to him, and said softly, "It is so stuffy inside. I had to come out for a breath of fresh air."

Hank gazed appraisingly at her, lifted a tanned hand, sought the delicate golden chain resting around her neck, and slowly followed its length down to where it disappeared inside her low-cut bodice.

His fingers toying with the medallion where it rested between her full breasts, he accused, "That's not why you came out here, Duchess."

Feeling the heat of his fingers brushing her skin, Claire smiled seductively, and said, "No. No, it's not. The truth is that if you don't kiss me this very minute, I shall think you do not like me."

Fourteen

Without a word Hank flicked his cigar away over the veranda's railing, wrapped a long arm around Claire's narrow waist, drew her to him, bent his dark head, and kissed her.

It was not a polite, gentlemanly kiss. It was at once the hot, commanding kiss of a highly sexual man who knew how to quickly set a woman on fire. Exactly the kind of man Claire was looking for.

His strong, encircling arm pressing her steadily closer to his tall, hard frame, Hank's masterful mouth moved aggressively on hers. Claire's lips eagerly parted and he took full advantage, his tongue thrusting deeply, giving to her, taking from her, dazzling her.

Trembling, shocked by how easily he could so excite her, Claire made a halfhearted attempt to pull away. Hank didn't let her go. He wrapped long fingers around the back of her head to hold her still.

And the long, hot kiss continued.

Even when voices from nearby announced that party-goers were spilling out of the hotel and onto the veranda, Hank continued to kiss Claire into sweet submission. While his heated lips hardened with passion and his sleek tongue stroked hers, Hank slipped his hand down from her waist, let it glide over the curve of her hip and move lower to cup and clasp her rounded buttocks through the folds of her full chiffon skirts. He pressed her pelvis against his, letting her feel exactly what she was doing to him.

Eyes closed, flushed face turned up to his, Claire knew she had to put a stop to this incredible kiss, lest they make love right here on the hotel veranda.

She lifted weak arms and began to push on his chest. Hank finally took his lips from hers, raised his head, and gazed down at her through smoldering eyes, confident she was now his for the taking.

But his passion turned to anger and frustration when she disappointed him again.

With a stifled yawn, Claire said, "Now good night to you, Mr. Cassidy."

And she turned and walked away, leaving him looking and lusting after her.

* * *

Claire unhurriedly crossed the veranda, went down the steps, and never looked back.

When she got into the waiting carriage, she released a held breath, leaned back against the soft leather seat, closed her eyes, and smiled with pleasure. In her twenty-seven years of life she had never been kissed the way Hank Cassidy had just kissed her.

Lips that kissed like that could surely overwhelm even the most jaded of women. So it wasn't surprising that his kiss had easily conquered her. Still, she had to remember that she was not the straitlaced Claire Orwell. She was the seasoned Duchess of Beaumont. It was important that she continue to behave accordingly. Which meant that once she had Hank alone in her suite, she could not demonstrate any traces of shyness nor could she be shocked by anything he said or did.

Claire's smile turned to a slight frown of concern. It had been relatively simple, so far, to convince Hank and everyone at the Springs that she was the sophisticated, fun-loving duchess. She'd encountered no Doubting Thomases. Had detected not an ounce of suspicion from anyone. Everyone took her at her word. But would she be able to play the part convincingly in bed?

Claire blushed at the thought. She knew very little about lovemaking. Her husband had almost been as reticent about making love as she. She had never been swept away on a tide of passion so intense it had made her lose all inhibitions. Had never spent blissful moments naked in bed with a thrilling lover. Had never made love with the lights on. Had never made love in the daytime. Had never made love anywhere but in a bed.

And she had never made love in any position other than the traditional one.

Claire sighed. She had never experienced the elusive mystery of orgasm.

By the time she reached the mansion, Claire was filled with self-doubt. At the same time she was almost giddy with anticipation.

Once inside, she lifted her skirts and hurried up the stairs. She took a couple of ivory roses out of their porcelain vase and rushed back down the stairs. She went out the front door and began plucking petals from one of the roses. She dropped the first petal on the wide front steps then moved back across the veranda toward the door, dropping petals as she went.

Inside she created an easy-to-follow path of ivory petals which went directly across the black-and-white marble-floored foyer to the grand staircase. Dropping at least one petal on each carpeted step, Claire was smiling mischievously when she reached the suite.

She dropped the remaining petals directly in front of the double doors.

She went inside and straight to the spacious bath. She undressed and took yet another hot bath. When she got out of the tub and dried off, she dabbed a drop of expensive French perfume behind each ear, between her breasts and behind each knee.

Naked, Claire walked into the suite's sitting room. She took three more of the ivory roses from their vase and moved to the bed. She scattered plucked petals from two of the roses over the satin sheets and pillows. She broke off the stem of the remaining rose and pinned the fragrant blossom in her hair just above her left ear.

Killing time, waiting for what she hoped would be an exciting sexual adventure to begin, Claire walked out onto the balcony and inhaled deeply of the clean mountain air. The night was cool. But she was warm. No, not warm. Hot. She was hot for the man who would soon walk right into the suite and take her in his arms.

Or would he?

What if she'd misjudged him? Had overplayed her hand.

Half-fretful, Claire turned and went back inside. From the foot of the bed, she picked up a beautiful ivory lace nightgown. The gown she had purchased solely for this momentous occasion. She lifted it up over her head and let it slip down her body to her ankles. She couldn't resist checking herself in the freestanding mirror.

She stepped before the mirror and bit her lower lip. She might as well have stayed naked. The lace gown concealed nothing. Claire glanced at the French mother-of-pearl clock resting on the white marble mantel.

She tensed. Hank should be receiving the note right about now.

Hank couldn't sleep.

It was past two in the morning, but he was still wide-awake. And agitated. He lay in bed, arms raised and folded beneath his head, staring at the ceiling, silently cursing the cruel beauty who so delighted in torturing him.

Hank frowned and raised his head off the pillow when he heard a knock on the cottage door. He sat up, threw his long legs over the mattress's edge and rose to his feet. He yanked up a black silk robe from the foot of the bed, slipped his arms in the long sleeves and loosely tied the sash at his waist.

"Coming," he called out and walked through the darkened cottage to the door. Irritated that someone would be bothering him at this late hour, Hank opened the door and said, "What the—?"

A smartly uniformed hotel employee held out a silver tray upon which was a sealed vellum envelope. Before the puzzled Hank could respond, the messenger turned and left.

Brow furrowed, Hank closed the door, went into the sitting room and lighted a lamp. He tore the envelope open. An ivory rose petal fell out and fluttered to the floor. Hank unfolded the note and read: "I can't sleep. And I know you can't. Come to my house now before the day breaks. Let's watch the sun come up together. Follow the white rose petals until you find me. Waiting. Waiting for you. Charmaine Beaumont."

Hank laid the note on a table, bent and picked up the dropped rose petal. He held it in his palm and debated whether or not he would go.

Would he show up at her place only to find himself shut out? Did she so enjoy making a fool of him that she would be watching from inside while he pounded futilely on a locked door?

To hell with her!

Who did she think she was dealing with anyhow? Some backward schoolboy who'd never had a pretty woman? He was no puppet on a string, for god's sake! He'd had enough of her and her tiresome routine.

But even as he told himself he wouldn't go, Hank was tossing off the robe and starting to get dressed.

Less than half an hour after the missive arrived at the cottage, Hank was alighting from a hired cab in front the Duchess's secluded estate.

"Stay here," he instructed as he paid the driver. "If I'm not back in ten minutes, you're free to go."

Hank turned and stared at the darkened mansion. He could hear his heart beating in his ears when he climbed the wide steps to the veranda. Rose petals led to the front door. He crossed to the heavy door, wrapped his fingers around the brass knob and held his breath.

He gave it a twist and it turned easily.

He pushed the door open and stepped inside.

He paused in the wide, high-ceilinged foyer. Overhead a chandelier burned low, giving off diffused light. Hank looked down at the black-and-white patterned floor.

And he began to smile.

There on the marble, scattered ivory rose petals made a path directly to the grand staircase.

Hank raised his eyes to the landing above, then stepped onto the base of the stairs. Silently he followed the trail of petals to a set of white double doors at the top of the stairs. He paused there, looked down. The trail of petals stopped directly in front of those closed doors.

Fifteen

Hank didn't knock.

He opened the double doors and walked inside. He quietly closed the doors behind him. He followed the petals across the white-carpeted sitting room and up three steps into the bedroom.

And lost his breath completely.

A lone lamp burned low on a night table, the white-frosted globe muting the light. The soft illumination revealed the beautiful Duchess of Beaumont kneeling squarely in the center of a large, ivory satin-sheeted bed.

An ivory rose adorned her glorious golden hair, which was loose and spilling down around her bare shoulders. She wore an ivory lace nightgown through which he could clearly see her large satiny nipples as well as the triangle of thick golden curls between her thighs.

Never taking his eyes off her, Hank kicked off his shoes and black stockings and followed the path of petals directly to the bed. He climbed onto the mattress and knelt among the scattered rose petals facing Charmaine Beaumont.

He gazed into her eyes for several long seconds before he asked, "How many times have I seen you, Duchess?"

"I don't know," she said with a smile of puzzlement. "A dozen. Two dozen. I'm not sure."

"You get more beautiful each time," he said honestly.

"Thank you."

"You're welcome."

Still half wary, wondering what she was up to, Hank finally relaxed when the duchess said, "It's warm in here, so warm. Take off your shirt, Hank."

Hank shook his head. "No, Duchess. You want it off, you take it off."

"With pleasure," she said. She reached out, and began deftly unbuttoning his shirt.

While her nimble fingers worked their magic, Hank told her in a low, caressing voice, "All I want is to make love to you."

"I know," she said like the confident woman she was portraying. "I know you do, Hank." She pushed the open shirt, leaned forward and began brushing soft kisses to his bared chest.

Hank held his breath and looked down on that golden head bent to him. He shrugged out of the open shirt, tossed it to the floor and reached for her. Clasping her upper arms, Hank urged her head up.

"Look at me," he said.

Preoccupied, Claire was admiring the ripple of muscles in his arms and chest, the growth of dark crisp hair that covered his torso in an appealing fanlike pattern, the amazing tightness of his flat abdomen.

"I said look at me," Hank ordered and Claire slowly lifted her eyes to meet his. He told her in tones brooking no argument, "Your game playing and my patience are at an end."

"I know," she said again.

"You summoned me. I came. You know what I'm here for."

"I do, Hank."

"To make love to you and for no other reason. Do you understand me?" Claire smiled and nodded. Hank didn't return her smile. He said, "If you had something else in mind, if you figure on tormenting me and then backing out at the last minute, you're now out of luck." With that Hank raised a hand, hooked his thumb under a narrow lace strap of Claire's nightgown and tugged it off her shoulder.

"I want you to make love to me, Hank," Claire

said, and did not flinch when he pushed the gown's other strap off her shoulder. "That's why I invited you here."

The lace bodice slipped low, but caught and clung to her full breasts. Supposing that he would quickly push it down to her waist, Claire was surprised when instead he took hold of her hand, sat back on his bare heels and gazed at her from heavily lidded eyes.

"You are one desirable woman," he said, examining her. "You have no idea how much I want you."

"And I you," she assured him. "There's just one thing."

Hank frowned. "Now what?"

Claire smiled at him. "It must be understood between us that this is to be but a brief summertime affair. Nothing more. No strings attached. No recriminations when it ends."

Hank grinned. "You picked the right boy here, Duchess," he said and meant it.

Slightly taken aback, Claire tilted her head to one side. "Oh? Are you so certain then that you won't fall a little in love with me?"

"Just as sure as you are that you'll forget me the minute you leave Saratoga. We're two of kind, Duchess. We understand each other perfectly."

Hank again rose into a kneeling position and drew her up against him. At once Claire felt her nipples tighten through the covering lace of her bodice.

"Let's stop wasting precious time," Hank said, "Kiss me, Charmaine. Kiss me."

Claire nodded, put her hands to his ribs and kissed him lightly on the lips. To her surprise, Hank's response was disappointingly tepid. Nonplussed, she tried again. Nothing. She playfully licked at his lips. She ran the tip of her tongue along the seam of his closed mouth. She bit his full lower lip. She tightened her arms around his waist and kissed him more aggressively, thrusting her tongue between his teeth to touch and toy with his. She kissed him over and over again.

Finally she took her lips from his, drew back a little, and anxiously asked, "What is it? What's wrong?" Then she caught the hint of devilment shining out of his beautiful blue eyes and knew that he was dallying with her the way she'd been dallying with him. "No more games, Hank, I swear it."

"In that case…" he said, easing her arms from around his waist and placing them at her sides, he peeled the lace gown down around her waist. A hot light instantly leaping into his eyes, he focused on her creamy breasts with their soft satiny nipples. But he did not touch them. Not yet. Instead he laid his hand on the outsides of her thighs and began to urge the lacy fabric of her nightgown up.

Claire helped free the gown, raising one knee, then the other. When it was no longer caught beneath her, Hank sat her back on her heels and pushed the lace garment up past her knees, but no farther.

Claire suddenly felt very vulnerable and uncertain. She was nervous as she'd never been before. She wasn't sure what would happen next. She trembled when Hank impulsively lowered his head and kissed her right knee. Her breath grew short when his fiery lips moved slowly up her thigh, his handsome face nudging the lace out of his way as he kissed her.

Terrified that he would keep going higher and terrified that he wouldn't, Claire released a pent-up breath when he lifted his head and smiled sexily at her.

Then wordlessly, they both rose up off their heels to put their arms around each other. Looking into her shining violet eyes, Hank said, "Kiss me again, Duchess, and this time I'll help a little."

Claire nodded and eagerly pressed her lips to his. Hank immediately took over, slanting his mouth across hers, parting her lips with his tongue, making her his own. Just as it had been on the veranda of the United States Hotel, Claire found his kiss thrilling beyond belief, so powerful and so shockingly intimate it was almost like they were already completely making love.

Her eyes closed, her naked breasts flattened against the firm muscles of Hank's broad bare chest, Claire knelt there on that rose petal strewn, satin-sheeted bed kissing the most exciting man she'd ever known. It was pure heaven. The thought occurred that if the two of them never did anything more than what they were doing right now, she would be totally content.

Claire felt as if she could never get enough of Hank's fiery kisses. The mastery of his mouth inflamed her, made the blood surge through her veins, made her bare nipples tighten and ache like never before. She hoped he couldn't tell just how much his burning kisses were affecting her. Hoped he wouldn't suspect that she was an inept novice whose sleeping passions he was all too easily awakening.

Claire became aware of Hank's tanned fingers caressing her throat and sliding down to her breasts as the scorching kisses continued. She felt as if her entire body were on fire. His kisses were at once playful, teasing and demanding. His tongue delved deep, exploring the inner recesses of her mouth while she trembled and melted in his arms.

After dozens of hot, penetrating kisses, Hank finally took his lips from hers. Claire's head fell back. Hank loosened his encircling arms, letting her go. She sank back down onto her heels, half dazed. Then looked up at him, filled with passion. Seemingly pleased with her response, Hank sat back on his heels.

He spread his knees wide, reached out and put his hands to Claire's waist. He drew her forward until she was inside the V of his open thighs. He then lifted her, leaned forward and whispered shocking words against her bare warm flesh as he kissed her throat and moved slowly down toward her breasts.

Claire sighed and held her breath as Hank's lips made a slow, tantalizing descent until at last they brushed a kiss to her tight left nipple.

At the touch of his lips, Claire emitted a little gasp of pleasure and automatically thrust both breasts forward. Hank gave the stinging nipple several plucking, playful kisses, then opened his mouth upon it and circled it with his tongue, licking it into a swollen bud of tingling sensation. Claire breathed shallowly and put her hands into his thick raven hair. She anxiously held him to her and laid her hot cheek atop his dark head.

Hank bit harmlessly at the rigid nipple, raked his teeth back and forth across it and gently pulled at it. Claire whimpered softly. Then he began sucking it until the nipple was swollen and erect and Claire's eyes were closing with rising ecstasy. She murmured his name and kissed his silky raven hair.

Hank moved across her chest to the other waiting breast. When he'd kissed and suckled it for several long seconds, he finally released the pebble-hard nipple. Claire took her lips from his disheveled hair and sank weakly back onto her heels.

Hank raised his head and looked at Charmaine. Never had he seen a more beautiful woman than this one. She sat there with the bodice of her lace gown down around her hips, her pale, perfect breasts bare, the nipples taut and gleaming wet from his kisses. Her golden hair was loose and spilling down around her shoulders, the white rose still stuck into the lustrous locks just above her ear.

Her eyes were shining with unmasked desire, yet there was, amazingly, a look of girlish shyness about her. Tremendously appealing. It made him want to take her in his arms and touch her tenderly and teach her patiently as though she were an innocent.

"Stay there just as you are, Charmaine," Hank instructed and with a fluid grace that caused Claire to blink in bafflement, he swiftly moved around her. The next thing she knew, he was kneeling behind her, drawing her back against him. After wrapping a strong forearm wrapped around her waist, Hank began kissing the side of her throat and the curve of her neck and shoulder.

Claire closed her eyes when his encircling arm loosened and his tanned hand spread on her flat stomach and slipped beneath the lace where it was bunched around her hips. She felt those fiery fingers on her bare belly, stroking gently, moving lower.

Claire sighed deeply, lifted an arm up and hooked it behind Hank's head. Her stomach was contracting sharply from the thrilling touch of his lean fingers.

Her heart was throbbing in her naked breasts. Her entire body was tensed. Waiting. Yearning.

The slow, sure descent of Hank's hand continued. Beneath the cover of lace, he gently stroked and caressed her quivering belly. And when he reached that triangle of golden curls between her thighs, he raked through the springy coils and possessively cupped her, his hand gently closing over her.

"Mine, for tonight," he said huskily. "Tell me this is mine."

"Yours, Hank. All yours," she said on a sigh.

He clasped her a little more firmly, his cupping hand lifting her a little, pressing her buttocks more firmly back against his pelvis. Hank kissed her temple and with gentle fingers spread the golden curls protecting that ultrasensitive feminine flesh between her open thighs.

"Ahhh," Claire sighed when his long middle finger lightly touched that tiny nubbin of flesh, swollen with desire, aching for his caress. "Hank, oh Hank."

With his middle and fore fingers, Hank began to slowly, gently circle that pulsing button of flesh, arousing Claire so carefully, so expertly she experienced an odd mixture of contentment and anxiety. She loved what he was doing to her. Loved the way she felt with his hand moving so coaxingly on her and the erotic sight of those lean dark fingers moving beneath the covering white lace. She hoped he would keep his hand there just where it was, that he would keep her at the thrilling level of ecstasy she was now enjoying.

At the same time she felt increasingly anxious, as if something were about to happen to her body over which she had no control. Something intense and frightening and foreign.

Hank was fully attuned to Charmaine's ever changing feelings. Keenly aware of her rapidly escalating state of arousal. She was so incredibly hot and excited it was surprising. It was as if this very passionate woman had been without a lover for a long time. That couldn't be, of course. But that's how her body was behaving.

Hank smiled with satisfaction. It was going to be one wild night.

Whispering encouragement, Hank continued to give the duchess what she wanted. It was—for now—too late to take his hand away, get undressed, press her down onto her back and bury himself deep inside her. He and his aching erection would just have to wait.

"Hank, Hank, Hank." Claire murmured his name in a breathless litany.

Hank continued to fondle and caress that most feminine part of her which was so distended, so fully aroused it was a throbbing point of pure sensation.

Hank coaxed a silky wetness from her and spread it from its source over the spot where she was burning. And while he caressed her, he whispered to her in a low, soothing voice, told her how he longed to keep her like this for as long as she'd let him.

"An hour. A night. Forever, darlin'," he said softly.

"Forever," she echoed.

On fire, more excited than she'd imagined possible, Claire squirmed and sighed and grew ever hotter as Hank's masterful hand pleasured her.

Feeling feverish and half-frightened, Claire again looked down and saw—partially concealed beneath the lace of her nightgown—that beautiful artistic hand moving between her open thighs. The sight of his lean brown fingers so expertly toying with her burning flesh was incredibly erotic.

Too erotic.

"Oh, oh, oh…" she began to pant and her eyes grew wide with fear and wonder. She felt as if she was going to actually explode, shatter into a million pieces and rain down all over the bed.

Hank kept her anchored with a forearm around her waist while his sex-wet fingers continued to caress and coax the coming orgasm from her. Within seconds the wrenching climax began and Claire cried out in ecstasy.

"Don't! Stop! Don't…don't ever stop!" she

pleaded almost tearfully, feeling as if she would surely die if he took his magical hand from her.

"Never, baby, never," Hank soothed and continued to gently stroke her until her wild elation reached that fearsome crescendo and she splintered in sweet eruption.

As boneless as a rag doll, Claire sank back against Hank's supporting chest, her breath coming fast, her hair in her eyes, her heart pounding. Throat dust-dry, body glistening with perspiration, Claire was struck with an overwhelming desire to laugh merrily because she was so incredibly happy.

She remained silent.

She didn't dare let Hank Cassidy know that she had just experienced her first sexual climax.

Sixteen

Claire wasn't sure when or how it happened, but as she came out of her lovely stupor, she realized that Hank was seated on the edge of the mattress with his feet on the floor and she was sitting on his lap. Her lace nightgown was missing. Where could it have gone? She had no idea. She was as completely naked while Hank, though bare chested, still wore his dark trousers. His arm was wrapped around her waist and his hand was draped across her knees.

"It's too warm in here," he said.

"Is it?"

"Let's go out onto the balcony and cool off."

Claire nodded happily. "Yes, let's. The balcony is totally private. We can't be seen out there."

Hank grinned. "You checked it out, anticipating this momentous occasion?"

"I did," Claire admitted, lifting a hand and touching his bottom lip with her fingertips. "From the first moment I saw you, my fondest fantasy has been to have you make love to me on this balcony in the moonlight."

"Duchess, it's about to happen," he said and rose to his feet with her in his arms. As he crossed to the open double doors, Hank told her, "I first saw you the day you arrived at the Springs. You were getting off the train at the depot. Your hair was shining like spun gold in the sunlight and I wanted you then and there."

Claire laughed and said, "I first saw you later that day. You were getting out of a carriage in front of the cottages of the United States Hotel. I stopped and stared. And I wanted you for my lover."

"I wish I'd known. You should have called out to me. We would have made love that very afternoon."

"I'm glad we didn't. The waiting has made this night a special one. Admit it, you want me more now than you did that first day."

Hank shrugged bare shoulders. "I wanted you then, I want you now." He carried Claire across the room and out onto the moon-silvered balcony. He went directly to the wide railing, turned about, leaned back against it, and kissed Claire. As they kissed, he slowly lowered her to her bare feet.

For several long seconds the pair stood there kissing in the moonlight while the night breeze rustled the leaves on the trees in the garden below and cooled their pressing bodies.

At once the kiss became abandoned, ravenous. Hank's hands moved eagerly over Claire's body. He clasped the twin cheeks of her bottom and pressed her into his pelvis.

Claire could feel his awesome erection straining the confines of his tight trousers. She provocatively rubbed herself against him and felt him surge and seek her warmth. At last she tore her lips from his, raised up on tiptoe, and whispered in his ear, "You going to leave those trousers on all night?"

She pulled back a little and, looking into his flashing eyes, put her hands between their bodies and unbuckled his belt.

Hank made no offer to help. He stood perfectly still, arms at his sides, while she unbuttoned his trousers. Once the pants were undone, Claire put her hands into the waistband at the sides. She waited for a heartbeat, then shoved the trousers down over his flat belly and slim hips, releasing him. He sprang free and Claire stared in awe as the trousers whispered down his long, leanly muscled legs and came to rest around his bare feet. Hank stepped out of them and kicked them aside.

He drew Claire back into his arms and held her.

Claire gasped at the feel of him, hot and naked against her. His rock-hard erection was pulsing against her bare belly, its insistence stirring incredible sensations in her responsive flesh. At once there were circles of fire around her breasts and a strong ache was starting between her thighs.

Hank slowly lowered his head and kissed her.

Her arms looped around his neck, Claire stood naked in the moonlight, weak and willing, with this magnificent man whose lovemaking was ten times more thrilling than any fantasy.

Claire blinked when finally Hank's lips left hers. His hands lifted, framed her face and he gazed at her, his eyes glowing like an animal's in the darkness. Those gleaming eyes mesmerized, hypnotized and she trembled against him, feeling their power, struggling to resist being too easily conquered by him.

"Touch me, Charmaine," Hank coaxed, his voice low, persuasive, and he set her back from him.

He dropped his arms to his sides again and waited. Claire didn't hesitate. She immediately began an intimate exploration of his tall, lean body, her hands moving over his muscled chest and down to his trim waist.

Determined to act like the libertine he thought her to be, she found it to be amazingly natural. This ruggedly handsome man had her behaving like a wanton whose only desire was to have his fiercely masculine body possess hers.

Claire slid her hands back up Hank's chest and

placed her warm palms directly over his flat brown nipples. She kept her hands spread upon him for several seconds, relishing the feel of the firm muscle, the smooth warmth of his skin. She moved her hands aside, leaned forward, put out the tip of her tongue, and licked him.

She felt his body tense.

She lifted her head, looked up at him, lowered her hand, and circled his navel with her forefinger. Then she traced the line of thick raven hair leading down his flat brown belly, purposely allowing the back of her hand to brush his bobbing erection.

Hank waited with baited breath, then exhaled anxiously when finally she wrapped slender fingers loosely around him.

Claire thrilled to the size and the heat of all that male power enclosed in her hand. It was now in her possession, hers to do with as she pleased. The thought struck her that she was not the weaker sex at this moment in time. She was the dominant one. She had total control over this big, strong man. She felt giddy with delight.

She said impishly, "You're throbbing in my hand, Hank."

"I know," he replied, hardly daring to breathe.

"I can lead you anywhere by your—"

"Yes," he groaned. "Do it. Lead me. Take me where you want me."

"Come this way," she said softly and, never releasing her hold on him, slowly, carefully walked backward until they reached the padded chaise longue. Claire asked him sweetly, "Will you make love to me here in the moonlight?"

"I won't be able to if you don't let go of me."

Claire smiled, pleased, and released him.

Hank immediately threw a leg over and sat down astride the comfortable chaise longue. He looked up at her. "Join me?"

Claire took a deep breath and sat down astride the chaise facing him. Hank reached out, took her chin in his hand, leaned forward, and kissed her. His mouth hungrily plundering hers, he drew her closer. Claire put her arms around his neck, arched her back, and brushed her breasts against his chest.

Their lips separated.

Hank put his hands beneath her knees, lifted her legs and draped her thighs over his. And drew her closer still.

Determined to conceal her sexual ignorance, Claire was flippant, saying, "There's only one thing between us, Hank."

"Which is?" he asked, brow furrowing.

She lifted her hand, licked her fingers until they were wet, and rubbed them over the smooth, hot tip of his thrusting masculinity.

"This," she said, toying with him. "I don't want it

to come between us, Hank." She licked her lips and added, "I want it to come inside me."

Hank anxiously brushed her hand away, lifted her and watched as she carefully guided the gleaming tip up into her. When it was just inside, she released her hold on him and put her hands atop his shoulders.

Hank stayed completely still while Claire cautiously impaled herself on him. Slowly, seductively she sank down onto his erection.

Blinded by the passion the duchess had so easily evoked in him, Hank felt her soft, wet warmth sliding sensuously down over him like liquid fire. He had to bite the inside of his jaw to keep from instantly exploding in her.

"You all right, sweetheart?" he finally asked when she'd settled herself upon him.

"Have you any idea how good you feel to me, Hank?" was her breathless reply.

"Ah, baby, you feel twice that good to me."

"Mmmmm. Love me, Hank. Love me well."

Leaning forward to capture a soft, warm breast in his mouth, Hank clasped her thighs and began the slow, rolling upward movement of his pelvis. Claire gasped at the initial thrust, then quickly found his rhythm and rode him with an expertise born of animal passion. She met each forceful driving lunge with her squeezing, gripping heat. She held nothing back; gave herself up to raging desire and abandoned carnal pleasure.

Her feverish body was completely open to his thorough invasion as he plunged all the way up inside her, stretching her, filling her, making her his own.

His mouth at her breast was greedy, intent. He suckled the diamond-hard nipple hungrily while Claire sighed and moaned and gripped his shoulders so hard, her nails cut into the flesh. She threw her head back and looked up at the moon shining down on them, silvering their enjoined bodies, exposing them with a heavenly radiance.

Claire imagined what the man in the moon could see as he shone down on them. An unashamed pair of wild, naked lovers coming together in the most unconventional way. In her mind's eye flashed the erotic image of the lunar view: Hank naked astride the chaise and she straddling him, the darkness of his skin and raven hair contrasting sharply with her pale flesh and light hair.

A beautiful, thrilling vision.

Wave after wave of incredible pleasure washed over Claire and she rode the rising tide of ecstasy like a woman possessed.

"Oh, Hank, Hank," she murmured, clasping Hank's head to her breast, bucking against him, feeling that frightening, joyous sensation beginning somewhere deep inside.

Hank's mouth released her nipple. She loosened her arms and he raised his head.

"I want," he said, pushing her tangled hair back, "to watch your beautiful face while you come."

Her eyes widening, she nodded, licked her dry lips, gripped his rigid biceps, and began to lose control. Hank held her and speeded his movements, his pelvis rising to meet the frantic slapping and grinding of her bare bottom.

"Oh, oh, oh," she murmured excitedly and he gave her all he had.

When she began to cry out, Hank wrapped a hand around the back of her neck, drew her face down to his and quickly covered her mouth with his own. While he swallowed up her shrieks of ecstasy, he joined her in paradise. He groaned into her mouth as he gushed up into her, the fierce pumping leaving him drained and weak.

Claire tore her lips from his, hugged his dark head to her, and sagged weakly against him. For several minutes they stayed as they were, arms around each other, bodies still joined, hearts racing, breaths short.

It was Claire who stirred first. She eased herself up, sighed contentedly, and smiled at Hank.

"How would you like me to draw you a nice, hot bath?"

He grinned. "How would you like to join me in that nice, hot bath?"

"I thought you'd never ask."

Both laughed as they rose and rushed inside.

After a long, leisurely soak in the suds-filled tub, the lovers stretched out on the satin-sheeted bed. They talked and laughed and played. And when dawn approached, they made love again. This time it was a lazy, unhurried coupling with Claire propped up against the pillows and lying on her back and Hank between her parted legs in the comfort of the big bed.

They even paused momentarily and watched the summer sun rise, since that was what Claire's note had invited him there for.

"Good morning, Duchess," Hank said and kissed her.

"Make it a better morning, Hank," she said and wrapped her silken legs around his back.

Seventeen

"Must you go?"

"I really must, sweetheart."

Claire sighed as she lounged naked against the stacked pillows. Despite her attitude of languid repose, she had the strongest impulse to pull the sheet up and modestly cover herself. But she didn't do it. She assumed that the Duchess of Beaumont would think nothing of lying about nude. And she was, for the time being, the duchess.

Claire stretched lazily and feigned relaxed nonchalance as she watched Hank dress. The sun had barely risen, but he explained that he was expected at the racetrack for the early morning workouts of his Thoroughbreds.

"You'll hurry back," she said.

Hank turned to look her and Claire felt butterflies take wing inside.

Lord he was exquisite.

Breathtakingly handsome. His face a study in male perfection. Strong, but beautiful. His sky-blue eyes were shadowed, predatory, fearless, but the mouth was soft, sensual, with an irresistibly provocative curve.

His body was as exquisite as his face. Tall, lean and dark. Broad, sculptured shoulders. Wide, deep chest. Slim hips, tight belly and tighter buttocks. Steely muscled thighs and long lean legs. A powerful, finely honed body.

And blessed with grace as well as strength. A lithe coordination of flesh and bone and muscle which was very, very attractive.

Earthy, sensual, passionate, he oozed sexuality. Just looking at him made Claire's pulse race.

"Is there a gauntlet to be run?" Hank asked, pulling her out of her reverie.

"I beg your pardon?"

"How many servants am I going to encounter on my way out of here?"

"It's dawn, Hank. No one is up." Claire got out of bed, went into the dressing room, and found a white silk robe. She slipped her arms in the sleeves, but did not tie the sash. She came back into the bedroom. "I'll see you out."

"Not necessary, Charmaine." Hank stepped close, took hold of her robe's silk lapels, ran his thumbs up and down the slippery fabric and told her, "I'll be back in a couple of hours. You get some rest."

Claire nodded, put her arms around his neck, stood on tiptoe and started to kiss him.

"No, don't do that," Hank warned, turning his head slightly, even as he slipped his hands inside her open robe. "If you kiss me I will never leave." He grinned, gave her bare bottom a harmless swat and released her.

Claire followed him from the bedroom into the sitting room and to the suite's double doors. There he turned and said, "Let's have breakfast together later this morning."

"Yes." Claire liked the idea. "But not here. Let's go to the finest hotel dining room in all Saratoga."

"In my opinion that would be the United States Hotel, Duchess."

"Then that is where we'll have breakfast."

"You realize, don't you, that the minute we're seen together—"

"Everyone will talk," she interrupted him. "Yes. They'll take it for granted that we're having an affair."

"You don't mind?"

Claire laughed merrily. "Dear, dear Hank. Surely you've heard the scandalous tales that follow me wherever I go." She toyed with a button on his shirt.

"My romantic liaisons—both real and imagined—have been fodder for the gossip mill for years now." Again she laughed. "Besides, I want it made clear to the ladies at the Springs that you have your hands full with me. They'll have to look elsewhere for male companionship."

"I like you, Duchess," Hank said with a devilish grin. "No pretense for you. You see what you want and reach out and take it. I do that myself." He paused. "That doesn't make us bad people, does it?"

"Most certainly not."

Hank put a hand inside Claire's open robe and caressed her breast. "We're two of a kind, you and I." He ran his thumb back and forth over her tightening nipple. "We want each other physically. Elemental sexual hunger and that's all. Nothing more, nothing less. We're of like minds on that score." He grinned as he added, "Or should I say like bodies."

"Mmm. Isn't it marvelous? No emotional attachments. No recriminations. No regrets. Just two healthy, hot-blooded people coming together for a few carefree summer nights of amour at a lovely mountain resort."

"I don't think I'll go to the track this morning," Hank said, his hand sliding down to her hip.

Again Claire laughed. "You silly boy, of course you must go." She pushed his hand away and drew her robe together. "Go watch your creatures run and be back here by ten sharp. I'll be dressed and waiting."

"I'd rather you be undressed and waiting."

"When we get back from breakfast, you can undress me at your leisure and we'll spend the long afternoon in bed. How does that sound?"

He brushed a kiss to her lips. "Like the best offer I've had all morning."

And with that the Silver King opened the door and was gone.

Claire closed the door behind him, sighed and returned to the bedroom humming happily.

It was incredibly thrilling to make love to the handsome, sun-bronzed Nevadan. And gloriously liberating to be the pleasure-loving noblewoman who went uncensured for her sexual escapades.

Claire doubted the duchess had ever made love to a man as physically beautiful as Hank Cassidy. And, oh, the things he had done to her. Such amazing pleasure! Claire blushed at the recollection.

Throughout the night of heated lovemaking she had pretended that she was not shocked by or reluctant to engage in wanton sexual behavior the kind of which—until now—she had been totally ignorant. After all, she was not Claire Orwell. She was the Duchess of Beaumont. Expected to take lovers. And to know what to do to excite and satisfy those lovers.

Claire sank down onto the love-rumpled bed, fell over backward across it, brushed a couple of wilted rose petals to the floor and flung her arms above her head. She exhaled slowly, stretched and smiled mischievously. She liked being the wayward duchess. She looked forward to the golden days—and nights—ahead. She could do just as she pleased, when she pleased, with whom she pleased. And the "with whom" was the gorgeous Nevadan.

She would cram a lifetime of pleasure into these fleeting days of summer. And when it was over, when the real duchess was to arrive, she and Olivia would silently slip away like two thieves in the night. She would leave Saratoga and the Silver King without a backward look or moment of regret.

Wasn't that how the very rich lived their lives?

One of the great activities of the day in Saratoga was a late breakfast at the United States Hotel. The event was a tremendous undertaking. The enormous saloon—actually four saloons at right angles to each other—could accommodate up to six hundred guests at one time.

Those hundreds of guests were waited on by one hundred and fifty waiters commanded by the consistently gracious maître d' hôtel.

The operation of finding proper places for the picky multitude was no trifling task. Once the guests were seated, waiters, dressed in spotless white jackets, extended their hands over silver domed covers and, at a signal from the chef stationed in the center of the saloons, removed them simultaneously.

Then came a great clatter of knives, plates and forks and spirited conversation. And waiters rushing hither and yon, bearing plates dexterously on their arms, marching to the appointed places. Then with their eyes on their commander-in-chief, they held the dish over the table, and set it down at the first signal. With another clap of hands from the commander a second dish descended. And finally at the third signal the tables were covered.

The entire exercise was immensely entertaining.

This drama that was breakfast at the grand hotel was well underway when, at twenty minutes past ten, the Duchess of Beaumont and the Silver King paused in the arched doorway of the crowded dining saloon.

Their presence was immediately noticed by people seated nearest the entrance. Those observant few stopped eating and stared. The domino effect quickly took effect as more and more breakfasters turned to see what the others were staring at. Soon the buzz of idle table conversation came to a halt. The clatter of silverware against china dishes ceased. The huge dining hall fell eerily silent.

Bowing and smiling, the slender, mustachioed maître d' stepped forward to greet Claire and Hank. He led the handsome pair through the filled tables to a choice spot at the very back of the room where the tall glass windows looked out on the verdant gardens.

The silence passed.

Everyone was now whispering and there was but one topic of conversation. The unexpected presence of the Duchess of Beaumont on the arm of Hank Cassidy.

Claire knew that this was to be an important outing, so she had dressed accordingly. Her hair was carefully arranged in a neat double row of plaits at her nape and atop her head was a saucy white straw hat banded with a wide navy grosgrain ribbon. She wore a stylish afternoon dress of navy-and-white striped poplin with frilly white collar and cuffs. On her small hands were snowy-white kid gloves. Expensive gloves imported from Paris. The gloves that Hank had caught her admiring in one of the hotel shops and bought for her.

Claire's fragile face looked as clean and scrubbed as a child's, save for the pale-pink rouge appealingly staining her full lips. Her violet eyes were aglow with good health and happiness. She was girlishly slender, her pale skin flawless, her taste impeccable.

A beautiful woman with presence.

The tall, dark man with her had no less a commanding presence.

On this perfect July morning Hank Cassidy looked exceptionally handsome. He wore a finely tailored suit of crisp white linen, a shirt of pale blue Egyptian cotton, and a neck piece of maroon silk. Bareheaded, his raven hair was neatly brushed and his tanned face was smoothly shaven. In his hand was a panama hat and on his feet were soft Italian leather shoes.

The radiant pair looked as guileless and innocent as a couple of naive children.

But everyone in that crowded dining hall, gentlemen and ladies alike, knew that nothing could have been further from the truth. It was at once a foregone conclusion that the lucky Silver King had successfully seduced the beautiful Duchess of Beaumont.

Or vice versa.

The gentlemen smiled and nodded and secretly envied Hank Cassidy his good fortune. The ladies were just as aware that the flirtatious standoff between Charmaine Beaumont and Hank Cassidy had come to a thrilling end. None were particularly shocked or surprised.

The majority of the married ladies exhibited no scorn or censure. Truth to tell they were delighted to have an exciting new topic of gossip. But the unmarried women were sorely disappointed that the brash duchess had snagged the most eligible bachelor at the Springs.

No sooner had the dazzling pair taken their seats than a smiling white-jacketed waiter appeared.

"I'm famished, are you?" Hank asked Claire.

"Starving," the duchess replied, eyes sparkling. "Let's order everything on the menu."

"Consider it done." Hank nodded to the waiter. "And a bottle of your finest champagne."

Minutes later a tempting array of hot and cold dishes graced the damask-draped table. Strong black coffee. Freshly squeezed orange juice. Ripe red strawberries. Heavy cream for dipping. Assorted sweet pastries, piping hot. Honey cured ham and crisp thick bacon and huge sausage patties. Soft scrambled eggs and cheese-filled omelets and eggs over easy. Dry toast and buttermilk biscuits and fluffy pancakes. Creamery butter and maple syrup and assorted jellies and jams.

And chilled champagne in tall crystal flutes.

Claire and Hank looked at each other and smiled.

"Shall I propose a toast?" Hank asked.

"By all means," Claire said.

He leaned halfway across the table and spoke in a low, soft voice so others couldn't hear. Claire heard every shocking word. And she blushed to the roots of her pale hair. Hank winked, clinked his glass to hers, and they drank.

Then the pair picked up their silverware and, with great appetite, eagerly began sampling a taste of this, a bite of that. Laughing and enjoying themselves, they had eyes only for each other. They made no effort to hide their fascination with each other, blithely ignoring the curious stares directed at them. They were oblivious to the whispers swirling about them.

And less than half an hour after walking into the dining room, Hank tossed his napkin down on the table. "Let's get out of here."

Claire nodded. Hank pushed his chair back, rose to his feet, and came around to help her up.

"Back to the estate?" she asked.

"Let's detour around to the cottages and spend a nice quiet afternoon there."

Eighteen

Hank ushered Claire up the steps to the private entrance of his cottage. Neither looked around or paid any attention to who might be watching. They didn't care who saw them.

Once inside Claire walked through the entrance hall and stepped into the spacious sitting room. Hank shrugged out of his suit coat, tossed it over the back of a chair and took off his tie.

Claire glanced curiously around. She fleetingly admired the handsome carved black-walnut furniture, the heavily flowered carpets, and the Brussels lace curtains over the tall windows.

She immediately crossed to the bedroom.

Dominating the room was a large square bed with a soaring black-walnut headboard. A counterpane of dark navy velvet covered the bed and a half-dozen big, silver-gray silk-covered pillows rested against the tall headboard. Across the room was an imposing black marble fireplace with a couple of easy chairs pulled up close.

Against the back wall were a black-walnut armoire and a tall, many drawered bureau. Directly opposite, at the room's front, a set of black-walnut doors stood open. But the gauzy transparent curtains had not been drawn. The diaphanous drapes were blowing outward in the breeze.

And, directly across from the bed was a large freestanding mirror.

Claire felt her face flush with heat.

She went back into the sitting room and smiled at Hank when he reached out and plucked the straw hat from her head.

"Excuse me for a minute, Duchess. I'll go turn the bed down," he said with a wicked grin and she nodded.

Continuing to explore, Claire took off her new gloves and laid them aside. She frowned when she saw a handsome, leather-bound book resting on a small end table. She picked the book up. Her eyes widened. A first edition of Anthony Hope's popular *The Prisoner of Zenda*.

She had, alone in P. Durkee and Sons Stationers and Books on her first day in Saratoga, admired this very book, wishing she could own it. Now Claire carefully opened the beautiful book and found just inside a handwritten message on blue vellum note-paper: "If you're reading this, you'd better be the duchess, because I bought the book for you. Hank."

Claire smiled with pleasure. She pressed the open book to her chest and called to him. "How did you know I wanted this particular book?"

From in the other room she heard, "What book?"

"You know very well what book. *The Prisoner of Zenda.*"

"I'm a mind reader."

"Were you following me that day?"

No reply.

Claire laughed and, continuing to hold the book close to her heart, crossed to a set of open double doors. She stepped out onto the private veranda and was instantly enchanted. The small terrace over-looked the hotel's huge, beautifully landscaped park. All manner of exotic blooming flowers and lush manicured greenery perfumed the air and were pleas-ing to the eye. Big arching elms spread their shading foliage over a white octagon-shaped bandstand that stood in the center of the park.

Soon Hank came up behind Claire and slipped his arms around her waist. She leaned back against him and sighed.

Nodding to the white bandstand, she asked, "Will a band play there today?"

"Five bands play there daily," Hank told her. "At precisely 11:30 a.m. the second of the five concerts begins."

"It's almost eleven-thirty, isn't it?"

"It is. By the time I get you undressed, the band should be playing."

Claire smiled and teased, "I thought I might spend the afternoon reading my book."

Hank took the book from her. "No, you didn't."

She turned about and smiled at him. "Shall we leave the sitting room doors open to the veranda so we can hear them serenade us?"

"Sure," Hank said, adding, "If you want to make love to a rousing John Philip Sousa march."

Claire laughed gaily. "Who knows? It might be inspiring."

Hank laid the book down on a small metal table, gently clasped her upper arms and looked into her eyes. "I need no inspiration. I want you more than you could ever know. I can't get enough of you."

"I know," she coolly replied. Then lowered her lashes flirtatiously and added, "You promised to undress me."

"I did and I will."

"And I need not lift a finger to help?"

"The privilege is all mine," he said, taking her hand and leading her inside.

When he released her, Claire made a move toward

the bedroom. Hank stopped her. "Let's stay here for a while."

Claire couldn't keep from frowning. "We're to undress in the sitting room with the veranda doors wide open?"

"Why not? The only place we could be seen is from the veranda and it's private. No one can be on it but the two of us."

"It seems a bit bizarre for us to…to…" Her words trailed away as she watched Hank shove a high-backed leather wing chair into place facing the open double doors.

Claire blinked in surprise when he sat down in the chair. His summer-blue eyes gleaming, he looked up at her and said, "Come here." Claire moved closer. "Make yourself at home right here on my knee," he said and reached for her.

Claire drew a shallow breath and sat down on his left knee.

"You're certain no one can see us?"

"Positive. Trust me. Relax." She nodded. "Now, first things first," Hank said, taking the pins from her hair, upbraiding the twin plaits. When he was finished, when her hair had fallen in shiny golden locks around her face and shoulders, he said, "Before this afternoon is over, I want to feel all this glorious golden hair spilling across my chest."

He slipped a hand under her hair and wrapped

it around the back of her neck. He drew her face down to his and kissed her, his tongue parting her lips and delving between her teeth. Claire sighed as his mouth urgently explored hers, tasting and teasing.

At the same time he was unfastening her dress. When the long, drugging kiss finally ended, Claire was half-surprised to find that her dress was completely undone.

She remained totally docile as Hank deftly urged the dress off her shoulders and down her arms to her waist. He leaned up and brushed a kiss to her right nipple through the covering satin of her lace-trimmed chemise.

At that moment the band outside struck up the rousing *Washington Post March*. Hank raised his head and laughed. Claire laughed with him. The concert continued throughout Claire's disrobing. But not all the tunes were marches. Interspersed were some sweetly romantic ballads that were the perfect counterpoint to this thrilling prelude to lovemaking.

Hank continued to leisurely, lovingly undress her, no matter the tempo of the music. His was a slow, sure hand and Claire was soon breathless as he dexterously disrobed her.

When at last she was totally naked, when all her clothes lay in a colorful heap on the carpeted floor, she laid back in his arms and sighed softly. Then she purred and squirmed as Hank began to make sweet, tender love to her.

Her head fell back on his supporting arm and she anxiously arched her back when his mouth slipped over her chin and to the hollow of her throat. His lips followed the descent of the delicate gold chain around her neck. His mouth opened over the medallion where it rested warmly between her bare breasts. Claire trembled in anticipation of his hot lips enclosing an aching nipple.

But to her surprise, he ignored her breasts. His strong arms lifting her up, he kissed a hot, wet path down the center of her chest. When his tongue circled her naval, Claire felt a great infusion of heat surge through her body. And when he brushed a kiss to her silken belly, Claire grabbed a handful of his hair.

Hank lifted his head and gazed at her through passion-clouded eyes. He said huskily, "You want to make love to me?"

"Yes," she whispered. "Oh, yes."

"Then you'll have to undress me."

"Gladly."

"Think you can get my clothes off while I continue to sit here?"

Claire smiled, tightened her grip on his lustrous hair, urged his head back, and kissed him hotly. Her lips against his, she said, "I know I can."

And then began to prove it.

* * *

The duchess scrambled up off Hank's lap and knelt before him. She took off his fine Italian leather shoes and stockings, then rose to her feet and slid down astride his lap. She began unbuttoning his shirt. Bottom lip caught between her teeth, she tugged and pulled while Hank laughed and teased her.

Enjoying himself, finding it tremendously arousing to have this beautiful naked woman crawling all over him, Hank was almost sorry the game was over when finally she managed to get the last of his clothes off.

The duchess exhaled heavily as she tossed his trousers aside. She was on her knees between his legs. She gave him a triumphant look, leaned up to him and put her arms around his waist.

"I told you I could do it," she whispered and pressed her cheek against the firm muscles of his chest.

Hank cupped the back of her head and said, "I never doubted you for a minute, Duchess."

For a long, enjoyable moment they stayed as they were, Hank seated in the chair, Claire kneeling between his legs, head on his chest, the crisp black chest hair pleasantly tickling her nose and mouth.

The band began to play "A Bicycle Built for Two." Hank eased Claire's head up, kissed her and urged her to her feet. He rose, lifted her up into his arms and carried her into the bedroom. Claire instantly noticed that the heavy velvet counterpane had been stripped from the bed as had the top sheet and all the silk-covered pillows. The discarded bedding was stacked on the chairs before the fireplace.

Hank lowered her down onto the bed and stretched out beside her. His weight supported on an elbow, he leaned over her and kissed the corner of her mouth. "You're beautiful," he said. "So beautiful I want to watch you make love to me." As he spoke, his hand moved down her body, touching, caressing, exciting. His fingertips circling her naval, he said, "I want to see you—every naked inch of you—when I enter you. I want to watch us make love until we both climax and are totally sated. But only if you want that, too."

Dazed, on fire, eager to do anything and everything with this man who evoked such wild passion in her, Claire murmured, "The mirror?"

"Yes, sweetheart, the mirror."

"All right." She boldly gave her permission.

And then with that swift fluid grace that was so much a part of him, Hank had Claire up facing the mirror, kneeling in the center of the bed while he knelt behind her. At his coaxing Claire raised her arms and clasped her wrists behind his head. He nudged her knees apart and moved his between. His jaw resting against her temple, he put his hands on her hips and drew her back against him. Claire felt his heavy erection throbbing against the crevice of her bare bottom.

Their eyes met in the mirror and held.

Hank began to slowly, seductively arouse the duchess to a fever pitch while they watched themselves in the mirror. For Hank it was incredibly erotic to see their reflections. Hers was an exquisite body, the breasts firm and high, the satin nipples now peaked into luscious points of temptation. Her waist was small and her hips flared with just the right curvature. Her belly was girlishly flat and between her pale thighs, the triangle of crisp curls shone like spun gold, concealing the treasure he sought.

Hank's hand gently raked through those coils to touch and tease that tiny button of slick female flesh which was the key to all her wild desire. Both watched as his hand slipped farther between her legs and he dipped his fingers into the silky moisture flowing freely from her.

When his fingers were shiny wet, he spread that moisture upward and rubbed it all over and around that swollen button of pure sensation.

When he had her so hot she was on the verge of climax, Hank took his hand from her and gently urged her over onto all fours. At her stage of high arousal, it seemed perfectly natural to Claire.

Claire wasn't sure when it happened exactly, but the next thing she knew, Hank had taken hold of her shoulders and drawn her back up into a kneeling position. He sat her back on his spread thighs and she felt his hard hot flesh buried deep inside her. Hank made urgent love to her while they watched in the mirror.

Her inhibitions had melted away in the blazing sexual heat. Claire found it tremendously thrilling to engage in this wild, abandoned lovemaking while they watched themselves. And mating in the middle of the day while a band played outside and laughing people promenaded in the gardens directly below and only the sheerest of curtains covering the open doors to the veranda made the shameless lovemaking all the more exciting.

Her hips gyrating against his thrusting pelvis, Claire murmured breathlessly, "I don't want this to ever end, Hank. I want us to stay like this for a long time."

As Hank surged more deeply into her, he whispered, "Yes, baby. We'll stay just as we are all afternoon."

"That's what I want, and...I...oh...Hank, Hank..."

"I know, darlin'," he soothed, "It all right, I've got you, I'll take care of you." He swiftly changed the rhythm, thrusting faster, driving more deeply until she began to lose control.

Hank watched her beautiful face flush with intense heat as orgasm overwhelmed her. She was wild, frenzied, her body gripping his, her hair whipping around her face. She cried out in ecstasy and called his name again and again. Hank did his best to continue watching even as his own climax began. But the ecstasy was too great, the incredible orgasm too draining.

His eyes closed and his hands covered her full warm breasts as he frantically bucked up against her, driving forcefully up into her, spilling himself high inside her.

When the tempest had passed and the spent lovers were too weak to move, too breathless to speak, they again gazed into the mirror at the perspiring naked pair that was them.

Her pale hands resting on the bronzed arms wrapped around her waist, Claire sighed, smiled and told him frankly, "I can't remember when I've enjoyed a summer noontime more."

Hank said, "And the fun's only just begun. There's still that book to be read."

Claire laughed and so did he.

Nineteen

"They went into his cottage before noon," confided a smiling Lillian Titus, her eyes twinkling.

"And they haven't come out?" asked a clearly jealous Caroline Whit. "They've been inside all afternoon?"

"Indeed!" Lillian gleefully confirmed. "My dear husband Horace told me not an hour ago that he'd heard that three waiters delivered a full gourmet meal to the cottage around four this afternoon but swore they saw only Hank, not a glimpse of the duchess."

"Oh, dear me," said Maxine Delaney, a bejeweled matron with snow-white hair and impressive social standing. "I do hope they surface long enough to come to my dinner party this evening."

The ladies were gathered on the veranda of the

Grand Union, enjoying a late afternoon interlude of refreshing iced drinks and spirited conversation.

"They can't stay in Hank's cottage forever," snipped Caroline Whit. "The races start tomorrow and Hank Cassidy has a half-dozen Thoroughbreds running."

"Think she'll be with him at the track?" asked Lillian Titus, eyebrows lifted.

"No, she will not," Caroline stated with great authority. "Surely you remember that the duchess *never* went to the track. Not even when the duke had horses running."

"Why, that's right," agreed Lillian. "I had forgotten. And the duchess made no secret of the fact she does not like horses or racing."

"Ah, but then she never liked the duke, either," offered Maxine with a girlish laugh, adding, "My eyesight is failing, of course, but doesn't it seem that the duchess is more beautiful than when last she was here?"

"Oh, now, Maxine, it's been seven or eight years since the duchess was at the Springs. You've just forgotten—"

Interrupting, Maxine leaned up and said, "My memory is just fine, thank you very much, Lillian. And I say that the duchess is prettier and happier."

"Yes, well you'd be prettier and happier, too, if you were forty years younger and that handsome devil, Hank Cassidy, was after you," Lillian said with a smile.

Maxine chuckled and nodded her agreement.

Caroline Whit didn't laugh. With a wave of her hand, she said, "She's just a novelty. Hank will tire of her soon enough."

In a darkly paneled billiard parlor just off Broadway, the talk among the gentleman was much the same as it was with the ladies.

"They went into his cottage before noon," said Horace Titus, chalking his pool cue, watching his opponent prepare to take a difficult shot.

"And they haven't come out yet? Good God, it's after six," said Reed Wheatly, an affable, middle-aged millionaire from New York City. He took his shot, sending the round white ball skittering across the green felt table and into a side pocket. He straightened, then shook his graying head. "That lucky rascal, the Silver King."

Horace Titus nodded his agreement. "I'm told three waiters delivered a full gourmet meal to Cassidy's cottage around four this afternoon, but swore they saw only Hank, not a glimpse of the duchess."

"Well, they can't stay in there forever. The races start tomorrow and Hank has a half-dozen ponies running, doesn't he?"

"Yes, he does," Horace confirmed. "Think the duchess will be with him at the track? She never went with the duke."

"Hank's not the duke. Eight to five says she will be with Hank for the races."

"I'll take that wager."

And so it went.

The whispering had begun the minute the pair had entered the dining room of the United States Hotel that morning. By late afternoon the Saratoga gossips—both men and women—were having a field day.

At Maxine Delaney's dinner party that evening, the pair—noticeably absent—had become the talk of the town.

The word had quickly spread.

By nine that night everyone knew that the couple had gone inside Hank's hotel cottage and had remained there all day. And all evening. Speculation on when they would emerge became an entertaining game for the gentlemen. Bets were taken on the exact hour when the lovers would finally surface.

An informant was paid to discreetly stand guard across the street from Cassidy's cottage and to report back as soon as the two were seen leaving.

That informant had a long wait. Too long. He fell asleep around midnight.

"I've entered Red Eye Gravy and Eastern Dancer and four other mounts in tomorrow's opening day racing program. Tell me you'll go to the races with me."

"I'll go to the races with you."

Hank smiled, then sighed with contentment.

Naked, he lay stretched out on his back with an arm folded beneath his head. The duchess, also nude, lay on her stomach across the bed, her cheek resting on his belly, her long unbound hair fanned out across his bare chest.

The summer sun had long since set, but a wide swatch of moonlight spilled in through the sheer curtains covering the open balcony doors and fell across the bed where they lay.

Clutched tenaciously in the curve of Claire's bent arm was her leather-bound copy of *The Prisoner of Zenda.* "Hank, it was so sweet of you to buy this book for me."

"I'm a sweet guy."

"Yes, you are," she said, then accused, "but you're also rather presumptuous."

"Could be. The truth is I bought the book hoping I'd get the opportunity to give it to you. And I did, didn't I?"

"Yes, you did. Shall I read to you?"

"Some other time."

Claire laughed and playfully bit his bare belly. "Well, you couldn't have given me anything I would treasure more. How can I ever thank you?"

Hank grinned. "Maybe I can help you think of something."

* * *

"You know, don't you," Claire asked as they lay lazily stretched out in the moonlight, "that you and I are missing—have missed—Maxine Delaney's dinner party."

"She'll live," Hank said. "Unless you want to get dressed and go."

"I want to stay right here."

Hank swept a hand over the golden tresses tickling his chest. "Me, too." After a long comfortable pause he said, "Tell me about yourself, Duchess. I know a lot about your body, but very little about you."

Claire still didn't stir. "What's to know, Hank? I'm a widow. My late husband, the Duke of Beaumont, left me comfortably wealthy which makes it unnecessary for me to ever marry again. Thank heaven. I have no family to speak of, but scores of good friends. I used to come to the Springs with the duke, but it's been several years since last I was here." She sighed and added, "I like it here. I like the clean mountain air and the grand hotels and the glittering parties and the Thoroughbred races." Claire finally raised her head and laid her precious book aside. "I like you, Hank Cassidy."

"How much do you like me, Duchess?"

Claire laughed gaily and whipped her hair back off her face. "Enough to spend every hour with you for as long as I'm here at the Springs."

"You'll be staying until the end of August, won't you?"

"No. I'm leaving the middle of August."

Hank made a face. "Why? The season's not over until the first of September."

"I know, but I must get back to London."

"Then you won't be here for the Travers Stakes," he said, scowling. "I've got Black Satin, the finest Thoroughbred I've ever owned, entered in that race. I'd like you to be with me when he wins."

"Sorry, darling."

"You have to change your plans, Charmaine. You have to—"

"No," she cut him off. "I said I'm going and I am. Don't try to pin me down, Hank. I don't like being pressed."

Hank made a face. "Sorry, darling."

"You're a fabulous playmate and we'll continue to have fun together until the middle of August. Then I'm leaving. Not because I have to, but because I choose to." She spread her hair back across his chest, leaned up, kissed his chin, and said, "Now it's your turn, Hank. Tell me everything there is to know about you."

Hank shrugged. "I'm thirty-two years old, in good health, have never been married, made a fortune in the Nevada silver mines. Like you, I have no family, but my home is in Virginia City, Nevada. I was born and raised there and plan to die there when I'm a very

old man. I have a place in New York City where I sel-
dom go and a horse farm outside Louisville, Kentucky. I came to Saratoga for the first time six or
seven years ago and have been here every summer
since. I like horses and bourbon and good food and
pretty women. I like you, Duchess." He pressed her
closer. "Spend the night with me?"

"Love to, darling."

"And go to the races with me tomorrow?"

"Love to, darling."

"And make love to me right now this very minute."

"Love to, darling."

Twenty

"They're off!"

The much anticipated Saratoga racing season had officially begun. It was exactly 11:30 a.m.

At five minutes to post time, a red-jacketed gentlemen had stepped onto the racetrack directly in front of the finish line, lifted a gleaming gold-plated bugle to his lips and sounded the familiar call to the starting gate.

Thirteen sleek Thoroughbreds had moved, one by one, into the gate. As soon as the last Thoroughbred had been boxed, a pistol was shot into the air and the starting flag dropped. The full field broke from the gate and onto the oval track.

The crowd of five thousand spectators came to their feet and began to cheer wildly in the beautiful slate-roofed grandstand. A second floor stairway led up to the clubhouse where a balcony ended in the Queen Anne circle with a bright lawn running down to the track. It was here that the well-heeled turf set gathered to watch the races.

In a private box on the finish line in the Queen Anne circle, Hank Cassidy was up out of his chair. With him in the box was a radiant Claire. She, too, was on her feet and cheering madly for Red Eye Gravy, the big bay stallion sporting bright green-and-white silks, Hank's official racing colors. Red Eye Gravy was rounding the first turn, sixth behind the leaders.

Whistling and applauding, Hank leaned down and said in Claire's ear, "Don't worry. He's in a good position, right where he should be."

"You sure? Looks like the others are pulling away from him."

"They'll burn out and then we'll take 'em after the turn. You'll see!"

Eyes focused across the oval track to the sprinting Thoroughbreds, Claire followed the flash of green and white and nodded, hoping Hank was right.

"Look, sweetheart," Hank said as the field raced into the far turn and Red Eye Gravy began to make his move. The big bay passed a couple of contenders, moving swiftly up on the outside.

Now there were only two horses ahead of him.

Claire's hands went to her cheeks when the daring jockey riding Red Eye Gravy edged the big mount up between the two front runners as they raced down the front stretch in a fight for final position.

For the next few thrilling seconds the three Thoroughbreds raced neck and neck, so close together there was not enough room between them to slide a sheet of tissue paper. The screams from the crowd were deafening. Hank was whistling and beating on the rail of the box with his rolled-up copy of the day's racing program.

Just when it looked like the race would end in a three-way dead heat, Red Eye Gravy slipped between the other two as if his big body was greased. He surged ahead and thundered across the finish line, first by a nose.

Laughing, happy, Hank grabbed Claire up in his arms, swung her around and declared, "We won, baby, we won!"

"I know, I can't believe it!" Claire said, eagerly embracing him. When he set her back on her feet, she said, "Hank, that was so exciting, I'm actually breathless."

"Makes two of us," he said. He took her hand and placed it over his hammering heart.

Claire felt the rapid rhythmic beating and warned, "We better sit down and calm ourselves."

Hank nodded.

They sat down at the small square table where an

array of tempting delicacies had hardly been touched. Hank took a bottle of chilled champagne from a silver bucket of ice. They toasted the winning stallion and Hank said proudly, "No surprise the big boy won. His sire was the great speedster Red River Valley who won the Kentucky Derby a couple of times back in the early eighties. And his dam was a fine sorrel filly who has foaled a half-dozen fast colts."

Interested, eager to hear him talk about his horses and this sport which he clearly loved, Claire said, "What about this next race? Do you have a contestant?"

"You bet we do."

The second race was even more thrilling than the first. Eastern Dancer, a three-year-old chestnut colt Hank owned, led the pack from box to wire, making the entire outing look easy. Around the one-mile track, Eastern Dancer sailed on his own, leading all the way. Unpressured, he turned for home and repulsed all challengers through the front stretch, bounding across the finish line to win handily.

What fun they were having!

Hank and Claire laughed and drank champagne and cheered for Hank's mounts to come in on top. After watching five races, in which two of his horses had come in first and another second, an excited Claire asked, "Who do we like in the next race?"

Before Hank could answer, Caroline Whit stepped

up to their box and greeted them. Hank politely rose to his feet and acknowledged her.

"Afternoon, Caroline. I believe you've met the Duchess of Beaumont."

Smiling at Hank, Caroline said, "Please, sit back down." She turned her attention to Claire. "Yes, of course, I know the duchess. How are you, Charmaine?"

"Quite well, thank you," Claire said with a warm smile.

"Mmm, I'll just bet you are," Caroline replied. "I'm really surprised to see you here though."

"Why is that, Caroline? You're here. Many of the ladies are here."

"Yes, but you never came to the races when the duke was alive. As I recall you had a great aversion to horses. The poor old duke had to take a bath and change his clothes each time he had been anywhere near the stables." She looked at Hank, then back at Claire. "Why the extraordinary change? A woman who can't stand the smell of horses at a racetrack?"

"Ah, Caroline. How observant you are. I have changed," Claire said. She wrapped a possessive hand around Hank's biceps, touched her cheek to his shoulder, and added, "All credit due to Mr. Cassidy. Hank's teaching me about this fascinating sport of kings and I'm thoroughly enjoying it. Why, he's even promised to take me down to the stables one evening soon so I can get up close to the big beasts. Doesn't that sound exciting? I can hardly wait."

Caroline looked at Hank. Her tone was sharp when she told him, "The owners won't like it. Those stables are strictly a man's domain. Women have no business there."

"I'm an owner, Caroline," Hank reminded her. "And I've no objection to the duchess having a closer look at my Thoroughbreds."

Caroline shrugged and changed the subject. "Maxine Delaney was extremely upset that you two missed her dinner party last evening."

Hank started to speak, but Claire pressed his arm with her hand. She said, "It was unforgivably rude, I agree. However this morning we did send Maxine a large bouquet of roses with our humble apologies."

With her green-eyed gaze resting solely on Hank, Caroline said, "Surely you'll be attending tonight's ball at the Grand Union Hotel. Diamond Jim Brady and his glamorous girlfriend, Lillian Russell, are the hosts."

"We'll be there, Caroline," Claire said, and turning to Hank asked, "Won't we, darling?"

"If you say so, baby."

Caroline Whit exhaled with rising annoyance. "Then I'll look forward to seeing you both this evening. Save a dance for me, Hank." It was a statement, not a question. She turned and flounced away.

"I think she likes you," Claire said as Caroline returned to her box.

"Jealous?" he asked with a slow smile and wink.

"Should I be?"

Hank shook his dark head, put a hand under the table and found Claire's. Their fingers touched—a simple brushing together. But it was enough to make chills run up Claire's spine. Her thick lashes lowered flirtatiously over her shining violet eyes and she felt her face flush with heat as she recalled with vivid clarity what that slow masterful hand had done to her earlier in the morning. How his gentle touch on her flesh had so easily sent her into orgasmic ecstasy.

"This next race should be very exciting," Hank said, apparently fully aware of how the touch of his hand had made her breath grow short.

"Oh? Why is that?" she asked with a smile.

"It's the Saratoga Flash Stakes. One of the entries is a speedster called Onaretto and his jockey is none other than Alonzo Clayton." As Hank spoke, one of his fingers moved and touched hers lightly. It stroked the length of her index finger in a subtle, but suggestive way. "Alonzo Clayton was the youngest Derby winner at age fifteen on a mount called Azra back in '92."

"Is that a fact?" Claire said, attempting to pay attention to what he was saying as Hank's lean hand wrapped around hers, his fingertips rubbing her palm.

"It is and that's not all." His hand closed over hers

and she felt her fingers gently crushed in the warmth of his palm. "You want more?" he asked, the innocent question having a definite double meaning.

"You know I do," Claire said. She turned her hand over and wrapped her tingling fingers around the back of his.

"Last year at this very track," Hank said, coolly placing her hand over his trousered thigh, "a young jockey called James 'Soup' Perkins won five out of six races in one day. One day, mind you. And he was only fourteen years old…and then he went on to win the Derby atop a mount called Halma."

"Absolutely amazing," she marveled, then glanced anxiously into Hank's mischievous blue eyes as he pressed her open palm against his leg and let his hand rest lightly on hers. Beneath her fingertips was the hammered steel of his long-boned thigh. At her touch the firm muscles bunched and jumped, yet his expression never changed. Mindful of where they were, Claire behaved properly. She didn't slide her hand up close to his groin, but she allowed her fingers to stroke and caress his firm thigh through the fabric of his trousers.

Hank continued to sit there and very calmly educate Claire on the thrilling spectator sport of Thoroughbred racing. She listened and nodded and made the proper comments. And all the while a much more thrilling sport was going on between the two of them beneath the linen-draped table.

The duchess's gentle touch on his thigh was all that was needed to make Hank wish they didn't have to stay for the remainder of the racing program.

He glanced cautiously around, leaned close, and said, "Have you any idea what you're doing to me?"

"Excuse me, Hank. Madam," came a low masculine voice. The startled pair looked up to see a dapper, silver-haired gentleman standing before the box.

"Fox! My man!" Hank said as Claire quickly moved her hand to her lap. Hank jumped to his feet and shook his trainer's hand. "Sit down, sit down, there's someone special I want you to meet." Fox Connor remained standing as Hank introduced him to Claire.

"Fox, this lovely lady is the Duchess of Beaumont." To her he said, "Charmaine, my good friend, Fox Connor."

"A true privilege, Your Grace," said Fox, bowing slightly.

"I've heard so much about you, Mr. Connor. Won't you join us, please?" Claire said graciously.

"Thanks, but I need to get right back down to the stables." He looked at Hank. "I came up here to tell you we had to pull Silver Dollar at the last minute. Nothing serious. You know how temperamental he is. I can tell that he doesn't want to run today. No use forcing him."

"I agree. Maybe in a couple of days," said Hank.

"Sure. He'll be ready then."

"Black Satin? Going to take the big race for us? Win the Travers?"

"The stallion's in fine form," assured Fox. "He's a shoo-in to take the Travers. There's no doubt in my mind." Fox looked again at Claire, "An honor to meet you, Duchess. I hope I'll be seeing you again."

"You will," said Claire without hesitation.

After Fox had walked away, Hank gave Claire a look and asked, "What are you thinking about?"

She smiled. "The same thing you're thinking about."

Their abrupt departure caused a buzz of astonishment among the turf set.

All agreed that it was a first.

Hank Cassidy had *never* left the track before the final race had been run.

Twenty-One

Claire returned to the estate late that afternoon to dress for the evening's ball at the Grand Union. When the carriage stopped in the circular drive directly before the mansion, she kissed Hank goodbye and told him to come back for her at eight-thirty.

She stood unmoving and watched until his carriage was out of sight, then turned and raced up the front steps and crossed the veranda, calling Olivia's name. Olivia, her cane tapping before her, came hurrying through the wide hallway to meet Claire. Laughing, the two women embraced, glad to see each other.

Finally releasing the older woman, Claire said, "You weren't worried about me, were you?"

"Not in the least," Olivia assured her. "I knew where you were. Who you were with." With a sly grin, she ventured, "I assume you have been enjoying yourself with the handsome Mr. Cassidy."

"Oh, Olivia, that is an understatement," Claire replied. "I am having the time of my life!"

"Good for you, you deserve it," said Olivia. "Judging by the sparkle in your eyes, I suppose you intend to see the young man again very soon."

"In exactly two hours," Claire said with a pleased smile. "We're going to a dance tonight hosted by a gentleman known as Diamond Jim Brady. Have you heard of him?" Olivia shook her head. "Well wait until you hear this," said Claire, eager to share what the gossips said about the colorful Jim Brady and his paramour, the actress Lillian Russell.

"As you might surmise," Claire told her friend, "Jim Brady is filthy rich!"

"I would assume so," said Olivia.

"And he loves diamonds. He owns at least twenty-thousand of them. Twenty thousand! Can you imagine?" Claire laughed then and confided, "they say the buttons on his underwear are fashioned out of diamonds."

Olivia's eyebrows lifted and her eyes twinkled. "For heaven's sake! You have to be joking."

"Not at all. And I've seen Miss Russell, her diamonds flashing in the sunlight, riding about the boulevards astride a gold-plated bicycle Diamond Jim gave her."

"Will wonders never cease!"

"No. Not here in Saratoga, they won't." She laughed merrily and added, "This should be a very interesting evening."

"And I'll want to hear all about it," said Olivia.

At twenty minutes of nine Hank Cassidy knocked on the mansion's front door. Jenkins admitted Hank and directed him into the sitting room.

"The duchess will be down shortly," Jenkins announced and disappeared.

Before Hank could sit down, Olivia came into the sitting room and smiled warmly at him. "You must be Mr. Hank Cassidy."

"In the flesh," Hank said with a grin.

"I'm Olivia Sutton, companion to the duchess."

"A genuine pleasure to meet you, Olivia," Hank said, adding, "May I call you Olivia?"

"By all means. Please—" Olivia extended a hand toward a sofa "—won't you sit down? Charmaine shouldn't be long."

"Only if you'll sit and visit with me," said Hank, promptly winning Olivia's full approval.

The two sat on the sofa together and talked easily about the springs, the mineral waters, the races, the casinos and the colorful people who came to Saratoga in the summertime. They laughed together as Hank shared stories he'd heard about the free-spending Diamond Jim Brady and his legendary gambling losses. And of Brady's constant companion, Lillian Russell, the blond, blue-eyed darling of Broadway.

But both abruptly stopped laughing when Claire stepped into the wide arched doorway and, without saying a word, commanded their undivided attention.

The two were momentarily awed into silence by her pale blond beauty. She looked ethereal, not of this world. More like an angel stepping out of the clouds. Her hair fell lose around her shoulders and was held back off her face with an oyster shell comb.

She wore a ball gown of shimmering sky-blue taffeta with double flounces of lace around the low-cut, off-the-shoulder bodice. Her waist was incredibly small and attractively accentuated the full swell of her bosom.

Olivia knew Claire's secret.

She had helped her dress. Beneath the blue taffeta gown was a tightly laced corset, an embroidered and beribboned corset cover, two frilly petticoats and, skimpy lace-trimmed satin underwear and silk stockings.

Claire swept into the room and smiled at Hank as he rose to his feet and stared at her. She turned about in a complete circle, then asked, "Do you approve?"

Hank needlessly cleared his throat. "You know I do," he managed to reply, finding it hard to keep his hands off her.

"You look exceptionally beautiful this evening, Duchess," Olivia said. "You'll be the fairest lady at the dance."

"Not necessarily," Claire said. "Lillian Russell is a lovely woman and—"

"Miss Russell pales in comparison with you," Hank said. "I assure you, you'll be the most beautiful woman there."

Claire plucked a fresh red rose from a nearby vase, broke off the stem, stepped up to Hank and tucked the fragrant blossom into the lapel of his elegant white dinner jacket.

Looking into his indigo eyes that were flashing with ardent intensity, she said, "And I'll be with the handsomest man." She turned away from him. "We'd best be going," she said as she leaned down, kissed Olivia's cheek and whispered in her ear, "I'll probably see you sometime tomorrow." She straightened.

"Have a wonderful time, you two," Olivia said, rising from the sofa.

"Nice to meet you, Olivia. You must join us for dinner one evening soon," Hank said.

"Why, thank you, Hank. That would be nice."

Hank took Claire's arm and ushered her from the room.

Outside the handsome pair hurried down the steps and Hank handed Claire up into the waiting carriage.

He climbed in, stepped across her, sat down close beside her and put his arm around her.

"You sure you want to go to the ball?" he asked and for a moment Claire was hypnotized by his penetrating eyes, beautiful mysterious eyes darkened with raw passion. His fingers toying with the gold chain bearing the medallion she always wore, he whispered, "We could just skip the ball, go back to the cottage and—"

"Later, Hank," Claire softly interrupted. "We've the whole night ahead of us." She fanned her fingers over his smoothly shaven jaw. "Let's go to the dance and stay until midnight." Hank frowned and she explained, "It'll be thrilling. Think about it. Sweet agony. The entire time we're there we'll be eagerly looking forward to midnight. Counting the minutes until—" she smiled seductively "—at the stroke of twelve, we escape to your cottage and spend the rest of the night sipping champagne and making love."

Hank's hand released the golden chain. "You're a cruel woman, Charmaine." But he smiled and kissed her with tender restraint. His lips on hers, he reached up and thumped the top of the barouche, signaling the driver atop the box. They were immediately on their way.

A phalanx of carriages were lined up on the west side of Broadway just outside the well-lit six-story

Grand Union Hotel. The barouche had to wait its turn to pull up before the hotel's canopied entrance. Claire and Hank didn't mind. They held hands and talked of their day at the races and of their plans to go to the track again tomorrow.

It was well past nine when finally they entered the big ballroom and were met at the door by the beaming Diamond Jim Brady. The flamboyant Brady lived up to his reputation. Diamonds flashed from his collar buttons, shirt studs, necktie pin, cuff links, belt buckle and watch chain.

At his side, the buxom actress, Lillian Russell, was no less jewel adorned. Garbed in a gown of signature white satin, she had diamonds glittering in her upswept blond hair, dangling from her earlobes, caressing her bare throat and sparkling from her fingers.

When Hank and the Duchess were introduced to their host and hostess, Diamond Jim took his diamond-studded eyeglass case from inside his breast pocket, slipped on his spectacles with their diamond-trimmed frames, and reached for his diamond-adorned pencil, explaining that he'd heard Hank had some fine ponies running and he wanted the names of a couple so he could make wagers. Diamond Jim pulled out his leather notepad with its diamond clasp.

"Black Satin and Silver Dollar are my fastest, soundest Thoroughbreds, Mr. Brady," Hank said.

"Jim is so forgetful," offered the husky-voiced

Lillian and raised a diamond-decorated white feather fan to stir the still air. "Aren't you, sugar?"

Diamond Jim laughed good-naturedly. Clearly mad about the beautiful actress, he agreed that he was. "Now you young folks enjoy yourselves, you hear?" he said when he'd jotted down the Thoroughbreds' names.

"We will, Mr. Brady," said Claire. "And thank you for inviting us."

"Call me Diamond Jim, Your Grace," he said. He slapped Hank on the back and added, "There's all kinds of food and liquor at the far end of the ball room. Help yourselves."

His hand enclosing Claire's elbow, Hank guided her through the crowd toward a long mahogany bar. They nodded and exchanged pleasantries with stellar guests that included Rockerfellers and Morgans and Vanderbilts. Many of America's wealthiest gentlemen were in the Grand Union ballroom on this warm summer night.

The presence of such notables meant nothing to Hank and Claire. They didn't care who was at the dance. They only had eyes for each other. When finally they reached the bar and were handed crystal flutes of French champagne, they silently toasted each other, then turned and leaned back against the bar to drink the chilled wine.

They stood very close together, their bodies touching, brushing, their free hands clasped between them. When they'd finished the champagne, Hank ushered Claire onto the dance floor. The orchestra struck up the popular tune, "The Band Played On." Hank smiled, drew Claire into his embrace, and began to slowly turn her about on the crowded floor.

Neither noticed that Caroline Whit, in the arms of Parker Lawson, was aggressively maneuvering toward them.

"Now, you listen to me, Parker," Caroline was saying in his ear, "You're not to take no for an answer."

"Caroline, I really don't think it will do either of us any good to cut in on them."

"It may do *you* no good, Parker, but I know how to make the most of a dance, if you know what I mean."

"Maybe you do, but apparently the duchess has the same talent. Take a good look at Cassidy—she's got him wound up tighter than a ten-day clock."

"Parker, you get me over there and into his arms!"

"Fine. We'll give it a shot."

Parker deftly danced Caroline through the crowd and purposely bumped into Hank's back. Hank paused, turned and looked around.

"Oh, sorry, Hank," said Parker with an apologetic smile. "Guess I've got two left feet."

"Hello, Duchess. Hank," Caroline trilled, looking only at Hank.

Hank and Claire nodded politely and went back to dancing. Caroline made a mean face at Parker and shoved him forward.

"Shall we change partners, Hank. What do you say?"

"No," was Hank's one word reply.

Frowning, Caroline reached out and grabbed Hank's arm. "You're being rude, Hank."

"I know," he said and drew Claire closer.

Caroline turned her attention to Claire. "Your Grace, won't you honor Parker with one little dance?"

"Not tonight," Claire said and never took her eyes off Hank.

Hank smiled and commandingly spun her away, leaving Caroline Whit muttering in frustration and Parker Lawson shaking his blond head.

"What did I tell you?" Parker said. "The duchess has Cassidy wrapped around her little finger. And she seems to be totally smitten with him, as well."

"That haughty British bitch," Caroline snarled under her breath. "Coming over here to America, grabbing the man I want! Who does she think she is? And why did she come back to the Springs after all these years?" Caroline gritted her teeth as she watched the couple dancing away.

Lost in each other, eyes half-closed, Hank and Claire swayed sensuously, bodies pressing, hearts beating as one. Desire flared and quickly escalated. Each gliding step, each gentle undulation was incredibly arousing. Claire could feel Hank's thighs brushing hers through the taffeta of her gown, his pelvis sliding sinuously against her own.

Her arms looped around his neck, her head on his shoulder, she drew a shallow breath when, as they turned in perfect tempo to a slow romantic ballad, Hank's knee became insinuated between her legs. Her response was immediate and involuntary. Her tense, tingling body sought the temporary balm his trousered thigh offered. She pressed herself against it and wished the crowd around them would magically disappear.

His hand flattened on her back, Hank drew Claire closer and whispered in her ear. "I can't wait."

"Nor can I," she murmured. "Let's leave. Go to the cottage and—"

"Too far away," he said, and she heard the urgency in his voice. He abruptly stopped dancing, took her hand, and led her through the crowd toward the ballroom's front entrance.

Dancers paused to stare and whisper as the pair rushed out into the lobby. There, too, guests who were taking a short breather from the dancing stared and shook their heads, supposing that Cassidy and the duchess were leaving at this early hour.

But they were not leaving.

Hot for each other as only the young and vigorous can be, the golden couple simply could not wait until they reached the privacy of his hotel cottage.

Claire saw Hank glance around as he handed her into an empty cloakroom. He followed her into the darkened room and hurriedly locked the door behind them. Unable to see in the pitch blackness, she heard him say, "Come here to me."

She did.

At once they were kissing hotly and anxiously undressing each other. In the stygian darkness, they couldn't really see each other, could only feel. It was enough. It was exciting. It was erotic.

In seconds Claire had Hank's shirt open and pushed apart. While she pressed kisses to his warm bare chest, Hank was deftly lifting her rustling taffeta skirts and shoving her lace-trimmed satin underwear over her hips and down her belly.

As the satin whispered down her weak legs Claire's hands went to the waistband of Hank's dark trousers. Working to unbutton the snug black pants, she eagerly stepped out of her undies and kicked them aside.

Before she could release him from the confines of his trousers, Hank tore her hands away. Then he puzzled her by turning her so that she stood at a right angle to him. Her skirt bunched up around her waist, he put one hand on her flat belly, the other on her bare bottom.

"Hank," she whispered softly, wishing she could see his face. "What are you—?"

"Shhh, baby," he murmured as both his hands slipped possessively between her legs, one from the back, the other from the front.

His hands met and his tapered fingers began stoking the fires of her passion. Claire's breath caught in her throat and her heart pounded with excitement. She momentarily wondered if Hank would ever run out of novel ways to swiftly arouse her to a fever pitch. She was sure that he wouldn't. Thank heaven.

The cloaking intimacy of the darkness made this forbidden lovemaking all the more thrilling. That and the laughter and talk from the foyer just beyond the locked door. For Claire it was incredibly thrilling to have her dark lover's fingers stroking and probing and doing all kinds of marvelous thing to her while only a few short feet away, guests milled about in the foyer.

"Ohhh," Claire sighed as Hank expertly stroked her pleasure points, teasing her, toying with her, making her squirm and sigh and tingle.

The next thing she knew Hank had turned her about and was pressing her back up against the locked door. Without a word being said, she reached down, freed him from his opened trousers, and felt him surge against her bare belly.

Hank put his hands under her bare bottom, lifted

her up and was immediately inside her. She released a held breath and said his name on a sigh.

She clung to the strong column of his neck and wrapped her legs around his waist as he pounded forcefully into her. They kissed and hunched and bucked and gasped and all too soon exploded in wrenching orgasm. When the violent waves of ecstasy had passed, they sagged tiredly against the door.

Coming to her senses little by little, Claire began to smile. Then to softly laugh. Hank laughed, too. They were laughing at themselves for misbehaving so disgracefully.

"You should be ashamed of yourself, Duchess," Hank teased as she lowered her feet to the floor. "Seducing a respectable, naive gentleman during a crowded dance."

"I? What about you, Mr. Nevada Silver King? Dragging a helpless female into a darkened cloakroom to ravish her!"

They stayed there in the pitch-black darkness for a few more minutes, laughing, kissing, enjoying each other. Then they straightened their clothes and hunted for Claire's discarded underwear.

When finally they were presentable and exited the cloakroom, they disregarded the turning of heads and censuring looks that were shot their way.

They left the gala and stepped out into the warm summer night. Hank raised a hand to signal the carriage. While they waited, Hank turned and looked at the beautiful flushed woman beside him. He grinned. A scarlet petal from the crushed rose in his lapel was sticking to the swell of her left breast.

"What?" she asked. "What is it?"

"Nothing, sweetheart. Just that you're adorable and I'm glad you're here with me."

"I'm glad too, Hank." Claire smiled then and said, "What a lovely night."

"And it's about to get lovelier, Duchess," he said and squeezed her narrow waist.

Twenty-Two

It was Sunday evening.

Olivia had not seen Claire and Hank since they'd left for Diamond Jim Brady's dance on Saturday. Twenty-four hours ago. Olivia understood completely. The handsome pair were clearly in the first thrilling throes of a grand passion and wanted only to be alone together.

Olivia was delighted for Claire.

There was a new radiance about her and Hank Cassidy was responsible. There was no doubt in Olivia's mind that Claire Orwell was happy as she'd never been in her life.

Might never be again.

Olivia knew all too well how fleeting such euphoria could be. Or how love lost was never regained, never forgotten. Olivia shook her head worriedly.

Despite all her protestations to the contrary, Claire was in danger of losing her heart to the handsome man from Nevada.

But for now, and for at least another week into which she would cram all the living and loving possible, Claire was absolutely ecstatic. It was obvious that she wouldn't have traded places with anyone on earth. When it came down to it, how many people were ever lucky enough to make that statement?

Smiling now as she mused it over, Olivia closed and locked the front door. She turned, thrust her silver-headed cane forward, and walked unhurriedly through the silent house. She went into her room, picked up a book and sat down to read.

She read only a couple of pages, closed the book and laid it aside. She rose with the aid of her cane and left her room. She went out onto the back veranda, leaned against a porch pillar and sighed.

It was a beautiful evening. Warm, but not hot, with a slight breeze from out of the east. The subtle scent of roses was in the air. With twilight just beginning to fall, a few stars appeared in the sky.

Olivia took a deep breath and slowly released it. And she frowned. She was, she realized, lonely. She knew no one at the Springs. The only places she had been in Saratoga were a couple of small, out-of-the way casinos. In neither of those gaming establishments had she spoken to anyone. And no one had spoken to her.

She had not been invited to any of the resort's many social events, nor should she be. She was, after all, a paid companion to a British duchess. Her position placed her one peg above the household servants. Paid attendants were not included on anyone's guest lists. And, truth to tell, she wouldn't have wanted to go to the dances and parties. That sort of thing was for young, energetic people. She was neither young nor energetic.

Olivia shook her head and silently lectured herself. What a foolish, ungrateful old woman she was! She had never in her life had it this easy. She, Olivia L. Sutton, formerly an inmate in Newgate Prison, now lived in a duchess's opulent mansion. Her teeth had been fixed, her graying hair styled, and she had nice clothes. She could come and go as she pleased and spend money as if it were her own. For the first time in years she did not go to bed hungry and dirty and sick and afraid of being attacked.

Who could ask for anything more?

Olivia smiled and went back inside.

In her room she crossed to her neatly made bed. She reached beneath a pillow and took out the purple velvet drawstring bag which Claire insisted she keep in her possession. From the bag Olivia withdrew their closely guarded stash of money. She carefully counted it as she did every night.

She took several bills, laid them aside.

She put the rest of the money back inside the velvet pouch and returned the stash to its hiding place beneath the pillow. She picked up the bills she had taken and stuffed them in her reticule.

She went to the tall bureau and looked into the mirror atop it. She frowned, pinched her cheeks, bit her lips, and picked up a long-handled hairbrush.

When she put the brush down, she laid out her finest dress.

Fox Connor felt his heartbeat quicken when, at shortly after dusk on that same Sunday evening, he stepped into the dark vestibule of Canfield's casino. An elegant establishment with tall windows and a French Renaissance interior, Canfield's provided plush little parlors on the left, a large gaming room on the right and an elegant dinning room at the rear.

Upstairs were private rooms where white chips valued at $100 were the minimum. The worth of each succeeding—red, blue, yellow—chip raised to $100,000 for the brown.

In the gaming rooms tuxedos or tails were required. The ladies wore so many jewels, Canfield hired a private detective to mingle with the crowd to protect them against thieves.

Dressed in the required evening wear, Fox went directly to the downstairs gaming room. He paused at the entrance, looked about and smiled with pleasure. Soft tapestries, silk-upholstered chairs, massive mantels and black-walnut woodwork made the room inviting.

At this early hour there were few players. Before the evening was over, the place would be packed with gamblers.

Fox heard the familiar sound that never failed to excite him. The swirl and clatter which accompanied the tiny white ball as it spun around and around the varnished wheel of the roulette table.

A trio of players were there. A couple of rowdy, inebriated young men, and a quiet, well-dressed lady of advanced years.

Standing behind the table was a tall, unsmiling man with a pencil-thin mustache and sallow complexion. "Twenty-three black," the croupier announced in a flat monotone and the two young male players groaned. The lady remained silent. Her expression did not change.

Fox approached the table as the ball went whirling around the wheel once more. "The number is even. Twelve red," the croupier announced, deadpan.

Nobody won.

Fox took a seat on a silk-covered chair between the young men and the gray-haired lady. He laid a couple of bills on the green felt. The croupier scooped up the money and shoved a stack of chips at him. His fellow players began placing chips along the layout.

The lady waited until the white ball was again flying around the wheel, then unhurriedly reached out and laid a blue ten-dollar chip on number eleven. Fox glanced at her, rubbed his chin thoughtfully, then placed a yellow one-hundred-dollar chip directly atop her chip.

The spinning wheel began to slow, the white ball skittered and jumped, landing first on red seventeen, popping out, dancing dizzily around and falling into red thirty-six before ricocheting up and down. The two young men were clapping their hands and counting their winnings when the fickle white marble bounced up out of thirty-six, tumbled crazily around the slowing wheel and finally came to a final rest in black eleven.

Fox and the lady exchanged pleased looks, sharing the thrill of winning that only fellow gamblers can fully understand.

"Black eleven. Odd," announced the dead-eyed croupier and thrust a stack of blue chips at Olivia.

Fox looked at her. "What number shall we take this time?"

"You choose," she said.

"Not on your life. Be my lucky charm."

Olivia nodded and laid two blue chips on black number eight. Fox followed suit, dropping two yellow chips atop hers. A camaraderie was quickly developing. Enjoying themselves, they were soon laughing and joking like two old friends.

And they were lucky.

Very lucky.

When Olivia had won more than five hundred dollars, she pushed her chips across the table and said to the croupier. "Cash me in."

"Same here," said Fox, his winnings ten times what hers were.

He rose, smiled at Olivia, and said, "You are my lucky charm and I don't even know your name."

"Sutton. Miss Olivia Sutton. Companion to the Duchess of Beaumont."

"Ah, then you must know Hank Cassidy. I understand that he and the duchess are—"

"Indeed," Olivia replied with a knowing smile.

"I'm Fox Connor, Miss Sutton."

Olivia nodded. "Hank's friend from Kentucky."

"One and the same," he said, then added, "It's as if you and I already know each other well." He reached for Olivia's cane. He handed it to her, took her arm and ushered her toward the door. "Have you had dinner?"

"Why, no, I—"

"Nor have I. Dine with me," he said. Olivia blinked in surprise. He smiled and gently coaxed. "It's too early to end such a lovely evening. Have dinner with me and later, if we're in the mood, we can return to the tables."

Feeling wonderfully gay and lighthearted, Olivia

smiled and told him, "Only if you'll agree to come to the estate some evening this week and have dinner with me."

"Is tomorrow evening too soon?"

"Tomorrow would be perfect, Mr. Connor."

"Fox," he said with a charming smile. "Call me Fox, Olivia."

Twenty-Three

The fevered impromptu lovemaking in the darkened cloakroom of the Grand Union Hotel during a crowded social function was not the first, nor would it be the last time the hot-blooded Hank and the fiery Claire would behave so recklessly.

Hank had a powerful hold on Claire.

And she on him.

Together they were passionate, irresponsible, dangerously daring.

Seductive, sinfully handsome, with a smile that could melt the coldest of hearts, Hank knew how to draw Claire to the edge and dangle her over. And Claire, breathtakingly beautiful, vibrant and alluring, could have snapped her fingers, demand he kneel and worship her and Hank would have dropped immediately to his knees.

A highly incendiary affair.

A look, a touch, a whispered confidence and their teasing flirtation would instantly erupt into flame and blaze out of control.

There were many a quick exit. An anxious search for a nearby place to be alone, and then a frenzied coupling in the most implausible of venues.

Up at the lake where they'd gone for a fish dinner at Moon's, then decided they had no appetite. At least not for food. On an iron lace settee in the private gardens of the duchess's estate. Most uncomfortable, but ultimately satisfying. And even including a strictly man's domain, the Thoroughbred stables behind the oval racetrack.

It happened on an evening that had begun innocently enough. A late dinner at the Congress Inn where the two had enjoyed a delicious meal which began with cups of cold consommé followed by Lobster Newburg and a crisp green salad. Dessert was tutti-frutti pudding with Kümmel sauce. And finally pineapple cheese and Albert crackers.

Pleasingly full and relaxed, they lingered over their coffee and brandy. Then the two of them, in no particular hurry, left the hotel and leisurely strolled back toward the cottages commenting on the coolness of the evening, the brilliance of the stars in the inky night sky.

Halfway there, Hank paused and asked Claire if

she'd mind walking out to the track with him. Said he'd like to look in on a couple of the Thoroughbreds entered in the next day's races. And he wanted to check on his prized stallion, Black Satin. See if the big fellow was feeling well and was relatively calm.

"You think it will be all right?" Claire asked, tilting her head to one side. "As I recall, Caroline Whit said women are not welcome at the stables."

"My woman will be welcome," Hank said with such possessive authority Claire felt her heart skip a beat.

His woman.

She was his woman. At least for now. She liked being his woman. Liked him being *her* man. Wished he could be her man forever.

At that moment Claire experienced an unexpected twinge of dread and melancholy. It struck her that in only a few short days this would all be over. She would awaken from this lovely dream to face stark reality. She would kiss Hank Cassidy good-night as though nothing were amiss, then rise with the dawn and flee Saratoga without saying goodbye.

And Hank—*her* Hank—beloved by all the ladies and admired by all the gentlemen, would no longer be hers.

Claire didn't realize she was frowning until Hank's low, soft voice broke into her troubled reveries.

"What is it, Duchess? If you'd rather go back to the cottage and wait for me there, I'll—"

"No," she almost choked. "I want to go with you. I want to *be* with you. Every hour. Every minute."

Hank laughed, took her hand, laced his long fingers through hers and drew their clasped hands up to rest against his chest. Against his heart.

"Darlin'," he said, "you couldn't get rid of me if you tried."

Claire smiled, pleased with his statement. She affectionately pressed her head against his muscular shoulder and sighed. Soon they neared the stables and Claire heard the soft whinnying of horses, the shuffling of hooves against wooden stall floors.

Just outside, a big, tough-looking man was stationed directly in front of the entrance to the sprawling structure. His feet wide apart in an assertive stance, his arms crossed over his massive chest, clearly alert to any sound or sight, he stood blocking access to the stables. His assignment was to keep out any and all visitors who didn't belong there, with a discerning eye for undesirables who might threaten harm to the valuable Thoroughbreds inside.

"Hey, Jim," Hank greeted the guard. "How's it going? Anyone inside tonight?"

Jim recognized Hank, smiled, uncrossed his arms, and shook Hank's hand. Then he shrugged his beefy shoulders. "Bristow and Cooper and a couple of the other owners came by earlier in the evening. But no one's here now. I don't look for anybody else to show up at this late hour." He quickly amended, "Except for you, Mr. Cassidy. You going inside?"

"We are, Jim." Hank introduced Claire, then assured the hired watchman, "We shouldn't be long. A few minutes. Half an hour at the most. Just wanted to check in on a couple of the colts we have entered in tomorrow's races, then look in on Black Satin. He's been high-strung and fidgety since arriving in Saratoga. I'm hoping he's beginning to calm down and will be ready to run in the Travers Stakes."

"Sure. Go right on in," said Jim. "Stay as long as you want. I imagine your groom and the other stable boys are asleep."

"We'll be extra quiet," Hank said with a smile. "No need to disturb anyone's slumber."

Jim moved aside and Hank and Claire walked past him. Claire immediately blinked in the shadowy passageway. On the floor, low-burning lanterns were evenly spaced along the wide alley. But they gave off little light.

Speaking quietly, mindful of waking the grooms, Hank explained, "My Thoroughbreds are stabled at the far end of this long alley." Claire nodded and glanced about as they silently walked down the dimly lit lane, hand in hand, saying nothing.

"Here we are," Hank finally whispered as he stopped before a large stall.

Claire looked around. Several yards on down the

corridor, a young boy was curled up on the wooden floor, sound asleep. She saw no one else.

She automatically jumped back and winced when a sleek black horse abruptly poked his great head out of the stall.

"How you doing, Satin?" Hank asked as he ran a gentle hand over the Thoroughbred's gleaming neck. "You feeling okay tonight? You rested and calm? Want to run for money in a few days?"

Standing at Hank's elbow, Claire asked, "May I pet him?"

"He'll be angry if you don't," Hank said. He momentarily urged her back out of the way, and opened the stall's wooden gate. Addressing the stallion, he said, "Move so the lady can come inside and visit."

The Thoroughbred threw back his head and nickered, but did not move an inch. Hank reached up and gathered a handful of the creature's long mane, urged his head down, and laid a spread hand on the stallion's face. Resting the heel of his palm squarely between its eyes, he firmly pressed.

"Back up, Black Satin," he gently commanded.

The Thoroughbred obeyed. Hank praised him, released him, and turned his back on the big steed. He extended a hand to Claire and drew her inside. He shut the gate behind her. Half afraid of the big, powerful beast, half eager to get up close and touch him, Claire hung back.

"He won't bite," Hank said and gently drew her over to stand between him and the stallion.

The colt pricked up his ears and danced nervously. Claire sank back against Hank, hesitant.

"He looks dangerous," she said.

Hank smiled, wrapped his arms around her waist, pressed his cheek against her temple, and said, "He's stirred up. Too nervous to rest. But he would never hurt you, sweetheart."

"You sure?"

"Very sure."

"And what about you, Hank?" she asked as she tentatively reached out her hand and touched the big stallion. "Would you?"

"Hurt you? You know better than that," he said, his arms tightening around her. "I'm as harmless as this stallion and you already have both of us eating out of your hand."

Hank loosened his arms, allowing her to step closer to the big beast. Skittish, high-strung, the ebony colt's eyes widened and he anxiously danced about, moving away from her, attempting to escape. He pricked up his ears and tossed his head around, his big body shaking.

Claire sensed the stallion's anxiety. But she followed as he moved to the back of the stall. She murmured to him and stroked him and assured him that she was his friend. In no time the stallion was nick-

ering softly and nuzzling her shoulder. Warming to
him as he to her, Claire put a hand to his velvet muz-
zle and pressed her face to his jaw. She whispered to
him, placated him, caressed him.

Hank watched the duchess work her magic on the
black colt. He was amazed and intrigued by what he
saw. This big powerful beast mastered by the touch
of the pale fragile woman. As Charmaine ran a soft
hand over his glistening withers, Black Satin quiv-
ered with pleasure and excitement.

Hank swallowed hard. He couldn't believe what
was happening.

This golden-haired dazzler had conquered both
man and beast. Hank's lean body tensed like that of
the Thoroughbred as he watched the duchess's soft
white hand glide sensuously over the stallion's
gleaming black coat. Hank was mortified. She was
sexually arousing him by the innocent act of stroking the stallion.

Hank felt himself stir.

He gritted his teeth as he watched Charmaine
wrap her arms around Black Satin's neck and press
her slender body close to the trembling stallion's
powerful frame. Hank ventured a glance down beneath the colt's belly and was not surprised at what
he saw. The stallion was fully aroused.

Damnit! He should never have brought the duchess to the stables. The only thing to do was to get her out of the stall immediately and wake the stable boy, tell him to rub the beast down and get him calmed enough to rest.

Hank knew he wasn't going to do that. He clenched his hands into tight fists at his sides and swore under his breath. He, too, was fully aroused. And he was going to take the duchess right here in this stall no matter how much it might upset the stallion.

He had to have her.

Now.

He couldn't wait another hour, another minute.

She must have sensed it.

Suddenly the duchess took her arms from Black Satin, turned away from the stallion, looked up at Hank, and spoke his name without sound. In the shadowy light Hank could see her breasts lifting and lowering with her quick breaths, saw the pulse beating rapidly in her pale throat and the dilation of her violet eyes.

At once she was in his arms, kissing him, clinging to him, knowing what was going to happen. The stallion knew, too. His nostrils flared and he whinnied and snorted excitedly and kicked at the rear wall of the stall.

"Darling, we can't, not here," Claire murmured, heart racing. "The stable boy…"

"Sound asleep. He won't wake up," Hank said, not

caring if it was true. He was already frantically raising Claire's skirts.

"But the stallion," Claire warned. "Will he—?"

The sentence was never finished. Hank's lips covered hers, conquered hers. His tongue delving deep into her mouth, Hank held her with one encircling arm and managed to get his hand up under her dress and inside her satin underwear.

She sighed into his mouth as he touched her, teased her, readied her to receive him. He abruptly ended the kiss, lifted his head, and maneuvered her to the far back corner of the shadowy stall where the floor was strewn with loose hay. He released her, yanked his shirttails out of his trousers and furiously unbuttoned his shirt, dropping it on the hay. Claire eagerly followed his lead. Anxiously they undressed, eager to be naked.

In a matter of seconds they came into each other's arms and kissed and embraced, unmindful of the agitated horse attempting to bite his master's bare shoulder. Shrugging off the stallion's halfhearted attempts to inflict pain, Hank sank to his knees, taking Claire with him.

There in the straw, they knelt on their spread clothes, holding each other, continuing to kiss until they were out of breath and their hearts were racing in their naked breasts. Upset and excited, the colt nickered and paced back and forth in the small enclosure, his sharp hooves barely missing the pair kneeling on the hay.

"Hank, we're torturing the poor stallion," Claire murmured in Hank's ear as she glanced up at the huge black colt.

"Better him than us," Hank replied, too aroused to concern himself with Black Satin's distress.

He eased Claire over onto her back and, with a well-placed knee, urged her legs apart. He came between her legs and immediately entered her, certain of the level of her arousal. Claire exhaled as he slid into her, his erection rock hard and huge.

"Ahhh," she gasped, suddenly unsure if her body could accommodate him.

"Take it all, baby," he entreated, his hands going to the insides of her thighs, raising her knees, pressing her legs wide apart. Bent on opening her fully, his need to fill her completely spurred him on.

Claire loved it.

Never had they been more intimate. Never had Hank been more totally hers. She could feel him thrusting and throbbing inside her, greedily possessing her, taking her with a primitive hunger that was both frightening and thrilling. And she, led by innate passion and determined to make him hers, skillfully used the muscles of her young, firm body to squeeze and hold and give him exquisite sexual pleasure.

"Baby," Hank gasped, his eyes closed, perspiration glistening on his chest. "Sweet, so sweet."

A secret little smile playing at her lips, Claire clung to his biceps and rocked with him. Giving. Taking. Making hot, uninhibited love. She was as primal as he, as wild in her quest for sexual nirvana. Glorying in the joy of their total surrender to each other, Claire lay there on the hay, accepting each hard driving thrust from her randy rutting lover. Tilting her pelvis up to accept the rhythmic strokes, she bit her lip, turned her head, and caught sight of the black stallion rearing up, agitated.

She saw what Hank had observed earlier.

The big beast was aroused, ready to mount a mare. She should have felt sorry for the poor stimulated creature. Or repulsed by the frightening sight. But caught up in the throes of consuming carnal lust as she was, she found the shocking spectacle exciting.

It was incredibly thrilling to have the big aroused stallion just a few short feet away while she and Hank made love beneath him on the hay. It struck her that this big lusty lover pumping furiously into her was every inch as much the well-hung stallion as the black colt. The way Hank filled and stretched her, his was surely as huge as the stallion's.

It was one of those shameful secret thoughts that made Claire blush with guilt while triggering her coming climax.

Somewhere in her foggy brain Claire knew that what they were doing was unforgivably rash. Perhaps even dangerous. Should the stallion bring those sharp hooves on Hank's back it could harm them both.

So be it.

She couldn't stop.

With Hank loving her with complete abandon, Claire clung to him and thought she might die of an ecstasy so intense she was nearing sexual hysteria. With her arms and legs wrapped around Hank and the pungent scent of horses and hay and sweat and sex assaulting her senses, Claire found heaven.

She began to sob Hank's name.

His mouth quickly silenced her. While he kissed her she exploded in wrenching orgasm, frantically clasping him to her, her mouth, her body, her very soul laid open wide to him.

When finally the wondrous shared climax ended, Hank tiredly collapsed atop Claire.

"Black Satin?" came a boyish, sleepy voice from very near, "Is that you making all that racket? Somebody in there with you?"

"Stay where you are, Theo. It's Hank," Hank called out, then put his finger perpendicular to his lips, silently telling Charmaine to remain quiet. "You go on back to sleep."

"Satin okay? He was putting up an awful racket. Woke me up."

"I know, but he's fine now," Hank assured, jumping up and reaching for his clothes. "Just a little nervous. Nothing to worry about."

"Want me to come on in there—"

"No. Thanks, but it's not necessary."

"Okay, then." A pause, and the boy said softly, "Mistah Hank?"

"Yes, Theo?" Frowning, Hank had one foot in his pants leg while Claire cringed in the corner with her clothes pressed to her body.

"You ain't mad at me for sleeping on the job?"

Hank grinned. *Thank God you were.* "No, not at all."

Twenty-Four

Overnight they became friends.

Good friends.

They met at the roulette table, but Olivia Sutton and Fox Connor soon found that they had a great deal more in common than just their love of wagering.

Accepting Olivia's invitation to come to the estate and share a quiet supper, Fox stayed past midnight. Comfortable with each other, genuinely liking one another, they talked and joshed and laughed like a couple of youngsters, enjoying themselves immensely. They shared a like sense of humor, slightly acerbic. What one found amusing tickled the other.

Near the end of the evening as the pair sat on the white lace settee out in the garden, the easy, inconsequential conversation took a more reflective turn when Olivia casually said, "You know, Fox, all evening we've talked about everything under the sun, except each other. I like you very much, but I know so little about you. Other than the fact that you are Hank's Thoroughbred trainer from Kentucky and his dearest friend. And, that you're entertaining company."

"Why, thank you, Olivia," he said. "May I return the compliment?"

Not to be deterred, she prompted, "Tell me about yourself. About your family, your wife and—"

"I have no wife, no children," he said in a casual, matter-of-fact manner. After a brief pause, somewhat wistfully he added, "The truth is I never married because the woman I loved wed somebody else."

"Oh, Fox, I'm sorry, I—"

"Don't be. It was a long, long time ago. My young, shattered heart has long since healed." He smiled easily then and told her, "I'm perfectly content, my dear. I love Hank as if he were my own son. I enjoy what I do and I'm good at it. I have a most satisfying life, thanks to Hank."

"You've been together a good while, I take it."

With an affirmative nod, Fox said, "I've known Hank Cassidy since he was a boy. From the start we shared a love of fine horses." Fox laughed and told her, "Back then I worked on a ranch in Nevada and Hank, well, bless his heart, didn't even own a pony. Had to walk everywhere he went. But I'd see him in town on Saturdays and take him out to the spread so he could pet and feed and ride the horses. He loved it. He'd say—blue eyes sparkling in that innocent young face—'one day, Mr. Connor, I'm going to have a horse of my very own!'"

Touched, Olivia said, "And now he owns lots of horses."

"That he does," Fox said, smiling at the recollection, then continued. "We're family, Hank and I. I'm all the family he has. Hank was an only child. His mother died giving birth to him. His father was killed in a mining explosion when Hank was seventeen. Hank grew up fast and he…" His voice became so soft that Olivia had to strain to hear. Fox spoke with pride and great affection about the successful young man he loved more than his own life. He conceded that Hank had his faults and that many a disappointed young lady had cried to her mother that Hank had no heart, but he knew better.

Hank had a heart as big as the state of Nevada and was kind and generous to a fault. He genuinely cared about his employees as few mine owners did and he never forgot a man who worked for him. Or, the man's family. Concealing his good deeds as others hid their blackest sins, Hank quietly financially took care of many a downtrodden family.

Olivia nodded and listened and noted that the articulate Fox Connor was telling her about Hank Cassidy, but saying little about himself. She didn't press him. She was, in fact, learning a great deal about Fox from listening to him speak so fondly of Hank.

"…and then a dozen years ago Hank bought the Greenway Horse Farm and asked if I'd run the operation for him. I agreed to give it a try. I left Nevada and I've lived in Kentucky ever since," Fox concluded. Then he shook his head and said, "Listen to me, I've talked your arm off about myself. What about you, Olivia? Is there a Mr. Sutton and perhaps some beautiful grandchildren back in London?"

"No. No, there's not. I never married, either."

"Well, now I can't believe that," Fox said, truly surprised. "There must have been—"

"Yes," she interrupted, "there was…somebody."

"Tell me about him."

"Oh, I can hardly remember—"

"Yes, you can."

Olivia was silent for a moment, then said; "Yes. Yes, I can. He was…" Olivia began to talk about the unforgettable man she had loved. Smiling as she spoke about him, she recalled with vivid clarity exactly how he looked, how he moved, how he sounded when he spoke her name.

"And you were swept away."

"Mmm. A foolish virgin I was…well foolish, anyway," she said with a self-deprecating laugh. Fox laughed, too.

When their laughter subsided, Olivia's mood

turned somber and she exhaled wearily. Gazing out into the lush, darkened gardens she told her avid listener that the only man she had ever loved was killed in a boating accident before he could marry her and give a name to the child she was expecting.

Olivia fell silent once more.

Fox waited. Said nothing.

When she spoke again Olivia told him that her beautiful daughter, the light of her life, had died at age eleven.

"Oh, my dear, I'm so terribly sorry," Fox sympathized. He lifted an arm and put it around her thin shoulders in a purely comforting gesture. "A childhood disease?"

"Yes," Olivia said with unmasked bitterness. "Malnutrition."

Fox frowned, horrified, but did not comment. He just patted her shoulder soothingly. He didn't prompt or pry, but waited for her to explain if she chose to do so.

She didn't.

Olivia stopped short of revealing anything more and wished she could take back what she had said. Due to the circumstances—the ruse she and Claire had concocted—she couldn't dare tell Fox the whole truth. Couldn't reveal how, alone and with a child to support, she had quickly fallen on hard times. Nor could she declare that while Great Britain was the most powerful nation on earth and the richest, scullery maids still started at sixty dollars a year.

And even those positions were hard to come by since more than twelve million people—including her and her child—were constantly hungry and on the verge of starvation. She couldn't confess that she had stolen to feed her sickly child. Or that the frail little girl had perished when she, Olivia, had been nabbed stealing fruit from a street stand and thrown in jail. Couldn't weep and burden this kind man with how she'd lost her will to live after losing her daughter, how she had survived on the mean streets as best she could until her petty thievery had finally landed her in the infamous Newgate prison.

She couldn't tell him that she had languished in Newgate for many years until the summer evening when an elegant young woman with golden hair had ended up in that terrible hellhole. How she had managed to save Claire from a brutal attack by a pack of murderous inmates and in so doing had altered her own fate.

"…and since she was well aware of my credentials," Olivia said, carefully sticking to the story she and Claire had contrived, "the Duchess of Beaumont asked if I would accompany her to America." Olivia lifted her shoulders, smiled and said, "And here I am."

"And I'm glad you are," said Fox.

Twenty-Five

In a roomy, specially built one-seated surrey with fringe on top that was drawn by a pair of high-stepping matched bays, Hank and Claire rode down traffic-clogged Broadway. The rush to the Saratoga racetrack had already begun, although it was a full hour and a half until the eleven-thirty post time.

Like the rest of the fashionable turf set, Hank and Claire preferred arriving at the track early. It was pleasurable to drink their morning coffee and juice and then leisurely enjoy a sumptuous brunch while they studied the day's racing program.

The genuine Duchess of Beaumont—so Caroline Whit had peevishly reminded Claire—had never attended the races with her late husband, the duke, when they visited the Springs. So heads always turned when Claire showed up each morning on

Hank's arm. Race enthusiasts mused that judging from the way the duchess studied the form and focused her binoculars on the field and loudly cheered for Hank's entries to cross the finish line first, she'd had an amazing change of heart.

Playing her part with ease, Claire had admitted to Hank that she had never been interested in horses or racing, so she knew very little about the sport. He would have to educate her. He was, Hank had assured her, happy to be her tutor.

And so she had learned a great deal about Thoroughbred racing in the short time she'd been at the Springs. She had learned even more about Hank Cassidy. Hank positively loved horses and it showed when he talked excitedly about his prized Thoroughbreds.

He told Claire that he had promised himself when he was a boy that one day he would own the finest stallion in Nevada.

"And now I own dozens," he had said with a satisfied smile.

"Mmm. They're all fine horses, but Black Satin is my favorite," she had replied with coquettish smile, subtly reminding him of their frenzied lovemaking in the stallion's stall.

Hank had winked her and said, "Well, now, I don't know, Duchess. Maybe you ought to give Silver Dollar a look-see some night soon."

"You naughty boy," she accused with a throaty

laugh. Then added, "A man after my own heart." Hank laughed. She said, "Tell me more about the Thoroughbreds. Educate me, darling."

He nodded and spoke with authority and knowledge about bloodlines. He proudly told her that there were at least twenty-five stallions working as studs at Greenway Farm in Kentucky and a herd of the bluest-blooded broodmares in the world.

Eyes flashing, Hank stated emphatically that he didn't condone the whipping of horses to win races, no matter how important the race. Not a single one of his Thoroughbreds had ever had a whip flourished over them or felt the grating of a spur.

"How do you know they haven't?" she had asked, skeptical.

"Because I know Fox Connor. He runs the entire operation with an ever-watchful eye. Fox would never tolerate such behavior from a jockey," Hank replied. "Every rider we've ever hired has been firmly warned against the slightest mistreatment of an animal."

"But many jockeys do apply the whip if they think it necessary?"

"Most really good jockeys cajole their mounts. Others occasionally apply the whip, but lightly, not really harming the colt or filly." His lean jaw tightened and he admitted, "However there are a handful who have been known to beat the hell out of the horse."

"That's terrible. You'd think the mishandled mount would rebel and—"

Interrupting, Hank told her about a speedster called Domino that hated his jockey. "The only way they could get Domino quiet long enough to get a saddle on him was to hold a rubbing cloth over his eyes."

"The poor creature."

"Amen." Hank nodded. "A few unscrupulous owners have even been accused of using electric prods and narcotics on their horses. The cruel bastards!"

Claire saw the sudden flushing of Hank's tanned face and the narrowing of his beautiful blue eyes. She felt her heart squeeze with affection and respect. He was so gentle, kind-hearted.

Now as the pair approached the oval track where a sea of carriages were discharging passengers, Hank exhaled with agitation. He was silent. Claire was quiet, as well. The surrey sat unmoving in a long queue of carriages.

As if on cue, they turned and looked at each other. Claire lowered the wide brim of her straw bonnet slightly, shading her fair face from the morning sun. She smiled at Hank. Hank smiled back. Holding his gaze, Claire removed her gloves, dropped them into her lap, and laid a soft hand on his trousered thigh. She felt the muscles bunch and jump beneath her palm. She lifted her chin a trifle, licked her bottom lip wetly, and saw the sudden flare of passion in his expressive blue eyes.

For a long moment they stared at each other.

Finally, Hank spoke. "It's a beautiful morning, isn't it?"

"Absolutely perfect."

"Tell me, Duchess, which would you rather do on this perfect morning? Watch a bunch of Thoroughbreds race around the track—" his gaze dropped to her lips and lingered "—or make love to me?"

"What do you think?" Claire said, lowering her lashes.

Hank liked her answer. "I think you feel the way I do."

She nodded. "Back to the cottages?"

"Look at the traffic," Hank said, glancing behind them. "It would take us a half hour just to get turned around."

"What are we going to do?" she asked, brow furrowing, knowing him and herself all too well where the subject of sex was concerned. Now that the topic had been broached, neither would be able to think of anything else until they made love.

Hank waited impatiently until the carriage directly in front of them inched slowly forward, leaving an open space of thirty or forty feet. Seizing the opportunity, he managed to skillfully turn the surrey out of the line of carriages. He blithely ignored the shouted questions his actions incited.

"What's wrong, Silver King? You not feeling well? Too much champagne last night?" called a fellow owner from a landau just behind.

"Hey, Hank," shouted another, "you so scared my colt will beat your filly, you going to hide back at the hotel?"

Hank laughed good-naturedly, lifted a hand high in the air and waved away their taunts. He was temporarily, but thoroughly, distracted. For the moment he had lost interest in friends and breakfast and Thoroughbred races.

This golden-haired enchantress beside him was all, was everything. And he wanted her as if it had been weeks, not hours, since last he'd had her.

A short mile away from the oval track Hank turned the surrey off the road and, ducking tree limbs and bumping up and down on the seat as they rolled through thick underbrush, drove to a secluded spot amid the tall, sheltering pines.

The minute the carriage came to a stop, Hank tossed the reins aside, turned, plucked the straw hat from Claire's head and took her in his arms. They kissed and from the instant his lips touched hers their simmering desire exploded into searing sexual heat. Hank's arms tightened around Claire, drawing her closer, flattening her breasts against his chest. Her hands on his shoulders, she felt the muscles slide and flex beneath the fabric of his fine linen jacket.

His tongue deep inside her mouth, stroking, arousing, he deftly gathered up the skirts of her bronze poplin suit. His deep, intrusive kiss continued to dazzle and weaken her and before she realized what had happened, Hank had relieved her of her lace-trimmed underwear. Suddenly she felt the warmth of the sun on her bare stomach and thighs.

When finally he ended the prolonged kiss, Hank raised his head and looked at Claire with such intense ardor she was spellbound. So utterly transfixed by him it frightened her. His heavily lidded blue eyes had darkened with lust and there was a sexily succulent curve to his gleaming bottom lip.

He looked at her as if ravenously hungry for the taste of her.

But he didn't kiss her again. He just gazed unblinking at her while he flipped open the tiny covered buttons of her suit's tight bodice. A muscle flexed in his tanned jaw when he pushed the opened jacket apart. He slipped a hand around the side of Claire's throat, put a thumb beneath her chin and gently urged her head back. Then he bent to the swell of her pale bosom which was rising and falling rapidly beneath the low-cut silk chemise.

With his hot face, Hank nudged the shimmering

silk down until his lips covered a stiffened nipple. But to Claire's dismay he only brushed a couple of close-mouthed kisses to it, then raised his head, looked into her eyes, and said, "Say you'll let me love you in any way possible." Before she could reply, he added, "Say you want me to love you in every way possible."

"I do, Hank," she murmured. "Any way. Every way."

But she was puzzled when, instead of quickly un-buttoning his snug trousers and taking her, Hank swung off the leather seat, turned about and sat down on the surrey's floor, facing her.

Heart pounding, not knowing what to expect, Claire, her knees firmly pressed together, gave him a questioning look. "What on earth are you—?" The sentence was never finished. "Ohhh," she gasped as Hank gently pushed her knees apart, leaned up be-tween and let his lips graze and skim over her trem-bling belly.

"I have to," he said, his lips moving against her tin-gling flesh, "kiss you. Taste you." He drew a ragged breath and added, "Love you in every way possible."

He didn't wait for her permission. He sat back a little, wrapped his hands around the backs of her knees and opened her legs wider. Feeling shame-fully exposed, Claire automatically lowered her hands to cover herself. Transfixed by that sexually hungry expression still curving his mouth, she felt the blood rush to her cheeks when she fully realized his intention.

Did lovers actually do such shocking things? Did this incredibly sensual man really mean to…to…

Hank gently swept her hands away and brushed hot, moist kisses across her belly and up and down her thighs where the pale flesh was exposed atop her gartered stockings. Claire squirmed and gripped the leather seat and couldn't believe that she was behaving so shamefully.

But she didn't ask him to stop.

Hank gave the duchess every opportunity to say no. To insist that he quit. To tell him she didn't want this, wouldn't allow it.

Her intoxicating feminine scent making it almost impossible for Hank to restrain himself, he continued to patiently sprinkle nonthreatening kisses across her silken belly and down the insides of her thighs. Butterfly kisses that tickled and teased and taunted.

When she began to whisper his name and softly sigh, Hank knew she had surrendered. His hot cheek pressed against her cool belly, he stayed as he was for a heartbeat longer. Then he slowly turned his face inward and kissed her naval, dipping the tip of his tongue into the tiny indentation. His face slowly slipping lower, he nuzzled his nose in the springy golden curls between her thighs. He inhaled deeply then blew on the crisp blond coils, stirring them, stirring her.

The duchess stiffened and gripped the leather seat more firmly when Hank lifted a hand and parted the golden curls, completely exposing her to his hot eyes, his hotter lips. With the tip of his lean index finger, he lightly touched her and Claire's eyes closed with pleasure and expectation.

Hank saw her wince and hold her breath when he took his hand away. He waited for Claire to calm a little. He stayed perfectly still, did nothing more than warmly envelop her with his mouth. He knew, could tell by the subtle lifting of her pelvis, the very second when she wanted more.

He kissed her then. Gently. Sweetly. His tongue barely touching her. He didn't stroke, lick or circle. He simply kissed her until the slick female flesh warmly enclosed in his mouth was throbbing and a silky liquid was flowing from her, moistening his lips, wetting his tongue.

"Sweet, hot baby," he murmured huskily and began to love her as she needed to be loved.

Hank eased one of Claire's legs up and draped it over his shoulder. He urged the other slender limb outward, bending her knee and placing the stockinged leg in an open, cocked position. He put his hands beneath her bare bottom and drew her to the very edge of the surrey's leather seat.

Again he bent to her, this time burying his face in her. Claire felt his mouth open on her, over her, enclosing her. Setting her afire.

He began to stroke her lovingly. Claire moaned and shivered and couldn't believe what was happening to her. But she loved it, loved him doing this to her, loved the way it felt.

When Claire began to anxiously press herself closer to the promise of his mouth, Hank lifted her, his hands spread beneath her, and licked and lashed and loved her while she gasped and trembled and clasped his head in her hands, frantically clutching him to her.

Never had she felt anything like this!

The sun hot on her face, Claire sat on the edge of the surrey seat with her skirts up around her waist while the handsomest man she had ever known showed her a brand-new kind of loving. His strong hands holding her to him were possessive, masterful. His mouth enclosing her was hotter than the summer sun. His stroking tongue was a raging fire, licking her with its flames.

And she, shamefully open to him, totally held in his thrall, was a dormant volcano, threatening to erupt at any minute. And powerless to stop the spouting gusher.

Claire didn't want that to happen.

Not yet.

She selfishly wanted to keep Hank where he was for a long, long time. To spend all day just as they were at this minute. To keep him doing just what he was doing. To make him go on loving her in this shockingly unorthodox way forever.

Claire shuddered with building ecstasy. Strangely, it was as if she were both a willing participant and an invited voyeur. She was right here with Hank experiencing all the wonderful sensations from his incredible lovemaking, but at the same time she was watching the two of them as if they were pagan strangers performing for her benefit.

The players in the amorous drama were perfect for their roles. The handsome, immaculately dressed man seated on the surrey floor between a swooning blond woman's parted legs. The woman with her dress pushed up and naked to the waist. The man's head bent to her, his tanned face pressed into the blond curls of the woman's groin.

What an erotic performance!

Voyeur and participant merged when Hank's stroking tongue took Claire closer and closer to the edge.

"Hank, Hank," she began to plead, lunging up off her spine, gripping the leather seat tightly, squeezing Hank's head in the vice of her thighs. "Please, please…yes…oh, darling yes…oooh!"

And then she was crying out in ecstasy and rocking back and forth until her gripping thighs weakened and fell apart while Hank coaxed the last bit of splendor from her.

When he came back up onto the seat beside her, she sighed and sagged against him, totally spent. Hank wrapped his arms around her and pressed her head to his supporting shoulder. Claire closed her eyes and gratefully rested there.

But only for a moment.

Sighing contentedly and modestly pushing her skirts down, Claire slowly raised her head. She looked at Hank and saw the fire still blazing in his eyes. His lips were gleaming wetly. A vein was throbbing on his forehead. She laid a hand on his jaw, tilted her face up, and kissed him. She tasted herself on his mouth and started to pull away.

He wouldn't let her. His hand cupping the back of her head, he deepened the kiss and she then tasted only him.

When their lips separated, she looked at him through a fog and said, "Thank you, darling, for—"

"It was my pleasure," he said, his voice rough with emotion.

"Tell me," she then said, softly, "that I may love you in any way possible." Her hand went to his waistband. "That you want me to love you in every way possible."

Looking directly into his eyes, she unbuttoned his

trousers and released his throbbing erection. While Hank held his breath, she popped her index finger into her mouth and sucked on it. Then she lowered the moistened finger and ran it over the smooth tip of his thrusting masculinity.

And almost gave Hank a heart attack when she slipped down off the surrey's seat and turned about to face him.

Twenty-Six

The affair between Claire and Hank continued to blaze brightly. They were well suited for each other. Carefree. Passionate. Fun loving. They didn't care what others thought or said about them.

On their very first night together, they had agreed that this summer romance would remain just that, a summer romance. Neither wanted a lasting relationship. No strings. No expectations. No fidelity. Footloose and fancy-free they were and would happily remain.

But…the heart does not always listen to the mind.

Claire found herself dreading the day she would lose her handsome prince of love. Hank caught himself wondering how he could possibly return to Nevada without his regal sweetheart.

Claire refused to believe that she had been foolish enough to fall in love with a man who made no secret of the fact that he had no intention of ever being tied down to one woman.

Hank laughed sardonically at himself; what kind of fool was he that he was falling in love with an independent noblewoman who did exactly as she pleased and needed no one. He had to remember that the duchess was a lively, luscious libertine who'd had many lovers before him and would have many after.

And so would he.

A love affair like theirs was intense, tempestuous, exciting.

Commitment and marriage were something else again. Something neither wanted or needed.

Or did they?

The warm golden days and cool silver nights passed too quickly. Claire wished that she could wave a magic wand and have time stand still. That she could command the hands of the clocks to stop moving this very minute.

It had all been so wonderful and she didn't want it to end. Incredible as it seemed, she had managed to fool everyone. She had effortlessly convinced them that she was the spirited Duchess of Beaumont. And in so doing had enjoyed the most exciting summer of her life.

But the fairy tale was about to end.

On this lovely August Sunday night, the eve of the

real duchess's arrival, Claire lay in Hank's arms knowing what he didn't suspect. That this was to be their last night together.

She would never again wake up to find him in her bed.

Already there was a dull ache in Claire's breast. How she had loved waking each morning to find Hank beside her. All that rugged, muscled power at rest and tousled midnight hair falling over his forehead. And those darkly lashed, beautiful blue eyes closed.

In repose he looked appealingly peaceful and vulnerable and innocent. More than one morning she had awakened and quietly studied him, thankful for the opportunity to admire him in all his naked male beauty.

Now Claire's arms tightened around Hank and she pressed closer to the heat of his long lean body. They lay lazily stretched out on her bed in the estate's upstairs master suite. The balcony doors were open. It was a still night, no hint of a breeze. The sounds of soft music and merry laughter carried on the thin mountain air from somewhere down below in the village.

His free hand toying with the unique medallion she always wore, Hank absently ran the pad of his thumb over the smooth mother-of-pearl disk with its embossed gold profile. He had noticed the striking medallion the first time they'd met. Claire had told him that the profile was her mother, that the medallion was precious to her and that she wore it everywhere, even to bed.

"You're quiet tonight sweetheart," he said now with a yawn. "Something bothering you? Something I should know about?"

"No, darling, not a thing," she replied, giving a performance that Bernhardt herself would have been proud of.

Early next morning, a soft knock on the suite's double doors awakened Claire. Hank slept on. Annoyed that the butler would dare disturb her when Hank was here, she cautiously slipped out of bed. She drew on a robe, reached up and lifted her loose hair free of the robe's satin collar, tied the sash and crossed to the sitting room.

Easing the door open a crack, Claire blinked when she saw Olivia standing before her, an unreadable expression on her face. In her hand was a telltale yellow envelope which had not been opened.

"This just came by messenger," Olivia whispered, nodding to the telegram. "I thought it might be important."

Claire immediately tensed with apprehension. She stepped out into the corridor, and quietly closed the door behind her. She reached for the yellow envelope, anxiously tore it open, and took out the missive. It read: "Mrs. Claire Orwell, Have had change of plans. Will not be arriving in Saratoga on August 19.

Am delaying arrival until Monday, August 26. Charmaine Beaumont."

Claire read and reread the telegram.

And she began to smile when she handed it Olivia. Olivia quickly read the message and she, too, smiled. Her eyes shining, Olivia opened her arms and Claire eagerly embraced her.

"Not cast out of paradise just yet," whispered Olivia against Claire's ear.

"Allowed to play in the Garden of Eden a while longer," Claire replied. She gave Olivia a squeeze then stepped back. Inclining her head toward the closed door, she added, "And the innocent Adam is just inside waiting for me to wickedly tempt him."

Unable to contain her joy, Claire began to laugh. Olivia made a face and put her index finger perpendicular to her lips. It did no good. Claire couldn't quell her laughter, so she clamped a hand over her mouth and skipped down the stairs. Olivia, now laughing, herself, thrust out her hickory cane and followed.

Staring at the two as if they had lost their minds, the butler sniffed with indignation when they burst out the front door and onto the veranda. There they dropped down onto the front steps, laughing so hard tears rolled down their cheeks.

When finally they'd calmed, Olivia, wiping her eyes, said, "Eve, you better get back upstairs before Adam awakens."

Claire nodded, hugged her friend once more, rose to her feet and went inside.

She was overjoyed. An unexpected reprieve. A few more precious days to spend with Hank. Another full week with the handsome lover of her dreams—168 more hours with the one man she knew in her heart she would never forget.

Claire silently vowed to make the most of it. She would spend every moment with Hank. Not let him out of her sight!

"Duchess, I need to go into the city one day this week," Hank announced later that same Monday morning. "I'll go this Wednesday. We have no entries in Wednesday's racing program. I'll take the train down early in the morning and be back up by dinnertime."

"New York City for the day? Sounds exciting," Claire said. "I'll go with you."

"Ah, no, no, duchess," he said, shaking his head. "You stay here and relax." He smiled disarmingly and suggested, "Maybe take Olivia out for a late lunch at one of the hotels."

"Darling, I'd rather go with you," Claire said, a feeling of unease swamping her. "We could—"

"Sweetheart, this is strictly business," he interrupted. His tone sounded slightly strained when he shrugged and added, "I'll be pretty much tied up the whole time I'm there."

* * *

New York City
Monday afternoon, August 19th

In a stately stone mansion across from Central Park, the wealthy, handsomely gowned madam of the city's most renowned brothel had called together a half-dozen of her most beautiful girls.

Miss Abigail, the rotund, milky-skinned, raven-haired madam, had christened her establishment Palmetto Palace in honor of her Alabama roots. An aging southern belle, Miss Abigail had made her way east after the War Between the States had left her once prominent family destitute.

Intelligent, charming, and a shrewd business-woman, Miss Abigail had turned the world's oldest profession into a near respectable livelihood. Palmetto Palace had earned a reputation for employing only the most ravishing of women. And the most expensive. A gentleman without a large bank account need not venture into the establishment.

But if a visitor was wealthy enough and generous with that wealth, he would find that his carnal tastes—no matter how depraved—would be cheerfully indulged by some of the most beautiful women in the world. Sexual fantasies became thrilling reality behind the closed doors of the plush upstairs boudoirs in the imposing park-side mansion.

Now as the madam invited six carefully hand-picked girls to take their seats on the tapestry-covered French sofas and armchairs in the drawing room, she was bubbly with excitement.

The women, in varying states of undress, were annoyed that Miss Abigail had interrupted their slumber. None had gone to bed—at least not to sleep—until well past dawn. They were accustomed to sleeping late into the afternoon. It was not yet 1:00 p.m. Yawning and stretching, they grumbled that they hadn't gotten enough rest.

"Girls, girls," Miss Abigail scolded, clapping her hands for quiet. "You'll be glad I awakened you once you hear my news." Beaming, she looked from face to face and announced, "On Wednesday of this very week we will be welcoming a most generous guest back to Palmetto Palace. The wealthy gentleman will arrive sometime around—"

Interrupting, a regal beauty with pale shimmering tresses that reached to her waist, asked, "Do you mean the patron we've all heard so much about? The notorious Dr. Clean?"

"The very one," assured Miss Abigail. "Now you know what that means. His taste in women is varied. One year he prefers only redheads, the next brunettes. This year, he has informed me through his trusted emissary, it is the blondes who rule."

The girls looked at each other and nodded. All were blondes. Both the gleaming locks on their heads and the short curly coils of their groins were regularly bleached by a professional to varying shades of blond.

"I have chosen you six because you are blond and bold and gorgeous. I shall inform Pierre that he is to come in tomorrow to carefully lighten any dark roots he might find among you." The girls groaned and muttered, hating the time-consuming procedure. Miss Abigail ignored the protests. "Once you are blond all over, the gentleman caller will be more than pleased with any or all of you."

A leggy amazon in a black kimono said, "Cherry told me a girl can make more money in just one night with Dr. Clean than she can in—"

"It is true," the madam confirmed. "The girls who have pleased him have had princely sums settled on them."

"Of which you took the lion's share," needled Simone, the Palmetto's cynical comic.

The girls giggled.

So did Miss Abigail.

"As an added bonus," Miss Abigail said, her round cheeks dimpling, "Dr. Clean's been known to gift the lucky lady or ladies with a precious gem or two."

"I want emeralds!" stated the lovely Lulu, sweeping her shimmering blond hair back off her face.

"I prefer diamonds," said the young, angelic-looking Jennie.

"If I may finish…" said Miss Abigail. "This year,

some of you will be joining the gentleman in Saratoga Springs. Suites have been reserved at the cottages of the United States Hotel." She again looked from face to face and said, "While you'll be wearing expensive gowns and dining on caviar and champagne, you will not be allowed to go outside your assigned cottages. He'll want you waiting at any hour of the day or night that he might desire your company."

"I've never been to Saratoga," said Lulu.

"I want to go," said Jennie. "I'll make him like me so—"

Interrupting, Miss Abigail said, "I'm quite sure he'll like you, Jennie. Very, very much." Jennie smiled, pleased. "The rest of you may go back upstairs now. Jennie, you'll kindly stay behind for a moment, please."

"I sure will, Miss Abigail," said Jennie, visions of a handsome client making thrilling love to her then showering her with diamonds filling her head.

When the others were gone, Miss Abigail sat down on the French sofa beside the glowing Jennie. She took Jennie's hand in hers and said, "Aren't you the fortunate one? You will be the first to entertain the esteemed guest who, as you may have noticed, the girls refer to as Dr. Clean."

Jennie's large eyes grew larger still. "Then he's a prominent physician? A handsome and immaculate doctor with a surgeon's beautiful, artistic hands?"

"Not exactly," Miss Abigail said with mysterious smile. "But just remember, my dear, you'll be paid handsomely for the evening. And, you will not be expected to work again for at least three months."

Jennie frowned, puzzled. "But why, Miss Abigail? I don't understand."

The madam squeezed Jennie's hand. "You will when I explain what Dr. Clean expects."

Twenty-Seven

It was nearing noon on Wednesday when a shiny black carriage rolled to a stop before the majestic Waldorf Hotel in New York City. Two baggage-filled conveyances followed close behind.

The hotel's smartly uniformed doorman quickly snapped to attention, summoning a platoon of bellmen before rushing forth to meet the illustrious arriving guests.

Smiling sunnily, he was reaching a gloved hand out to the carriage door when it burst open, hitting him in the chest and very nearly knocking him on his backside. A chubby young boy with uncombed brown hair and soiled white shirtfront leaped out and laughed when he saw the pained expression cross the doorman's face.

Tumbling out behind the ill-mannered youth was

another boy, this one two or three years younger. This lad was even more pudgy than the first and more unkempt, though the clothes both wore were noticeably expensive. The knee of the younger boy's dirty trousers was ripped and buttons were missing from his stained shirt. He giggled and kicked the doorman in the shins, then stuck out his tongue.

"Now you boys behave yourselves," came a none-too-stern voice from inside the carriage, a command neither child obeyed. "I'll make you go without dinner," threatened the father of the unruly pair as he swung down out of the carriage with a groan and a grunt.

"Welcome to the Waldorf, Lord Nardees," said the doorman, bowing grandly before the corpulent baron who wore an expensive, finely tailored suit which, unfortunately, was too small. The jacket could not be buttoned over his massive girth and the trousers rode low beneath his huge overhanging belly. Worse, the costly clothes were smudged with grease and grime.

"Kindly give Lady Nardees and my sweet little daughter a hand," ordered the obese lord, scratching an itchy underarm through the fabric of his wrinkled jacket.

"Certainly," said the doorman. He leaned in to offer assistance and was once again assaulted when a tubby little girl leaned out, grabbed him around the neck and jumped onto him like a monkey swinging onto a tree limb.

As diplomatically as possible, the doorman unwound the dirty-faced child's short, gripping arms from around his neck and gingerly set her on her feet. Her nose running, she stood there right at his elbow, refusing to move back, tugging on his uniform sleeve, whining.

"You're mean!" she accused, her face screwing up into a frown as if she might cry. "Why did you put me down? Pick up me! Carry me inside! I'm tired and I do not wish to walk!" She stomped on the doorman's foot, rubbed her runny nose on the sleeve of her soiled organdy dress, and said, "Father said I wouldn't have to walk!"

"Move back a little, Katherine, sweetie," said Lord Nardees. "Not to worry, someone will carry you inside." He patted her atop the head and said, "Let your dear mother get out of the carriage."

Maintaining the habitual calm he had over the years trained himself to project, the doorman reached in to assist the last discharging passenger. A woman as broad as she was tall. She was very short in stature, but so chunky she could hardly clear the carriage door.

A frown on her round, perspiring face, Lady Nardees, wearing costly designer clothes that looked as if she had slept in them, began scolding the doorman before her small feet ever touched the sidewalk.

"Don't just stand there," she snapped, "Help me out!"

"Yes, of course, Lady Nardees," said the dutiful doorman, offering her a hand.

She didn't take it. She shook her head, setting her drooping sausage curls astir, and huffed with annoyance. "Can't you see that I'm a tiny little woman? Do you expect me to jump to the sidewalk?"

"No, I—"

"Put your hands to my waist and lift me down, you dolt!"

The doorman wasn't sure where her waist was. But he gave it a shot. Only to be scolded again. Forcefully shoving his hands down a couple of inches, she snapped, "Not so high up! That's not my waist! I am highly insulted that you would attempt to touch me inappropriately! Must I inform your employer of this outrage and insist that you be let go? Surely the Waldorf does not condone such conduct."

"Lady Nardees, I humbly beg your pardon. I had no intention of—"

"You were attempting to get familiar with me and I'll not tolerate such behavior!"

"Again I offer my apologies, Lady Nardees," he said, hoping his face was not red with rising anger.

"Very well, but just be more careful where you put those reaching hands of yours! I shan't have the hired help groping me and patting me down as if I were a loose-moraled creature of the lower classes."

"I understand, Lady Nardees," he said.

He staggered under the weight when she leaned out, wrapped her arms around his neck, and fell into his arms, much like her daughter before her. Struggling to keep his balance, he took a couple of uncertain steps backward, then one forward, before gaining control and carefully unburdening himself of his heavy load.

The cloying scent of her sweet perfume combined with pungent body odor threatened to sicken him. He held his breath while she adjusted her wrinkled clothing, turned about and marched inside.

He shot a glance at the spoiled little girl still standing at his elbow and stiffened when she put her hands on her hips and said, "My father said you are to carry me up to my room!" She stamped her foot for emphasis.

The doorman looked up and signaled a big, burly bellman over. "Mac, the young lady wishes to be carried inside."

"Certainly," said the bellhop.

The hotel staff had been briefed prior to the arrival of the British nobleman and his family. It was not the first time the baron and his brood had stayed at the Waldorf. They had chosen the Waldorf two summers ago when it had first opened its doors. They had so enjoyed their stay, they had returned the next year. This was their third visit to the grand hotel.

Everyone knew what to expect of the visiting aristocrats. Three servants came with them, a number not sufficient to fully meet the demanding family's needs. Therefore, as ordered, a quartet of hotel employees were present, lined up to welcome the esteemed guests and to make their stay as enjoyable as possible.

The Nardees brothers raced around through the opulent lobby, shouting and chasing each other and raising eyebrows of other hotel guests, before the entire family was herded into the elevator and taken up to their suite of rooms on the hotel's top floor.

Insisting she wanted to ride piggyback, Katherine squealed with delight when the muscular bellman indulged her. Her arms clasped over his throat, her knees gripping his ribs, she kicked her heels into his sides as though he were her own personal pony.

It took a good hour to get the Nardees five settled into their various rooms. In the suite's two sitting rooms—one small and intimate, the other quite spacious—fresh-cut flowers and gold-covered boxes of fine Belgian chocolates graced polished tabletops. The four hotel employees were on hand to help the Nardees's personal servants unpack the many trunks and valises and to make the family comfortable.

Lord Nardees marched about barking orders at the harried staff. He informed the maître d' that he wanted a seven-course dinner served in the suite at precisely 7:00 p.m.

While the children ran through the rooms shrieking and roughhousing, Lady Nardees took off her hat, tossed it aside, and sank down into an overstuffed easy chair. Grumbling that it was too warm, she raised her rumpled skirts to her knees and, straining to bend over, rolled her garters and stockings down to her ankles.

Oblivious to the chaos around her, she reached for a box of chocolates and lifted the lid. She sighed with satisfaction as she popped a bonbon into her mouth, rolling her eyes with pleasure.

The children fought over which room would be theirs. The disagreement became so spirited, the two boys wrestled and punched each other as they rolled around on the plush wine-hued carpet.

In the fracas of gouging and kicking and hitting each other, the porky pair slammed into an antique drum table which had once graced the summer palace of Napoleon. The priceless piece overturned, toppling an expensive porcelain vase and sending it to the floor where it broke into a dozen pieces and scattered flowers and splashed water across the carpet.

Lady Nardees heard the crash, but didn't get up from her chair to investigate. She shouted, "What on earth have you two done now? I swear, you'll be the death of me yet."

Lord Nardees walked into the room where the boys were still fighting amid the broken porcelain and scattered flowers. He exhaled heavily, rubbed a hand over his big stomach, shook his head and called for a servant to clean up the clutter.

When finally the very last employee departed the suite, Lord Nardees withdrew his gold-cased watch from the linen vest which was riding up over his ballooning belly, revealing a wide portion of his rumpled shirt above his sagging trousers.

It was 1:00 p.m.

"Beatrice, where are you, my dear?" he called out to his wife.

"In here, Wardley," came the choking response.

He followed the sound to one of the suite's sitting rooms. His wife looked up when he entered. Smears of chocolate ringed her mouth and the gold-covered box at her elbow was half empty. She smiled at him. Her teeth were coated with chocolate.

"I have to go out for a while, my dainty pet," he said.

She reached for another piece of candy, popped it into her mouth and chewed. Her mouth full of chocolate, she said, "Very well, dear, but have you seen to dinner?"

Twenty-Eight

At one o'clock on that Wednesday, Claire, Olivia and the dapper Fox Connor were having a late lunch served on the estate's side veranda overlooking the lush private gardens.

Fox ate with gusto, commenting that the broiled salmon sprinkled with toasted almonds was absolutely delicious. Olivia wholeheartedly agreed, then graciously pointed out that the bottle of chilled white wine that Fox had brought along complemented the succulent fish perfectly.

Claire nodded, smiled at them both, but didn't speak. She picked at the salmon and green salad, but had no real appetite. She sipped the wine, but ate very little. Finally she gave up. She carefully placed her fork on the china plate, lifted her linen napkin, patted her mouth, and laid the napkin on the table.

"Will you two please excuse me?" she said, looking from one to the other.

Olivia frowned, "Why, Duchess, you've hardly touched your food. Is something wrong?"

"No, no, not a thing," Claire said. "Just not much of an appetite today. I think I'll take a walk in the garden."

Fox quickly rose to his feet. He came around to pull out Claire's chair and help her up. "My dear, if you're not feeling well, perhaps I should go and—"

"No, no, sit down, Mr. Connor," Claire said and smiled at him. "I'm fine, really. Enjoy your lunch and forgive me for being rude."

Fox stayed on his feet as Claire turned away. She left the table, stepped down off the veranda and walked out into the gardens, her arms hugging her sides.

Fox and Olivia exchanged glanced. Fox sat back down. The pair watched as Claire strolled away, ignoring Olivia's call to put on a bonnet lest she blister. Claire raised a hand and waved away Olivia's warning.

Olivia shook her head. "She's a trifle stubborn at times."

"Aren't we all, my dear?"

Olivia nodded. And the conversation quickly turned back to horses and racing. Since becoming friends with Fox, Olivia had developed a genuine interest in Thoroughbred racing. With Claire's permission, she had gone to the races on occasion, hurrying to the ladies' betting circle to make her wagers. Armed with tips from Fox, she had chosen winners almost every time and had won a respectable amount of money.

"…and in tomorrow's third race, we have Eastern Dancer entered. I expect him to go off at two to one odds."

"I'll have my money on him," said Olivia with a smile.

But even as the pair continued to discuss one of their favorite subjects, Olivia was distracted. She was growing increasingly concerned about Claire. She hoped that Claire was as impervious as she was stubborn.

When the two of them had cooked up this Duchess of Beaumont farce, Claire had vowed that, like the real duchess, she could take a lover, enjoy a brief affair, then walk away with no regrets. Olivia was beginning to doubt that declaration.

Nodding and listening as he spoke, Olivia wished that she could confide in the levelheaded Fox. She longed to tell him the truth about everything. But, of course, she couldn't. She didn't dare divulge to him or to anyone else that the golden-haired charmer claiming to be the whimsical Duchess of Beaumont was actually a straitlaced young woman who had never done anything like this before.

She wondered if Fox would understand if he learned the truth. She felt certain that he would. If she had judged him correctly, he would likely be amused by the ruse. What she knew for sure was that he was a kind man with whom she had already shared more personal secrets about herself than with anyone other than Claire.

But she could not unmask Claire.

She had no choice but to continue playing her part until the end, which was coming very soon. And when it did, she would have to leave without ever having leveled with Fox. Why did that bother her?

Olivia pushed her plate away and leaned back in her chair as she and Fox fell into a companionable silence. She looked out into the gardens and watched Claire stroll along the walkways that crisscrossed through the manicured shrubbery.

"Is something bothering the duchess?" asked Fox.

"Oh, no, I don't think so," Olivia replied, knowing better. She turned to look at him. "I suppose she misses Hank and can't wait until he returns." She tried to sound casual when she said, "I wonder why Hank went into the city today."

Fox shrugged. "No idea. He offered no explanation and I didn't ask for one."

"No. No, of course not. It was foolish of me to…" her words trailed away.

Astute, Fox leaned up to the table and said, "Olivia, Hank and the duchess know exactly what they are doing. They aren't children. Nor are they innocents. They are both sophisticated adults, are they not?" Olivia nodded. Fox continued, "They are having a pleasurable summertime affair and it is not the first for either of them. Nor will it be the last." He smiled and added, "I've seen Hank walk away from some of the most beautiful women in America. And it's well-known that the duchess has grown tired of and discarded many a handsome European admirer."

"Yes, of course she has," lied Olivia.

"Well, there you have it. No need for you to fret. The two are well suited. They are having a wonderful time, which both know will not last. Neither cares. Each will go on to someone else. So let's not worry about them."

Finally Olivia smiled. "You're right. I'm being silly." She shook her head as if to clear it, then asked, "May I tempt you with some dessert? I saw the cook dipping fresh strawberries in melted chocolate."

Twenty-Nine

"Stop! Stop right here," Hank said as his hired carriage turned the corner of Madison Avenue onto East Thirty-Fourth Street.

Hank jumped out before the wheels had fully stopped turning. He saw a shabbily dressed young couple making their slow way down the sidewalk in need of immediate help. A sandy-haired, worried-looking man and a very pregnant brunette young woman.

The man was supporting the woman, his arm was around her waist, her head on his shoulder. He was half dragging, half carrying her, his frowning face wet with perspiration. The young woman, obviously in labor, was grimacing in pain, tears rolling down her cheeks.

Hank hurried to the pair, giving the man a questioning look. The youth said, "We heard there's a hospital somewhere on this street."

"Yes, yes there is," Hank confirmed. "Four blocks on down. I'll drive you there."

"A friend told us the hospital would let us in even though we have no money."

"I guarantee it," said Hank. He scooped up the suffering woman and rushed to the carriage, calling over his shoulder to the young man, "Get in. Get in. We must hurry!" The man didn't argue.

"Mercy Hospital," Hank called to the driver, carefully settling the woman onto the plush leather seat. Nodding for the worried-looking man to slide in beside her, Hank said in a low, soothing voice, addressing them both, "It's going to be all right. Everything will be fine." He patted the crying woman's hand. "You'll be with a physician in less than five minutes."

The woman couldn't speak, could only nod her thanks before her eyes rolled back in her head as another wrenching pain tore through her body. She held her belly and bit her lips to keep from screaming.

When the carriage rolled to a stop before the big red hospital at East Thirty-Fourth and First Avenue, Hank leaped out and ran on ahead while the man helped his wife inside. Hank shouted for help and the staff immediately swung into action. A couple of white-coated orderlies came running. They were carrying a stretcher.

"We'll take over now," they said to the husband, carefully lifting the grimacing woman onto the stretcher and whisking her away.

The young man followed halfway down the corridor. Then he stopped, released a breath and turned back. Hands thrust into his pockets, he began to pace the corridor.

"She's in a great deal of distress," Hank was down the hall, buttonholing one of the physicians, the white-haired Dr. Clive McLoughlin. "Doctor, you must get to her right away. She's very young and this is likely her first child."

"I'll deliver the baby," Dr. McLoughlin said, recognizing Hank. "But afterward, we'll have to put the mother out in the hall. We have no choice."

Suddenly recalling that he had passed several occupied stretchers as he'd run down the hall in search of the doctor, Hank frowned. "You mean there's not a single room vacant?"

"Not a one," said Dr. McLoughlin. "Every bed is full. We've been turning away women unless it's an emergency, as with the one you just brought in." Dr. McLoughlin shrugged tired shoulders and said, "Now, if you'll excuse me, I better get into the delivery room."

"Yes, go on, go on. The poor woman needs you."

Hank walked back down the corridor. He frowned now as he again passed the patients who were forced to lie out in the corridor on stretchers. He felt for them. No privacy, no peace and quiet.

But he smiled when he looked up to see the worried man pacing nervously.

"She's with the doc now," he told him.

"Thank God," he said, relief flooding his face.

Hank took his arm and guided him into the waiting room. "Make yourself comfortable. I'll be right back."

Hank walked back out into the corridor and went directly to the hospital administrator's office for the appointment he'd been on the way to keep when he'd seen the young couple.

Hank told Davis Vance, the administrator, that he had seen firsthand what needed to be done. Davis Vance only nodded.

"The problem will be fixed," Hank assured Vance.

The two talked for a few minutes and Hank left the grateful Davis Vance with a handshake and a promise.

When he exited the administrator's office, he saw that the prospective father was again pacing nervously in the corridor.

He joined him and said, "She's in good hands. Dr. McLoughlin, one of Mercy's finest physicians, is with her and everything is going to be fine. In no time at all your child will arrive."

Hank's relaxed manner and air of confidence rubbed off on the young man. He released a sigh of relief, put out his hand, and introduced himself, "Spivey, sir. Louis Spivey."

"Hank Cassidy. Call me Hank."

"Hank, how can I ever thank you?"

Hank shrugged wide shoulders, shook the shorter man's hand and smiled. "No thanks necessary. All I did was give you a ride."

"You got us here in a hurry. Then you immediately got my wife a doctor." Louis Spivey continued to shake Hank's hand. "You helped us more than you'll ever know, sir, and I'm very grateful."

As they shook they heard, from somewhere down the hall, the squall of a newborn baby. A white-uniformed nurse stuck her head out into the hall and motioned to Louis. Hank and the younger man laughed and patted each other on the back.

"Congratulations, Dad," Hank said. "Now, go see your wife and child."

Eyes flashing with happiness, young Louis Spivey said, "Hank, I'm going to name my baby after you."

Hank threw back his head and laughed. "Then I sure hope it's a boy."

Lord Wardley Nardees was puffing and wheezing from the heat when he stepped into Tiffany & Co. on Fifth Avenue.

The baron was warmly greeted and immediately directed into a small private room. There he sank down into a comfortable chair before a mahogany table. He withdrew a handkerchief from inside his breast pocket and wiped his shiny face.

A little man with a pencil-thin mustache and thinning hair immediately brought in several velvet-lined trays filled with glittering jewels. On the table before Lord Nardees, the trusted employee spread out the trays.

The lord immediately dipped a pudgy hand into an array of diamond jewelry. He lifted sparkling chokers and bracelets and let them spill through his stubby fingers while he grinned wickedly.

He dropped the diamonds back into the tray, then ran his hands caressively over the mounds of precious stones. The employee stood beside the table, hands clasped behind him, watching as the wealthy client smiled and licked his fleshy lips and touched and toyed with the jewels in a manner that was somehow obscene.

"Ahhh," murmured Lord Nardees, his thumb rubbing back and forth atop a huge square-cut emerald. "Mmm," he wheezed as he drew a diamond bracelet across the back of his hand.

When he'd spent more than an hour fondling each valuable piece, the Tiffany's employee picked up a beautiful ruby-and-diamond necklace and suggested, "This, Lord Nardees, is an exquisite creation and one I'm sure Lady Nardees would love to receive."

The lord looked up, suddenly remembering that he was not alone. He realized as well that his presence at Tiffany's would likely be known around the city by nightfall.

"Yes," he said, "I'll take the ruby-and-diamond necklace. It will indeed look lovely around my wife's neck." He smiled, and then as an afterthought, said, "Perhaps this little diamond choker as well."

"Very good, Sir. Shall I wrap them together or separately."

"Wrap the ruby and diamond piece. I'll just put the other in my pocket."

Thirty

The sun was high and hot when Hank climbed the steps of a stately brownstone on Lexington Avenue. Inside, on the building's first floor, were the law offices of Brock, Bailey and Miller. The respected eastern firm had handled Hank's New York affairs for the last ten years and kept in close contact with Hank's Nevada attorney.

"Hank Cassidy, good to see you! Good to see you," said the smiling Barry Brock, hurrying out of his office to greet one of his most valued clients. "Enjoying your stay at the Springs this summer?"

"More than ever before," Hank answered truthfully.

Barry slapped the taller man on the back and laughed. "I don't doubt it. Fast horses and beautiful women. Who could ask for anything more?"

"Not me."

Barry ushered Hank into his richly paneled office and indicated a tall-backed leather chair. Hank plucked at the creases in his navy linen trousers and sat down. Brock circled the massive desk and took his chair facing Hank.

He leaned up, laced his hands atop the desk, and said, "What can I do for you today, Hank?"

Hank took a slim brown cigar from inside his suit jacket. "Do you mind?"

"Certainly not," said Brock. "Light up, my friend." Brock swiveled his chair around and indicated the row of heavy cut crystal decanters resting on a low bookcase directly behind his desk. "May I offer you a drink?"

Hank puffed on the cigar, inhaled deeply, and drew the smoke down into his lungs. He slowly released it and said, "A shot of bourbon would be fine."

"Good choice. I'll join you," said Brock. He rose and unstoppered one of the decanters.

He handed a shot glass across to Hank. "Whom shall we toast?"

"Charmaine," Hank said, lifting his glass.

Brock smiled and nodded. "Charmaine," he echoed.

Hank, liking the sound of her name, tossed the liquor down in one long swallow.

"Another?" offered Brock.

"No, thanks. I've a busy afternoon." Hank again drew on his cigar, then said, "Barry, I've just come from Mercy."

* * *

The lawyer nodded. His client was referring to the Mercy Maternity Hospital on East Thirty-Fourth. Hank was the hospital's sole benefactor. He'd had it built eight years ago, and had, since its doors opened, paid for its daily operation. During that time, hundreds of penniless young women had delivered healthy babies there. None had been asked to pay for their care or the services of their physicians.

"I think it's time we add a new wing," Hank said.

Barry frowned and shook his head. He had never understood why Hank had chosen a maternity hospital as his favored charity. It made little sense to him. Hank had no wife, had never had a child. It seemed odd that a single man would take such an interest in the fate of young pregnant women.

Hank had never told Brock that his mother, Maureen Ryan Cassidy, had died giving birth to him. He never mentioned it to anyone. But he never forgot it. And he always wondered if they hadn't been so poor, if his father could have afforded a physician to assist in the difficult birth, would his mother's life have been spared?

Hank hoped that building a maternity hospital that offered free medical care to those most in need would help save the lives of poor young women like his mother.

"Let's expand Mercy Maternity," Hank instructed his attorney. "Add a wing to accommodate at least another fifty beds."

"Fifty beds? That's going to cost a lot of money, Hank."

"I have a lot of money, Barry."

"I know, I know, but…look, I don't understand you. New York is not your home. You rarely even visit the city. You've spent very few nights in your Madison Avenue mansion. Why not help out the hospital in Virginia City? I'm sure they could use some capital."

"Can't do that," Hank said.

"Why on earth not?"

"Virginia City is a small town. Everyone knows everyone."

"So?"

"If I gave the Virginia City hospital five bucks, I'd be hearing about it before the sun set."

The lawyer again shook his head. "You could set it up the way we've done here. Have a proviso inserted in the legal instrument that the donor's name shall be kept strictly confidential."

Hank laughed. "There are no secrets in Virginia City. My Nevada attorney, bless him, is one of the biggest gossips in town. Now draw up the papers for me to sign. I've another appointment I must keep."

* * *

Fox Connor, thanking both Claire and Olivia for inviting him to lunch, left the estate around 2:00 p.m.

After Olivia saw him to the front door, she returned to the back veranda and Claire. She sat down in the glider beside her. After a few moments of silence, she said softly, "You want to talk about it?"

Claire looked up. "I don't know what you mean."

"Yes, you do. Something's bothering you and I think I know what it is." Claire said nothing. Olivia stated the obvious, "You're falling in love with Hank Cassidy."

"No, I…I…" Claire closed her eyes, opened them. "Why deny it? I am. Yes, I'm falling in love with a man to whom I mean nothing more than a meaningless summertime fling." She smiled sadly, looked at Olivia, and said, "Go ahead, say it. Tell me I'm the most foolish woman you've ever known."

"Not at all, child." Olivia said, "When it comes to love, we can all be quite foolish."

Claire frowned and idly twisted the golden chain around her neck. "I should never have supposed that I could behave the wanton and not pay the price. I'm ashamed of myself, Olivia. I was not raised to…to… My mother taught me better—she would be very disappointed in me."

"Would she?" Olivia said softly. "You might be surprised."

Claire was puzzled by the statement.

Olivia reached out and gently touched Claire's medallion, the 24-karat-gold profile of a beautiful woman in bas-relief against the mother-of-pearl disk. Unbidden, unwanted tears sprang to Olivia's eyes.

Stunned, Claire said, "Dear Olivia. Dearest friend. What is it?" She took the older woman's hand.

It had something to do with the medallion. She had caught Olivia staring at it before, as if it held some dark secret. Claire said, as gently as possible, "You have knowledge of me—something I do not know. Something you've never told me."

Their eyes met. Olivia said barely above a whisper, "Child, this likeness, this medallion." She paused, drew a slow breath and her voice broke when she said, "I was sworn to secrecy long years ago."

Claire's eyes widened with interest. She leaned over and embraced her friend. Patting Olivia's slender back, she whispered, "Now's the time, old girl. Our masquerade is nearly over. Tell me. Tell me all."

And Olivia began to do just that, the whole story pouring out while Claire clung to every word.

"In 1844, the Old Queen had been on the throne for several years. Bad times, hard times. Dickens tales, so cherished by the commoners who knew how to read, were happy fairy tales to those of us who experienced and endured.

"Starvation. Disease. No hope. But we, my old Mum, Willie Sutton and I, we were saved just when all seemed lost. Mum with consumption and me so frail you could read the *London Times* right through me. Weak…near death. Then comes a knock on the door.

"A tall, well-dressed man. He says, 'Willie Sutton? Mrs. Willie Sutton? Is she here?'

"Too weak to even deceive creditors, I said, 'And what if she is?'

"The tall gentleman doffed his hat and said, 'Tell her Nigel Bruce wants to talk to her.'

"'And who might Nigel Bruce be?' I asked.

"'Her son,' he said.

"And so we were saved.

"Seduced and abandoned at fifteen, my mother had her baby, a boy, taken by the authorities and put up for adoption. Archibald Bruce and his barren wife Joan, in service to Lord Ledet, adopted the child. Young Nigel was loved and doted on. Old Lord Ledet had no sons and liking Nigel, saw to it he had a decent education.

"There he was, my half-brother Nigel, thirty-two years old and a successful solicitor and personal assistant to the first Lord Northway, special counsel to the young Queen Victoria."

At the mention of Lord Northway's name, Claire's eyes widened and she felt as if she couldn't get her breath.

"Nigel sent Mum to hospital and had her nursed and nourished back to health. He fed us, clothed us and regaled us with tales of the rich and royal. With one provision—his birth, his relationship and all things connected with us, must never be mentioned by me or my mum.

"One day in the summer of '46, he showed us a photogravure cameo of a striking beauty. He said her name was Mellisand. He was taking it to London's—and the world's—finest goldsmith, Sir Rodney Atkinson at Cartier's. Atkinson's commission was to replicate this profile—" Olivia paused, looked at the wide-eyed Claire "—in twenty-four-karat bas-relief against mother-of-pearl. And Mellisand was—"

"My mother," Claire said softly.

"Yes, child. Your beautiful mother. I spotted the kinship—the high cheekbones and striking eyes especially—the moment you were dumped into Newgate."

"And your vow of secrecy?"

"No harm to tell it now. Dear Nigel was killed in Berkeley Square by a runaway carriage."

"And your mother?"

"My mum died the next month, a fever took her."

"And you?"

Olivia smiled. "I fell into bad company and enjoyed every minute of it." She sighed then and sobered. "You know the rest. I fell madly in love but he was killed before we could be married, before I gave birth to his daughter." Olivia shook her head sadly. "After that I didn't care what happened to me. I lived on the streets of London, was in and out of Old Bailey." She smiled again and, patting Claire's knee, said, "And then one hot summer night, you came into my life and saved me."

"You dear old girl," Claire said and hugged Olivia. When she released her, she said, making it more of a statement than a question, "My mother and the elder Lord Northway?"

"It was before your mother married your father," Olivia assured her. "They say she was the love of Lord Northway's life. As you know, your mother was, for a short time, a lady-in-waiting to the Queen. That's how they met, she and Lord Northway."

Claire nodded. "Why didn't they marry?"

"He was a wealthy member of Great Britain's aristocracy and already engaged to a viscount's daughter. When his love affair with your mother was discovered, she was cast out of the Queen's household and he was sent away to India. Three months later his intended arrived in India and she and Lord Northway were married."

"But I'm not…?"

"No, no. You're not Lord Northway's daughter," Olivia assured her.

"But my mother loved him and they—"

"Yes. They had an affair."

"And the kindly Lord Northway, the younger, that represented me, the barrister who got me out of Newgate, knew who I was? He knew that his father and my mother were once lovers?"

Using her walking stick, Olivia leveraged herself to her feet. She looked down at Claire. "Thousands whose mothers weren't are still rotting in jail."

Thirty-One

Claire stayed on the back veranda long after Olivia had gone inside to take a nap. Idly fingering the medallion, she thought about her mother falling helplessly in love with the first Lord Northway. Claire understood; she felt great empathy for her mother.

How sad to have loved a man who could never be hers.

Claire suddenly shuddered despite the warmth of the sun.

The same thing was happening to her.

She was falling helplessly in love with the Nevada Silver King, a man who, also, could never be hers.

Claire took a slow, shallow breath. Her lungs hurt. Her heart throbbed dully. It seemed too big for her chest. She bit her lip and blinked back unshed tears. But she promised herself she would never let Hank know that she loved him.

She would, just as planned, continue to behave the breezy, brazen lover who had not a care in the world nor a thought of tomorrow.

After all, that's what Hank liked most about the Duchess of Beaumont.

Hank hurried up Fifth Avenue.

Lost in thought, his head down, he turned into the wide door of Tiffany's and bumped squarely into a short, rotund man who was exiting the shop.

"I beg your pardon," Hank was quick to apologize and reached out to steady the fellow he had nearly knocked down. "Are you hurt, sir?"

"No, No, I'm— Cassidy? Hank Cassidy?" exclaimed the startled man, holding on to Hank's arms, fighting to regain his balance. "The Nevada Silver King?"

"Why if it's not Lord Wardley Nardees!" Hank said with a friendly smile. "We've been expecting you at the Springs."

"I'll be coming up," assured the baron. "You're going to be there for the final racing program at the end of August, aren't you? The Travers Stakes?"

"I just came down to the city for the day to take care of a little business," Hank said, shaking his head.

"I'm catching the late afternoon train back up. Will you be on the train?"

"Ah, no, I, too, have a bit of business to conduct here in the city," said Nardees. "However, I should be up by tomorrow evening. You have any promising Thoroughbreds running this year?"

"Several," said Hank with pride. "You? Bring any speedsters over this year?"

The lord nodded. "I've a bay stallion that's sure to take the Travers on closing day."

Hank laughed and shook his head. "Not if I can help it. I have a couple of the finest Thoroughbreds my Kentucky farm has ever produced." His eyes flashing, he said, "One's a three-year-old stallion called Black Satin. It'll take some mighty stiff competition to beat him." Hank put out his hand for the shorter man to shake. "Now if you'll excuse me, I'm in a bit of hurry."

"The devil take you!" exclaimed Lord Northway, frowning at the mere prospect of Hank's Thoroughbred beating his bay in the much publicized Travers Stakes. The baron was accustomed to having his way. "Cassidy, I want that horse of yours! I want to buy Black Satin. Right here and now."

Hank just laughed. "We'll talk when you get to the Springs. Good day to you, Lord Nardees." He stepped around the scowling lord and ducked inside.

* * *

A quarter past seven.

The evening meal in the Nardees's suite at the Waldorf.

It was more like a three-ring circus than a quiet family dinner. Timothy, the youngest son, had promptly turned over his glass the minute it was placed before him. Milk spilled across the table, soaking a great portion of the pink damask cloth and splashing the table's centerpiece, a huge bouquet of artfully arranged red roses. The drooping petals were now more white than red.

"Give me your milk, Malcolm!" the child shouted as he reached for his brother's glass.

"I will not!" Malcolm yelled and stiff armed Timothy.

Meanwhile, Katherine, the baby of the family, was up on her knees in her chair, reaching across the table for her father's stemmed wineglass. His utter self-absorption playing into Katherine's hands, he never even noticed.

His napkin tucked in beneath his double chin, sterling fork and knife firmly gripped in his hands, Lord Nardees was busy attacking a large platter of rare roast beef. A huge bite of the succulent meat disappeared into his mouth and he chewed, smacking loudly, grease dripping from the left corner of his mouth.

He was in heaven. Good food was one of his weaknesses. But not the only one.

Katherine drank down a half a glass of claret before her mother became aware. Preoccupied, a huge roasted turkey leg in her plump right hand, Lady Nardees reluctantly lowered her meat and began looking about for her napkin. She saw it had dropped to the floor, but wasn't about to stoop over and pick it up. Lifting a portion of the damask tablecloth, she wiped her mouth on it, and said, "Give me that glass, Katherine Anne!"

"No!" sassed Katherine. "It's mine and I—"

Malcolm grabbed at the glass. It and its contents went flying across the room. The glass did not break but the dark-hued wine quickly saturated a segment of the plush Turkish rug.

"There, that's better," said Beatrice Nardees and turned her full attention back to her half-eaten turkey leg.

The hotel staff scurried back and forth, clearing away dishes and fetching up new ones piled high with kidneys, ham, chicken, fish and lamb and too many varied kinds of vegetables to keep count.

The gluttonous five scrambled to beat each other to the loaded platters of food. There was much squabbling and reaching and slapping and grabbing. Each participant let out a shout of triumph when he or she managed to successfully snatch a piece of fried chicken or a hot yeast roll out from under another's nose.

While the hotel staff were horrified by the spectacle, it was a typical family meal for the Nardees clan.

Finally, after an hour of combat and full bellies all around, dinner was finished. The table looked as if it had been attacked by a pack of hungry wolves. Not a single family member came through totally unscathed. Little Katherine, half tipsy from the pilfered wine, was bawling loudly. Timothy had meanly pushed her face down into her plate of strawberries and cream.

Katherine's tears had little effect on anyone.

Lady Nardees sighed with contentment, unmindful of the gravy stains decorating the bodice of her expensive taffeta gown or the mustache of cream above her upper lip. Lord Nardees belched loudly and unbuttoned the first two buttons of his tight trousers. Dribbles of grease and dollops of gravy stained his shirtfront and vest.

The boys were up from the table and down on the floor, wrestling. Katherine bawled louder and louder, determined to get the attention of her parents. It didn't work.

Lord Nardees reached for his wife's hand, squeezed it, and got sticky whipped cream on his fingers. He withdrew his hand, wiped it on his napkin, and said with a smile, "I bought you a little trinket today, my love."

"What is it?" asked Beatrice, already growing sleepy from the big meal. "Give it to me this minute, Wardley."

"On one condition, my dear," he said, pushing back his chair and rising. "You'll promise to be understanding and supportive when I tell you I have a very important engagement with some fellow Thoroughbred owners this evening."

"If you must," Lady Nardees said with a yawn. "I'm so tired I'm going straight to bed." Then she turned in her chair to shout at her roughhousing sons. "You two stop that at once. And Katherine Anne, stop that crying. I can't hear myself think!"

Lord Nardees hurried to collect the small velvet box he had hidden earlier. When he handed it to his wife, she smiled at him and eagerly tore into the wrapped package. When she saw the exquisite necklace of ruby and diamonds, she beamed. "Why, Wardley, you dear boy. This will be perfect with the new scarlet ball gown I'm planning to wear on our first night in Saratoga."

Standing behind her chair and draping the necklace around her thick neck, her husband said, "Yes it will, Beatrice. You'll be my fair English rose, just as always." He fastened the necklace, leaned down and brushed a wet kiss to her chubby cheek.

Lady Nardees turned her face inward, seeking his lips with her own. She kissed him and said, "Take Malcolm with you this evening. He's twelve years old, time he started learning about the Thoroughbred business."

Displaying a parent's concern, Lord Nardees straightened and said, "Out of the question, my dear. It may be necessary for me to be out quite late and the boy's exhausted from our long ocean voyage. Malcolm needs his rest."

When Hank reached Saratoga, he hurried directly to the duchess's estate. The minute she saw the carriage coming up the drive, Claire rushed outside and down the veranda steps to meet him. Hank stepped down from the carriage and she came into his arms.

"I missed you," she said, clinging to him, inhaling deeply of his clean masculine scent, struck as always by just how handsome he was.

"Show me how much," Hank said, his lips against her ear, arms wrapped tightly around her. He added in a whisper, "Where's Olivia?"

"Out. Dinner with Fox," Claire said. "It'll be at least an hour before they return."

"We'll make the hour count," Hank said. He swung her up into his arms and carried her inside.

Claire laughed merrily as he climbed the stairs with her in his arms, taking them two at a time. Once he stepped inside the suite and closed the door behind him, Hank leaned back against it and kissed Claire. Not a hot, demanding kiss that instantly aroused her body. But an incredibly sweet caress that thoroughly touched her heart.

When Hank lifted his head and looked at her, she said softly, "I want you to love me the same way you kissed me."

Hank understood completely. He carried her to the bed, undressed her and himself, and took her with great tenderness. He was gentle and caring and sensitive. When at last he had skillfully coaxed her to a shattering climax and his own was coming as well, he whispered, "I love you, darling. I love you."

Claire did not reply, just clung to him, holding him tightly against her thundering heart. She didn't dare believe that he meant what he said. He was just caught up in the moment. He'd likely said those words to dozens of women.

After several long minutes of silence, Claire kissed Hank's shoulder and said, "Darling, that was the sweetest loving I've ever known."

A muscle flexed in Hank's tanned jaw. He tried not to think about the dozens of men with whom she had made love. What difference did it make? Why should he care how many there had been. He'd had a few himself.

He finally said, "And you're the sweetest lover I've ever known."

"Mmm," she murmured, stretching and sighing.

She told him again how much she had missed him, how the day had been interminably long without him. They talked about his trip down into the city, although he revealed little.

Claire turned over onto her stomach, draped her folded arms over his chest, and rested her chin in her hands. Toying with a long strand of her golden hair, Hank mentioned that he had bumped into one of her countrymen while he was in the city. A Thoroughbred owner who would be a competitor at this year's racing finals, the coveted Travers Stakes. He said the wealthy, titled nobleman, who owned a string of fine horses, would be probably coming to Saratoga tomorrow.

"You might know him, Charmaine," Hank said. "Nardees. Lord Wardley Nardees." Claire became short of breath. "You okay?" Hank asked. "Is something wrong, sweetheart?"

Thirty-Two

The plump, foppish Lord Nardees was sweating profusely by the time he climbed the stone steps of the stately three-story mansion across from Central Park.

In his haste to get to Palmetto Palace, he had not taken the time to bathe or change his soiled clothing after dinner. No matter, he simpered to himself. He didn't plan to keep these clothes on long once he was inside.

The obese lord drew a labored breath and rang the bell. He looked anxiously about, hoping no one would see him. He was relieved when the heavy door immediately opened and a tall, stone-faced butler admitted him with a nod.

"There you are, Lord Nardees," came that whiskey voice with its charming Southern accent. The smiling madam stepped into the spacious foyer.

"Miss Abigail," said Nardees and attempted to press a kiss on her cheek when she reached him.

She artfully evaded him, laughing and hurriedly lifting a perfumed handkerchief to her nose.

"Has all been made ready?" asked the eager lord.

"You naughty impatient boy," said Miss Abigail with a wink. "Indeed it is, milord." She took his arm and guided him to the carpeted staircase. "I've had a room specially prepared. Everything you need. Ready and waiting."

"The girl? Is she...?"

"Jennie is one of the most beautiful young ladies I've ever had," assured Miss Abigail as they climbed the stairs. "Twenty-two years old. Pale blond hair. Flawless porcelain skin." The lord's breath grew short, labored. Miss Abigail continued, "The face of an angel. The body of a—"

"Stop! Please, stop," cautioned Lord Nardees. "If you tell me more I shall have heart palpitations before I ever get to see her."

Miss Abigail laughed gaily. "Then suffice it is to say that you are going to be absolutely mad about Jennie."

"Is this lovely Jennie agreeable to...?"

"Certainly. She longs only to please you, but..." Miss Abigail paused, as if in thought.

Lord Nardees frowned. "What is it? There are restrictions? If so, I—"

"No, dear, eager lord," Miss Abigail assured him. "No restrictions. None, whatsoever. But since our beautiful Jennie won't be available to entertain other gentlemen for at least two or three months after her evening with you, I feel that she should be handsomely rewarded for her service. Over and above the sum you'll be settling with me."

Nardees nodded, reached into his trouser pocket and withdrew the dazzling diamond choker he'd purchased earlier in the afternoon. "Think this will pacify?"

It was Miss Abigail's turn to breathe faster. Expensive jewels were her only weakness. She almost envied Jennie.

Once upstairs, Miss Abigail ushered Lord Nardees down the wide, shadowy corridor. She saw that a couple of doors were open a crack, just wide enough for the curious girls to get a peek at the corpulent baron. Fortunately, he was so self-absorbed he never noticed.

The madam escorted the baron on down the hallway to the very last door and into an elegantly appointed boudoir. She indicated an interior door.

"Just in there is your…" She nodded and he understood. "The willing Jennie will join you here in a few moments. Make yourself comfortable, my lord. The caviar and champagne are right here on the table."

Lord Nardees sat down on a brocade sofa to wait. Excitement built with every passing moment. Would his companion be as lovely as Miss Abigail indicated? Would she be blond all over as he had requested?

Long minutes ticked away. The baron grew tense. Had the young lady changed her mind? Had she refused to comply with his wishes that she...

The lord struggled to rise. Just then the beautiful blonde stepped into the candlelit room. He smiled broadly at the exquisite young woman in a figure-hugging ball gown of shimmering blue satin. Jennie returned his smile, dimpling prettily. She eagerly came forward to meet her titled visitor, the British blue blood who was a man of great wealth and old enough to be her father.

Lord Nardees took both her hands in his, lifted one to his lips, and kissed the delicate knuckles. His eyes held hers for only a moment, then lowered to gaze at the magnificent body that was his to enjoy for the evening.

So ripe, so luscious. He thought about skipping the preliminaries—the sipping of champagne and nibbling on caviar, the polite small talk. But he would wait; he was not an animal. He was a baron, a cultured man of breeding who had invited a beautiful young lady to spend a pleasant evening with him.

"My dear," he said, his face red with excitement, "may I offer you a glass of champagne?"

"That would be lovely," Jennie replied and watched his hand shake as he poured the chilled wine into two long-stemmed crystal flutes.

For a few minutes the two sat side by side on the sofa, conversing politely. Lord Nardees did everything in his power to remain calm, to draw out the evening, to wait patiently.

But he felt like a small boy who had been given a beautifully wrapped package and he had to wait until his birthday cake was eaten to open the gift. The prospect of unwrapping six willowy feet of delicious femininity caused his heart to pound furiously.

And when he had unwrapped it and...

He could wait no longer.

"Darling, shall we retire to the other room?"

Jennie lifted a hand, pressed two red-nailed fingers to his fleshy lips, and said, "Give me fifteen minutes, Dr. Clean."

The lord thrilled to being called his secret name by this beautiful blond creature. The glint in her eyes told him she knew exactly what the name meant. There would be no surprises, no objecting, no refusing him.

"My dear, I will come in to you in exactly fifteen minutes."

Jennie smiled, rose and left the room, making sure he was watching as she walked away. She headed directly to the bath; there she undressed down to her silky skin. She bathed again although it had been only a couple of hours since her last bath. She stood and carefully dried her body and, naked, moved toward one of the many mirrored doors.

Most were closets.

One was not. It was this door that Jennie opened.

She stepped into a well-lit, windowless, sterile-looking room with a sheet-draped physician's couch at the center. On the small instrument table beside it rested a pair of scissors and a gleaming straight-edged razor. A low, round stool sat at the end of the couch. In the corner was a porcelain sink.

Jennie blotted all the moisture from her body and tossed the towel away. She shook out her long flowing blond hair and climbed up onto the physician's couch. She carefully spread the clean white sheet over herself, tucking it in under her arms. She lay quietly waiting, knowing exactly what was in store for her.

Lord Nardees entered the room. Gone were his stained shirt and wrinkled suit. He wore a doctor's starched white scrub gown and a surgeon's cap on his head. Over his mouth was a surgical mask.

Nardees said nothing to Jennie, but went right to work. He crossed directly to the porcelain sink and turned on the faucets. He picked up a new bar of strong soap, lathered his hands, then rubbed them vigorously together, scrubbing, washing, rinsing the short, stubby fingers. He reached for a small firm-bristled brush and worked on his ragged, dirty nails. He rinsed his hands once more and carefully dried them on a clean white hand towel.

Then he came to Jennie.

All business, he carefully removed the covering sheet, leaving her stretched out naked before him. He stood for a long moment admiring her. Then, pulling on a pair of rubber gloves, he reached out to the utility table, picked up a pair of sharp surgical scissors and made short work of cutting Jennie's long gleaming hair until it was no more than an inch all over her head.

He laid the scissors back on the tray.

He picked up a shaving cup and brush. He worked the soap into a rich lather and spread it over Jennie's shorn head.

She closed her eyes.

A silver-plated straight-edged razor glinted in the strong lamplight when Lord Nardees took it in his right hand. He sighed with erotic pleasure as he stroked a long, sure path directly across the middle of Jennie's head. In less than ten minutes the beautiful Jennie's head was bald as an eagle's.

The beaming baron meticulously washed all the lathery residue from her shiny scalp and felt his groin stir beneath his scrub gown.

"My dear, you are exquisite," he said. "Never have I seen a more perfectly shaped head on a woman."

Jennie said nothing. It was only the beginning.

Lord Nardees, locked in that light sterile room with razor in hand and dutiful blonde stretched out before him, spent the most exciting hour he had known since his last visit to Palmetto Palace a year ago.

He leisurely lathered and shaved Jennie's long, silky legs. Then her underarms. He checked the lush, full breasts for telltale signs of silky hair around the large nipples. There were none. He purposely prolonged the scraping away of the wispy little line of silken hair going from her navel down her flat belly.

Nothing left now but the part he most relished.

Savoring the joy, hating for it to end, Lord Nardees drew off his rubber gloves, tossed them aside, and slid a panel open underneath the couch. From inside he took a pair of stainless steel stirrups. He fitted the stirrups into the end of the table, turned and went again to the sink. He washed his hands, pulled on a fresh pair of gloves, and returned to Jennie.

With his toe, he dragged the low stool into place at the end of the table. He took a seat. Then he instructed, "My dear, lift your feet up into the stirrups." Jennie complied. "Good, good. Now slide your lovely bottom down closer to me and let your knees fall apart." Again she did as he asked. "Wider, my pet."

His breath now coming in loud, hissing spurts through the mask, Lord Nardees moved into position between Jennie's parted legs.

As a master craftsman shaping a rare work of art,

the stocky baron very carefully, very slowly shaved away all the crisp white-blond coils from Jennie's pubis. His hand was steady despite the fact that his eyes were gleaming demonically and his fleshy bottom lip was sucked behind his teeth in fierce concentration. Sweat dotted his forehead. And his white surgeon's gown was lifted, tentlike, away from his body by his rigid male member.

The blond woman, willingly parting with the last of her body hair, lay with her slender arms folded beneath her shiny bald head. She was as calm and relaxed as if the strange ritual were an everyday occurrence.

"Ah, there, there," the razor wielder finally said and reluctantly laid down his work tool. He rose, went back to the sink, and mixed a few small drops of iodine with warm water. He returned to lovingly bathe the newly shaven mons pubis with the soothing hygienic solution.

Beside himself now with sexual excitement, Lord Nardees peeled off his covering white surgeon's gown. Totally nude, his short, tubby body was every bit as hairless as that of the tall woman he had just shaved. Not one single hair on his chest, belly, or groin. Beefy arms and flabby legs as smooth and slick as silk.

Agilely, Jennie got up off the couch and preceded Lord Nardees out of the small, sterile room and into the plush boudoir. At the bed Jennie paused and turned to face Nardees. His pudgy hands clasping her upper arms, he leaned to her and kissed her, his lips open, his tongue thrusting against the barrier of his surgical mask.

He released her and climbed up onto the bed. He stretched out on his back. Jennie stood beside the bed, smiling at him. She ran her hands sensuously over her gleaming bald pate and her hairless body. Her slender fingers lingered on her full, high breasts before slowly sliding down to touch and cup her freshly shaved groin.

She licked her lips.

Then she got onto the bed.

Slowly, regally, Jennie stood up on the bed. She rose to her full imposing six feet, then stepped over the wheezing lord's portly body so that she was standing astride, directly above him with one bare foot on either side of his naked hips.

Then suggestively running the tip of her wet tongue around her open mouth, Jennie bent her knees and slowly squatted to him. And waited. Offering him an unobstructed view of his handiwork—that which so excited him. She also lifted her hands and erotically caressed her shiny shaved head.

While the baron stared, drooling, Jennie shifted slightly. A shaft of light from the bedside lamp caught and perfectly framed her temptingly slick female flesh. Lord Nardees gripped his painfully swollen shaft and shoved it up into the beautiful hairless Amazon.

Jennie had only to bounce up and down on him a few times before his neck bowed on the pillow and his eyes rolled back as hot semen squirted up into her. She slipped from him, turned, and slid off the bed.

She rose, turned about to face him, reached up and tugged down his surgical mask. She leaned over him, kissed his loose lips and asked, "Did I please you, Dr. Clean?"

He smiled dreamily. "My sweet, you have no idea." He pointed across the room. "Look in my trousers pocket. I have a little something for you."

Lord Nardees sighed contentedly as the bald beauty swayed across the room, grabbed up his trousers, and withdrew from the pocket the dazzling diamond choker. She hurried back to the bed and had him fasten the necklace for her. Then she got into bed and stretched out beside him.

Resting her weight on an elbow and fingering the fabulous stones gracing her pale throat, Jennie pressed her bare, hairless body close to his and whispered, "Take me with you to Saratoga?"

Lord Nardees caressed her gleaming bald head and smiled. "Perhaps next year, my dear."

Thirty-Three

Her final week at the Springs.

The old relaxed Claire was gone; she was now sick with worry.

Not only was the genuine Duchess of Beaumont soon to arrive, but the evil Lord Wardley Nardees was due in Saratoga any minute. Would he unmask her? Reveal her for the fraud she was? And if he did, would Hank despise her for deceiving him?

He would.

And she didn't blame him.

"Hank, would you mind terribly if I stayed in this afternoon?" she asked on that final Sunday when he came to drive her to the races. "I'm not feeling very well."

"Ah, Duchess, it won't be any fun without you,"

he said, looking for all the world like a disappointed little boy.

Touched, feeling for him more than she cared to, Claire laid a hand on his handsome face and said softly, "We have had fun, haven't we?"

"And we're going have a lot more. Come with me, sweetheart."

Claire looped her arms around Hank's neck and smiled. "Once again you've talked me into it."

Claire took her chances.

This would be her last day at the races. Her last day with Hank.

Tomorrow she and Olivia would leave on the early morning train. And twelve hours later the Duchess of Beaumont would arrive in Saratoga on the late afternoon train.

Claire went with Hank to the races, but she wore a broad-brimmed straw hat with a concealing veil covering her face. Once Hank had escorted her to their private box and ordered champagne and strawberries, he excused himself, explaining that he needed to go down to the paddock for a few minutes to speak with Fox.

"Be back before you can snap your fingers," he said and left her.

Alone in the box, Claire looked anxiously around for the portly baron. And her heart tried to beat its way out of her chest when she spotted the wicked lord in a box which was uncomfortably close.

Claire tilted her hat brim so that he couldn't see her face. She held her breath when, from out of the corner of her eye, she saw the baron abruptly rise and leave his seat. She quickly looked the other way and kept her head turned for several long seconds.

Finally she cautiously glanced back at his box. He was not there. She released a sigh of relief.

The red-coated bugler took his place below the grandstands and played the call to post. The crowd cheered as the parade of sleek Thoroughbreds came onto the track single file. Momentarily forgetting her troubles, Claire raised her binoculars and gazed through the gauze of her veil, smiling when she spotted Hank's green-and-white colors on the big gray-coated stallion, Silver Dollar.

When the horses had passed the grandstand and were heading toward the starting gate, Claire casually turned her binoculars on the crowd around her and felt her heart slam against her ribs when she spotted Lord Nardees in the box with Caroline Whit and Parker Lawson.

The lord was laughing and talking with Caroline. Claire froze when Caroline leaned close, whispered something to the baron, then nodded in Claire's direction. Quickly lowering her binoculars and looking away, Claire felt her stomach clench with alarm.

Caroline Whit had always made her nervous. It wasn't just that Caroline wanted Hank for herself and therefore disliked Claire. It was more than that. On a couple of occasions, Claire had caught Caroline staring at her intensely, carefully studying her, as if she suspected something.

Claire closed her eyes, opened them. She drew a shallow breath and told herself she must remain calm. Caroline Whit did not know the truth and as for the repulsive Lord Nardees, she would not be meeting him face-to-face.

She was, for the moment, safe.

But not for long.

After the longest half hour she'd ever spent, Hank finally rejoined her, and he immediately said, "Good news, darlin'. Lord Nardees, the baron I mentioned I ran into in the city…well, he's here. Right here at the races. He came down to the paddock and we got to talking. He's seen Black Satin and he's really interested in buying him."

"But I thought…aren't you running Black Satin in the Travers Stakes next week?"

"Yes, and he'll win it, too." Hank winked at her. "Then the asking price will go sky-high."

Claire nodded. "But you'll wait until then to sell the stallion?"

"I may never sell him, but I'm willing to consider a generous offer," Hank said, then added as an afterthought, "You know the baron, don't you, sweetheart?"

"Well, I…"

"He said you two are acquaintances, have attended some of the same social gatherings back in London." Claire could do nothing but nod and attempt a smile. Hank continued, "He's considering buying several of my Thoroughbreds, so we need to discuss it further. I invited him to drop by your estate after dinner."

"Discuss what further?" she murmured, her blood ice-cold.

Hank laughed. "Darling, you're not listening to me. The baron is genuinely interested in buying Black Satin and perhaps a couple more of my Thoroughbreds. He's coming out this evening."

"This evening?" Claire repeated, aghast, wondering if her face was as white as her summer dress.

"You don't mind, do you, Duchess?" Hank said, staring at her, looking concerned. "What is it, Charmaine? I didn't think you'd object. The baron won't stay long."

"No, I… No, of course not."

Claire couldn't get her breath. She felt sure she was going to suffocate. Lord Nardees was coming to expose her and there was nothing she could do about it.

Pleading a nagging headache, Claire insisted Hank take her back to the estate before the final four races had been run.

"No, darling, don't get out," she said, stopping him when the carriage pulled up before the house. "I need to lie down for a while."

"You sure you don't want me to stay?" he said. "You look pale. I'm worried about you, Charmaine."

"I'll be fine, Hank," she assured him. "Dinner at eight."

"I'll be prompt." He nodded, then said, "After dinner, once we've gotten Lord Nardees out of the way, I want to take you for a long ride in the moonlight. Away from the town, away from everyone. Say you'll go."

"I'll go."

Olivia laughed merrily as she stepped up to the betting window and cashed in her winning ticket on the last race of the day. She had been lucky all afternoon, thanks to the valuable tips from Fox.

Stuffing her winnings into her reticule, she made her way back to the rapidly emptying grandstands to wait for Fox. He had promised to drive her home as soon as he'd finished up at the stables.

Olivia sat down with a sigh of contentment. What a wonderful afternoon it had been. Hopefully, the fun and luck would continue. An evening at Canfield's seemed the appropriate way to end this lovely day.

Olivia glanced cautiously around, then took the wadded bills out of her reticule and carefully counted and recounted them. If she knew Fox, she wouldn't have to twist his arm to get him to take her to Canfield's tonight.

Olivia put her money away and tightened the reticule's drawstrings. She smiled with pleasure as she gazed out over the oval track where bits of fine dust raised from the day's final race still hung in the thin mountain air. Horses nickered from the stables out past the track, and trainers and jockeys walked back and forth, calling out, laughing and teasing each other.

Olivia loved the sights and sounds of the racetrack. The excited crowds cheering on their favorites. The sleek Thoroughbreds thundering around the rail. The miniature jockeys, sporting their owners' bright colors, up astride those big, snorting beasts. The trainers waiting behind at the barns, hoping for victory.

The thought suddenly struck Olivia that this would be her very last afternoon at the track. She was, she knew, a sentimental old fool, but the knowledge that this fairy-tale summer was about to end made her suffer a bout of melancholy.

She felt tears spring to her eyes and had to quickly blink them away when she looked up to see the smiling Fox Connor coming toward her.

"I hope you had your money on Eastern Dancer," he said when he reached her.

"Indeed I did," she said as he took her hand and helped her to her feet. "And that's not all." Gripping her cane, she leaned close and whispered in his ear exactly how much she won for the afternoon.

"Perhaps you could float me a loan," he teased, taking her arm and directing her out past the stables to the waiting one-horse gig.

"I don't know about that," she said, "but I'd sure be up for an evening at Canfield's. You interested?"

Fox gingerly handed Olivia up into the gig and climbed in beside her. "Sorry, old girl. Afraid I'll have to ask for a rain check."

"Oh? You get a better offer?"

Fox chuckled. "No, of course not. Don't you remember? I told you last week that I'm buying dinner for our jockeys this evening."

"Oh, yes, I had forgotten."

"It's something I do every year when the season's about to end. Just a little private celebration to show the boys my—and Hank's—appreciation."

"You're a nice man, Fox Connor."

"Be more than happy to take you to Canfield's tomorrow night, Olivia."

I won't be here tomorrow night, Fox. "Yes. Tomorrow night it is. I'll look forward to it."

The two chatted amiably on the way back to the estate. Once there, Fox helped Olivia out of the gig, took her arm and escorted her up the steps to the front door.

He said, "We haven't been to Moon's yet, have

we, Olivia?" Olivia didn't trust her voice. She shook her head.

"Well, then how about we drive up to the lake tomorrow evening, enjoy a fish dinner at Moon's, then come back to Canfield's. Sound good to you?"

Swallowing with difficulty, Olivia nodded.

"Then it's settled." Fox squeezed her hand, then released it. "Good afternoon, my dear. Until tomorrow."

"Until tomorrow," she managed to say, forcing herself to smile.

Waving, Olivia leaned on her cane and watched him skip down the front steps, climb into the gig and drive away. "Goodbye, Fox."

She exhaled heavily and turned to go inside.

"Wardley, will you kindly stop buzzing around the room like an annoying bumblebee! Sit down before you give me a headache," Lady Nardees scolded her husband as she reached for another cup of custard.

She was the only one still seated at the table after the huge Sunday dinner. The unruly children had been sent off to bed, but none had gone without a fight. The sounds of their protests carried through the suite as harried servants cajoled and pleaded and chased down their reluctant wards.

Lord Nardees never noticed the commotion. He was pacing the room nervously, filled with both dread and anticipation.

"Did you hear me, Wardley?" asked Lady Nardees. "What's bothering you this evening?"

"Why, not a thing, angel," he said. He stopped behind her chair and gave her plump shoulders an affectionate squeeze. He straightened and said, "Now remember, my sweet, I have an important business engagement tonight."

"I most certainly do not remember," she said, shoving her empty custard cup away and patting her full belly. "I thought we were going to the band concert at the Grand Union."

"I'd like nothing better, but Hank Cassidy has a couple of fine Thoroughbreds I simply must own. I have agreed to meet with him this evening and I'm late already."

"Well go on and have your meeting," said Lady Nardees, pushing back her chair. "Then come right back here and take me to the concert."

The lord rushed forth to help his wife struggle up out of her chair. When finally she was on her feet, he took her hand in his, kissed it, then made a face when a blob of custard clung to his lips.

He licked it away and said, "I wish I could, Beatrice. But I've no idea how long the meeting will last. I'm told Cassidy drives a hard bargain and I've no intention of letting him get the best of me."

Lady Nardess put her hands on her ample hips. "When will you get back, Wardley?"

"Don't wait up, my love," he said, hardly daring to breathe, hoping she wouldn't cause a scene. He was planning, after his meeting with Cassidy, to join one of the blondes he'd had transported up from Palmetto Palace. "It could be quite late, I'm afraid."

Lady Nardees frowned and shook her head, setting her curls to dancing. "You and those big ugly beasts. What a ridiculous pastime. I can think of many things that would be more enjoyable than watching a bunch of horses racing around a track."

The baron smiled. *So can I, dear, so can I.* "It's the sport of Kings, Beatrice, and therefore a fitting interest for a titled gentleman."

Beatrice shrugged, then yawned sleepily. "Very well, go. But don't you dare wake me when you come in."

"I'll be very quiet," he said, pressing his cheek to hers, and went for his suit jacket. Thrusting his short arms into the sleeves, he said over his shoulder, "Good night, dear. Sleep well."

He made a quick exit and once he was out in the wide corridor, he exhaled with relief. Then he smiled, pleased. She suspected nothing. She would sleep through the night without waking. She would have no idea that as she slumbered he would be down in the hotel cottages carefully shaving away all the golden hair from one of his four lovely blond ladies.

Lord Nardees's smile faded. Before he could

begin his evening of sexual pleasure, he had to keep his appointment with Hank Cassidy. He wished now he had turned down Cassidy's invitation to meet at the Duchess's estate.

The haughty Duchess of Beaumont had the unique ability to make him nervous and unsure of himself. They rarely saw each other in London, but on those occasions when they were at the same social affair, Charmaine Beaumont always looked at him as if she knew his guilty secrets.

That was foolish. How could she know? She didn't. She just didn't like him. Why, he couldn't fathom. He hadn't seen her since arriving here at the Springs and would just as soon have avoided her entirely.

But there was really nothing to worry about. The gossips said she was having a torrid affair with Cassidy. Said she was so happy she glowed and was so much lovelier than she'd ever been she was hardly recognizable.

The lord began to relax. The tart-tongued duchess would be on her best behavior around Cassidy.

Thirty-Four

"What shall I do?" Claire lamented the minute Olivia stepped into the house. "Hank has invited the dreadful Lord Nardees to the estate this very evening!"

"Dear lord in heaven!" Olivia exclaimed, placing her silver-handled cane in the umbrella stand. "I had no idea the two knew each other. And why on earth would Hank ask the baron to come here?"

She took Claire's arm and guided her into the sitting room.

"It's just my luck! Nardees has shown an interest in buying a couple of Hank's Thoroughbreds," Claire said, shaking her head. "He's coming out this evening to discuss it further. We have to leave, Olivia! Right now, this afternoon. Start packing and hurry. We can't wait until morning."

"It was a bit rude of Hank to invite Nardees to

your abode. Perhaps the ways of the West, but still…"

"Never mind that. Start packing!"

"It's too late, love," Olivia told her, resignedly. "The last train has already left the station."

"No more trains will…?"

"None going down into the city. The last train up from New York is due in at eight this evening." Olivia shrugged narrow shoulders. "Which will do us no good. After it discharges the passengers, the train sits in the station until early tomorrow morning. It's the train we'll be taking down tomorrow."

"No," Claire declared, exhaling with defeat. "No, no, no," she murmured, distraught. She sank down onto a chair and clasped her hands between her knees. "I can't even run away and avoid the inevitable. I deserve this," she said, brow furrowed. "I do, I deserve it. It's just punishment for an inexcusable deception. I cannot flee like the coward I am. I must stay here and be humiliated. Forced to witness the disgust in Hank's eyes when he learns the ugly truth about me."

Olivia sat down on the footstool facing Claire. "You're making too much of this. Be reasonable. Think it about it. If you have something to hide, so does Nardees. He won't tip his hand. Do you really suppose he wants you telling Hank what happened back in London?" Her thinning eyebrows lifted. "I don't think so."

"You don't know Nardees, Olivia. He's a vile, mean bastard and he'd like nothing better than to see me brought to my knees." She looked up at the older woman. "I can't do this. I *won't* do it. You will have to tell Hank that I've suddenly taken ill, am bedfast, too sick to come downstairs and—"

"I will do no such thing," Olivia folded her arms across her chest. "Tonight is the final performance in this well-acted drama and you will be at center stage to continue playing your starring role." Claire started to object; Olivia silenced her. "Tomorrow a sad, repentant Claire Orwell can be on that morning train. But tonight the carefree Duchess of Beaumont will laugh off any and all ridiculous accusations of the loathsome Lord Nardees. Then once the baron's gone, you'll spend the rest of the evening in the arms of the Nevada Silver King, the handsome young man who is simply mad about you."

"Hank is not mad about me," Claire said sadly. "He's mad about the Duchess of Beaumont."

"A mere quibble, child. No matter. Until dawn tomorrow, you are the duchess," said Olivia. "Now act like it!"

Shoulders slumping, Claire sat there mulling over what Olivia proposed. Soon her back straightened and her eyes narrowed with determination. She lifted her chin in defiance.

"You are absolutely right, you wise old dear. Until

tomorrow, I *am* the Duchess of Beaumont. This is *my* estate. And Hank Cassidy is *my* invited guest. I shall wear my most beautiful gown and have the most wonderful dinner served in the candlelit dinning room at precisely 8:00 p.m. And after dinner, when I have hurried Lord Nardees out of my house, I will go for a ride in the moonlight with my lover and…and…" She drew a shallow breath. "I will make it a night to remember for the rest of my life."

"Brava! Brava!" praised Olivia, laughing and clapping her hands.

"Why so nervous, Duchess?" Hank asked after dinner that evening as he sat comfortably on the sofa in the drawing room while Claire paced back and forth.

"I'm not nervous," Claire said, so nervous she was about to jump out of her skin.

Any infusion of self-assurance she'd briefly enjoyed earlier had long since faded and she couldn't sit still. Her heart had nearly stopped beating when, a half hour ago as she and Hank dined, she'd thought she heard a carriage coming up the drive. She had steeled herself for the inevitable, gritting her teeth and waiting for the doorbell to ring.

But it never had.

She was puzzled.

If it hadn't been Lord Nardees arriving, then who had it been? And why hadn't the visitor rung the bell?

"Hank," Claire stopped pacing and asked, "Did you hear a carriage in the drive a while ago?"

"I thought I did," he said, nodding. "Must have been wrong, though. Or maybe someone got lost, turned into the estate and then realized their mistake."

"I suppose," she murmured and went back to pacing.

Hank frowned. "What is it? I'll ask you again. Why are you so nervous?"

"Not nervous," she said. "Just restless. Must we stay in all evening? Why not meet with Lord Nardees tomorrow? You promised we'd go for a ride, drive far out of town. Let's leave now and—"

Hank raised a hand to silence Claire. "Hear that?"

"What? I don't hear anything." But even as she spoke, she heard the distinctive sound of a carriage rolling to a stop on the graveled drive out front.

"That'll be Nardees," Hank said, rising to his feet.

Claire didn't reply. She hurriedly crossed to the sofa and dropped down onto it, not trusting her legs to support her. At the sound of the loud knock she stiffened, balling her hands into fists on her lap.

Jenkins answered the door. He ushered the portly baron into the drawing room. "Lord Wardley Nardees," the butler announced with a bow.

"I say, Cassidy, sorry I'm late, but I was…I was…" He saw Claire and abruptly stopped speaking. His eyes widened and he blanched, then frowned.

"Doesn't matter," said Hank, reaching out to shake the baron's hand. "I believe you know my beautiful companion, the Duchess of Beaumont." He urged the baron forward. "Charmaine, you remember Lord Nardees."

Hank looked from one to the other. "Your Grace," said Nardees and reached for her hand. Claire felt her flesh crawl when he leaned over and pressed a wet kiss to the back of her hand.

"Milord," she said softly.

"Won't you have a seat, Lord Nardees?" Hank extended his hand, indicating an easy chair.

Once seated, Nardees paid little attention to what Hank was saying. He turned his beady eyes on Claire and licked his fleshy lips.

"Your Grace," he said with a smirk, and Claire's heart sank. "It's so nice to see you again, although I must admit, I hardly recognized you. You're more beautiful than ever."

"Thank you."

"Have you been in Saratoga long?"

"No, I have not," she said, her tone brittle as she lifted her chin and met his gaze, her eyes flashing a warning.

Hank spoke, drawing the baron's attention, but Claire could feel his eyes sliding back to her, knew he was enjoying himself at her expense. She didn't trust him to keep his mouth shut. She had more to lose than he, and he knew it.

If he managed to convince Hank she was not the Duchess of Beaumont, then certainly Hank would not believe her when she declared that the baron had tried to sexually assault her and, failing in the attempt, had had her thrown into Newgate. Once Hank knew she was a liar he would believe nothing she had to say. He would surely take the word of a genuine nobleman over a commoner governess.

Her head abuzz, Claire heard only bits and pieces of the conversation going on between Hank and the baron. She heard Hank mention Black Satin and a couple of his other Thoroughbreds. She was unaware of Nardees's reply.

But she snapped to attention when the baron, shifting his focus squarely on her again, said, slyly, "I say, Cassidy, my good man, I abhor dishonesty of any kind. Don't you?"

Hank scowled, insulted. "Sir, if you are questioning my integrity, I—"

"No, no, not yours, Cassidy. But…"

"Shall I serve the brandy in here, Your Grace?" interrupted a tall, blond servant in a parlor maid's uniform.

And, eyes sparkling devilishly, the real Duchess of Beaumont, dressed in a demure black uniform with white organza apron and matching cap, entered the drawing room. She bore a silver tray atop of which rested three snifters of cognac.

Immediately recognizing the duchess from photographs she'd seen in the *London Times* society pages, Claire stared in astonishment and felt all the blood drain from her face. Just then the devilish duchess turned her head and winked at Claire before approaching the sputtering Lord Nardees.

"Brandy, milord?" the duchess asked politely, stepping up to him, bending to offer the tray. He stared, speechless, mouth drooping open. "No?" the duchess said with a smile and a silent message in her glittering eyes. "What's that? You were just leaving? Then I must see you out."

Thwarted, the red-faced baron grabbed a brandy and downed it in one swallow. He wiped his mouth on the back of his hand, rose and began making excuses as he headed for the door.

Hank was totally baffled. On his feet now, he said, "Lord Nardees, no need for you to leave. We haven't really discussed—"

"Uh…I…I…just remembered," said Nardees, "I promised Lady Nardees I'd take her to a band concert this evening. You understand."

"Well, yes, sure, I understand." Hank quickly demurred, but he felt there was more going on here than met the eye.

"We'll get together sometime next week," said Nardees.

"Come along, milord. I'll see you out," said the impish Duchess of Beaumont, setting her tray down and taking his arm.

Out in the wide foyer, the duchess propelled the baron directly to the front door and slipped out behind him.

"What the devil is going on here, Charmaine?" he asked, fuming.

"Why, we're simply having a bit of sport is all." She laughed softly and added, "Isn't that why you frequently visit ladies of the evening? For a bit of sport?"

His round face rapidly turning scarlet, he threatened, "You dare say one word to—"

"Your dear trusting little wife? Why, Lord Nardees, you old silly, you. I wouldn't dream of exposing your countless infidelities." She laughed then and confided, "Wouldn't you know it? On the train coming up from the city I was fortunate enough to sit with a quartet of lively young blond women. So friendly they were, and such fun. Now why do you suppose they were coming to Saratoga?"

The baron frowned and tried to pull free of her. The duchess clung to his arm.

"Don't know? Then I shall tell you," she said, enjoying his discomfort. "A couple of the young ladies had silver flasks in their possession. It's a long ride and we got acquainted and they passed the flasks around." She shook her head. "It's amazing how a drink or two loosens lips, isn't it, Wardley?"

"What are you going on about, Charmaine? I am late for—"

"You're a betting gentleman, are you not, Wardley? As I recall, you are. I would wager this estate that you had those blond lovelies transported up to the Springs. Am I right? I am, I can tell by the look on your face. They are stashed away in the cottages at the United States Hotel for midnight visits, eh, Wardley?"

"So help me, Charmaine Beaumont, if you so much as—"

"Not a word shall pass my lips," she said with a naughty smile. "And you, I trust, will feel equally obligated to keep quiet about my young friend's harmless impersonation."

"That lying bitch in there—"

"Save your breath, you pompous pervert," Charmaine cut him off. "I know who the real liar is here. Say one word about this to that handsome young man in there and your vapid little wife will know about your quartet of blondes and what you have planned for them." He started to speak. She thrust out her arm and pointed to his waiting carriage. "You heard me, Wardley. You have the title, but it's Beatrice's fortune. She'd cut you off without a farthing.

Now leave quietly and don't come back." She laughed merrily then and said, "By the way, you have gravy on your vest, Dr. Clean."

She turned and hurried back inside. She stepped into the drawing room and asked, "Will there be anything else, Your Grace?"

"No, thank you, Claire," Claire said, and thanking the duchess with her eyes, added, "that will be all for this evening." Then she cleared her throat needlessly and added, "Mr. Cassidy and I were just leaving to take a drive."

"How lovely."

"Ah…there are some household matters I will need to discuss with you at first opportunity."

"Yes, Your Grace." The duchess nodded. "Whatever's convenient for you."

Thirty-Five

"It's cool this evening, almost chilly. Why not scoot over a little closer to me?" Hank coaxed as he and Claire drove slowly down busy, lamp lit Broadway.

Claire started to decline, but changed her mind when, stuck in traffic directly in front of the Grand Union Hotel, she saw Caroline Whit coming down the steps on the arm of Parker Lawson. Claire quickly moved closer, possessively looped her arm around Hank's and pressed her head to his shoulder.

"Now that's more like it," he said with a boyish grin. "I never want you too far away from me."

Claire peered around him and caught the frown that came to Caroline's face, and the false smile that immediately followed.

"Good evening, Duchess, Hank," Caroline merrily

called out, hurrying down the steps, dragging the reluctant Parker with her.

Hank turned his head and acknowledged them. "Caroline. Parker. Nice to see you."

"I've a marvelous idea," Caroline said, stepping up to the carriage, gazing only at Hank, "Why don't the four of us retire to the Congress Inn and have a nightcap?"

"Thanks. Some other time," Hank said.

"Hank's promised to take me for a drive in the moonlight," Claire needled.

"But it's so early," Caroline said. "You can take a drive later. Besides, in case you haven't noticed, there are clouds rolling in from the east. Looks like it might rain soon." She playfully plucked at the sleeve of Hank's suit jacket. "You don't want to get caught out in a summer storm. Let's all have some drinks and some laughs and—"

Interrupting, Parker Lawson said, "Caroline, can't you see they don't want company?" He took her arm and drew her back away from the carriage.

The traffic began to move. The carriage rolled away, leaving the disappointed Caroline behind, muttering under her breath.

"You're wasting your time, Caroline," Parker told her. "Cassidy only has eyes for the duchess."

Caroline yanked her arm free of his grasp. "I know

Hank Cassidy. He'll tire of her and I'll have him yet, you'll see. One way or the other."

"Could be. Until then, let's go to the bar in the United States Hotel and drink ourselves silly."

"Caroline wants you," Claire said as they reached the end of Broadway and began to move away from the traffic.

"I want you," he said without turning his head. "Nobody else. Just you."

"Hank, that's so sweet," she said and meant it. She tipped her head back and looked up at the night sky. A few high clouds had appeared on the eastern horizon and were slowly drifting closer. "Perhaps Caroline is right—it looks like we might get a few sprinkles within the hour."

"I don't think so," Hank said, gazing at the full white moon shining high overhead. He grinned and added, "I've asked the heavens to hold off any rainfall until we're back at the cottage later tonight."

"Oh, well, then it's settled," she said with a laugh.

They rode for a time in companionable silence, the sights and sounds of Saratoga quickly fading in the distance behind them. Hank took the road leading up to the lake, but turned off well before reaching the main body of water.

He stopped the carriage in among the tall pines. He grabbed the green-and-white lap robe from the back of the seat, came around, lifted Claire down, and took her hand. He led her through the trees, explaining that he had a secret place he wanted to show her, that he'd been saving it for a special occasion.

Such as tonight.

Claire felt her heart squeeze in her chest.

In and out of the moonlight they ducked, half of the time bathed in silver brilliance, the other half swallowed up in total blackness.

At last they stepped out into a grassy moonlit clearing and Claire was awed by the breathtaking panorama before them. They stood on a high cliff above a wide inlet of the lake. Fifty feet below, the foamy water lapped at the wall of sheer rock. Lights winked from across the lake and romantic music from a dance pavilion outside Moon's intermittently drifted across the water.

"Hank, it's beautiful. Breathtaking. I'm so glad you brought me here tonight."

Sinking to his knees to spread the lap robe out on the soft grass, Hank said, "I thought you'd like it."

When she walked closer to the cliff's rim, she heard him say in a tense voice, "Don't get too close to the edge, sweetheart. I wouldn't want to lose you."

But you're going to lose me, darling. We're going to lose each other. Claire turned back. Hank, still on his knees smoothing out the spread robe, put out his hand. She took it. She stood above, leaned down, cupped his face in her hands, and looked into his smoldering eyes. Hank raised his hands to her waist. He slowly drew her to him.

"Kiss me," he said, his head tipped back, hands clasping her waist. "Kiss me, baby."

"I will," she murmured and slowly sank to her knees to face him. She put her arms around his neck and lifted her face to his.

When her lips were a few scant inches from his own, Hank hesitated. A muscle working in his jaw, he looked at her for a long silent moment and Claire wanted to weep. In the flashing depths of his beautiful eyes was all the love, passion, and promise of commitment a woman could ever hope for.

Hank brushed his lips to hers, whispered her name and then kissed her.

They kissed kneeling there in the moonlight high above the lake and while Hank's smooth warm lips covered and conquered hers so sweetly, Claire anxiously pressed herself against him, achingly aware that this would be the last night she would ever be in his embrace.

Her eyes closed, her heart throbbing, she gloried in the feel of the powerful arms wrapped tightly around her and the hard muscled chest pressed against her breasts.

It was a night and a kiss she would never forget.

When finally their lips separated, Hank continued

to hold her and he said, "I'm glad we're kneeling, not standing. My knees are weak."

She smiled. "Mine, too."

"Let's sit down."

"All right."

Hank loosened his arms and released her. Claire sat back, crossed her legs under her and carefully spread her long skirts around her feet. Hank sat down facing her and he too crossed his legs beneath him.

He took her hand in his, held it, reached into his trousers pocket and withdrew a small velvet box.

He leaned forward and kissed her again. Then he took a deep breath, raised her hand up to his heart and said, "Feel how fast my heart is beating." Claire pressed her fingers to the firm wall of his chest and felt the rapid heavy thudding against her palm. He gently moved her hand away.

And then he totally caught her off guard when he said, "I love you, sweetheart. I've never said those words to anyone else, I swear it. I'm in love with you. Deeply, wildly, everlastingly in love with you. Marry me, Charmaine. Marry me." Hank flicked open the velvet box and held it up for her to see. The flawless brilliant cut diamond glittered blindingly in the bright moonlight. "I want to take you back to Nevada with me," he told her. "I want you to be my wife, the mother of my children, my companion in old age."

"Hank, I…"

"Say, yes, sweetheart. Marry me."

Knowing what she had to do, Claire called up all the resolve she could manage, laughed softly then, and said, "Why, Hank Cassidy, I'm disappointed in you. Remember how we said—"

"I know what we said," he interrupted, dropping the box and the diamond into her lap and taking hold of her upper arms. "I never meant for this to happen, but I'm in love with you and I believe you love me, too. This is not just a summertime affair, it's the love of a lifetime and we both know it."

As he spoke, his handsome face began to slowly disappear into enveloping darkness as high overhead a storm cloud slowly passed over the moon, blotting out the radiant light. Claire felt the first drops of rain pepper her head.

Hank never noticed the rain.

From out of the inky blackness, he said, "You don't want to live in Nevada? Fine. I'll go to England with you. I'll go anywhere with you. I love you, Charmaine Beaumont, with all my heart and if you'll agree to marry me, I'll do everything in my power for the rest of my life to make you happy."

The rain began to fall in earnest as jagged summer lightning streaked across the darkened sky and the following thunder rumbled ominously.

"We better get out of the rain," Claire said and started to get up.

"To hell with the rain," Hank said, catching her wrist and stopping her. He pulled her back down and said, "Did you hear me? I said I love you and I want to marry you." Anxiously, he searched for the dropped velvet box, took the diamond from it, and again held it up to her.

But there was no longer any light for it to reflect off of. The stone was as dark as his face. Hank shoved the ring onto his little finger, clasped Claire's upper arms and said, "I love you, darling. I love you."

Her face wet with rain, Claire drew a shallow breath and was grateful for the darkness when she said resolutely, "That, I'm afraid, is your misfortune."

"No, it's not," he said, his hands gripping her upper arms so tightly his fingers were cutting into the flesh, the rain plastering his dark hair to his head. "You love me, too, I know you do. Say it. Tell me you love me as I love you."

A flash of lightning illuminated Claire's wet face. "You're wrong, Hank," she lied, tears mixing with the rain. "I'm fond of you, of course, and we've had a lovely time, but—"

"Damn you, Charmaine Beaumont, look me in the eye and tell me that you don't love me."

Claire squared her shoulders and, her heart breaking, looked directly into his flashing eyes. The rain pounded them, soaking their clothes and drenching their hair. As the lightning flashed overhead, she said, loudly enough to be heard above the cloudburst, "I do not love you, Hank. I'm very sorry."

Thirty-Six

At just after midnight a morose Claire was packing when a soft knock came on the suite's door.

Claire braced herself to face the fully warranted wrath of the woman whose identity she had stolen. She crossed to the door, drew a spine-stiffening breath, and opened it.

The Duchess of Beaumont asked, "May I come in?" Then she grinned impishly and added, "Oh, I forgot, this is my home isn't it?"

Nodding, tears threatening in her sad violet eyes, Claire said, "Your Grace, I owe you my most humble apology. I will forever regret what I've done and I hope you can find it in your heart to forgive me. You won't believe this and I cannot blame you, but the truth is I have never done anything like this before. I am ashamed of myself and I know that I deserve any punishment you deem necessary."

"Well, I should think so," said the duchess, but her eyes gleamed with merriment. "Obviously you were not expecting me." Claire said nothing, just shook her head. The duchess laughed then and said, "I wasn't supposed to show up until tomorrow evening, but I'm so glad I arrived a day early and didn't miss out on all the fun."

Claire didn't share the other woman's mirth. She asked, "Are we to be arrested immediately?"

"Have you arrested? Good heavens, no," Charmaine Beaumont quickly assured her. "I have no such intention, so you may stop worrying."

"Thank you, Your Grace. I'm very grateful that you are not going to press charges," Claire said. "I'm aware that you would have every right to see me incarcerated."

"Ah, but you don't fare too well in prison, do you?" Claire's tear-filled eyes widened. The duchess nodded knowingly and said, "While you were out this evening, Olivia and I became friends. She is such a dear and she thinks the world of you. She told me everything."

"She did?" Claire blinked back tears.

Nodding, Charmaine said, "Olivia confided that the despicable Nardees had you thrown into Newgate because you rebuffed his advances."

Head bowing, Claire simply nodded.

"Look at me, Claire," the duchess commanded.

Claire raised her head.

The duchess said, "I am not surprised that the baron behaved so abominably. You're a very beautiful young woman and the spoiled, rapacious lord supposed that since you were in his employ and dependent on him for your livelihood that he had only to reach out and take you." The duchess made a face of disgust. "Wardley Nardees is an obnoxious boor and a cruel bastard." Her eyes narrowed when she said, "Attempting to sexually assault you and then bringing false charges against you. Absolutely reprehensible!"

"Yes, but what I've done is—"

The duchess cut her off. "My dear, there is no comparison."

Claire went on as if the duchess hadn't spoken, "Coming here, pretending to be you, occupying your estate and living your glamorous life. Can you ever really forgive me, Your Grace?"

The duchess laughed heartily and walked on into the suite. "Forgive you? Why I applaud you for coming up with such an ingenious idea. I've always admired creativity and imagination and you're obviously a very clever woman. I'm flattered that you would choose to be me." She crossed to a sofa, sank down into the comfortable cushions and patted the one beside her. "I trust I have enjoyed my summer holiday in Saratoga." Her eyes flashed and she smiled broadly.

Claire sat down beside the duchess. "You have." She finally managed a weak smile of her own. "Too much, I fear."

"Then why the tears?" The duchess withdrew a lace-edged handkerchief from inside the flowing sleeve of her satin negligee. She handed it to Claire. "Here. Dry your eyes and blow your nose. Then tell me all about it."

Claire dabbed at her eyes, but when she began to speak, fresh tears came. "The masquerade was a success. When I learned that you hadn't been to Saratoga for eight years or so, I was confident we could pull off the deception. I had seen photographs of you in the London newspapers and was aware of the resemblance. Same slender build, same light hair. I believe I did fool everyone. But I'm the real fool. You see I have fallen in love and—"

"Now that is foolish," the duchess agreed, nodding.

"I know, I know. I never meant it to happen," Claire sniffed. "But he's so wonderful and we've had such a lovely…an exciting…ah…an…"

"Affair? Is that the word you're searching for?"

"Yes. We've had a thrilling love affair and I—"

"Well, I'm sure it was enjoyable, but that's no reason to fall in love. I've had a number of affairs and never once have I lost my heart." She chuckled and added, "A fact of which I'm rather proud."

"I wish I were more like you," Claire said sadly.

"Well, you're not, so go ahead. Tell me about this extraordinary man who managed to steal your heart in three short weeks."

"He's the gentleman you saw here this evening. His name is Hank Cassidy and—"

"The Silver King," Charmaine interrupted.

"You know him?" Claire's eyes widened.

"No, Olivia told me who he was." Her throaty laughter again filled the room and she said, "I'd never seen him before this evening when I walked into the drawing room to serve the brandy."

Recalling that astonishing moment, Claire finally smiled through her tears. "May I compliment you. That was a stellar performance, Your Grace."

"Why, thank you, thank you. I was quite convincing, wasn't I? And didn't you like the way I managed to quickly usher Lord Nardees out of the house?"

"Priceless," said Claire with frank admiration.

"But we're getting off the subject," said the duchess. "Now, you were saying that you've foolishly fallen in love with the handsome Silver King?"

"I have," Claire stated. "Completely. Hopelessly."

"And he hasn't fallen in love with you?"

"No, he hasn't," Claire shook her head sadly. "He's fallen in love with the Duchess of Beaumont."

Hank shrugged out of his rain-soaked white dinner jacket the minute he walked into his cottage. He left it where it fell. He untied the black silk neck piece, pulled it off and dropped it. He unbuttoned the top buttons of the damp white shirt, which was sticking to his chest.

He didn't bother to change into dry clothes. He didn't even grab a towel to dry his sopping hair or blot the moisture from his face and chest.

He unstoppered a half-full bottle of bourbon and poured himself a whiskey. He turned to walk away, stopped, snagged the bottle between two long fingers and took it with him. He sank down into an easy chair and set the bottle on a small end table at his elbow.

It was dark in the cottage's sitting room, but Hank didn't bother lighting a lamp. The darkness suited his mood. He took a long drink of the whiskey, made a face and felt it burn down its way into his chest.

Good. Maybe it could burn her right out of his heart.

He lifted the glass again and drank it all down, then poured himself another. And another.

Hank frowned when he realized the bottle was empty. He turned it up and shook it, but nothing came out. He dropped the empty bottle to the carpeted floor, rose from the easy chair, and went directly to the row of bells. He rang the one which would bring a valet round to the cottage.

Thirty-Seven

"Yes sir?" the hotel employee, umbrella raised, asked when a brooding, scowling Hank answered his knock.

"Whiskey," Hank said, running a hand through his disheveled hair. "Bring me one, no make that two bottles of bourbon. Your finest Kentucky bourbon." The young man stood there and stared. That irritated Hank. "What the hell are you waiting for? I need a drink, man."

"Well, sir, I'm not sure we have any bourbon in the hotel kitchen. I'll have to go to the bar and—"

"I don't care if you have to go to Kentucky," Hank said, in no mood to quibble. "Bring me some bourbon."

"Yes, sir, right away."

The valet hurried away. He was out of breath when he reached the hotel bar, collapsed his umbrella, crossed the darkly paneled room, and anxiously motioned to the barkeep. Cupping a hand to the bartender's ear, he whispered that a clearly unhappy Hank Cassidy was drinking alone in his cottage.

"You mean the duchess is not with him tonight?" asked Wallace.

"No, she's not," said the valet. "And, furthermore, one of the porters saw Cassidy driving the duchess out toward her estate more than an hour ago. Then he came right back to the hotel. Alone."

The bartender's bushy eyebrows rose and he grinned. "She probably tired of him and sent him packing."

"Wonder who she'll choose next?"

While the two men quietly discussed Hank and the duchess, Caroline Whit and Parker Lawson came into the paneled room and walked directly up to the bar. Neither noticed the barkeep loading down the young hotel valet with two bottles of bourbon.

When the bartender stepped up before them, greeted them warmly, and asked what they would like to drink, Parker Lawson said, "We're just here for a quick nightcap, Wallace. Cognac for the lady and me."

"Cognac it is," said Wallace and smiled and nodded to Caroline.

She smiled back, then said to Parker, "I imagine Wallace hears all the hotel gossip."

Parker shrugged. "Perhaps. But I'm sure he's gallant enough to keep it to himself."

In seconds Wallace was back. He placed two snifters of the amber brandy before them and said, "You folks having a lovely evening despite the rain?"

"Yes, we are, thanks," Parker replied.

"Mmmm, so-so," Caroline corrected, lifting her snifter.

Parker joined her, raising his own and drinking thirstily. In minutes the snifters were empty and Wallace poured each another.

And another.

At 2:00 a.m., Caroline Whit and Parker Lawson were still holding the fort in the United States Hotel bar. Parker was drunk. Very drunk. His elbow resting on the mahogany bar, chin in his hand, he was silent, moody, reflective.

Caroline was tipsy, but as lively as ever. Bored with Parker's company, but not ready to call it an evening, she looked around for someone with whom she could have more fun than the glum Parker.

She saw no one of interest. Motioning Wallace to again fill her snifter, she leaned across the bar when he came forward, smiled seductively at him, and said, "Is it true what they say about bartenders, Wallace?"

"What do they say, Mrs. Whit?"

"That you hear all the interesting gossip." Wallace's eyes twinkled, but he said nothing. Caroline pressed him. Leaning more fully onto the bar, making sure her ample cleavage was appealingly displayed for Wallace's benefit, she whispered, "It's been such a dull, dull evening for me. Could you share some little tidbit? Something you heard here tonight."

"Oh, ma'am, I couldn't do that," Wallace stated emphatically. "I could lose my job if I—"

"Why, Wallace, I'd never tell a soul. Not a single soul." Wallace nervously looked from her to Parker. Caroline waved away his concern. "He's too drunk to worry about. Now tell me, what have you seen or heard that I might find interesting?"

Wallace glanced warily around the near empty bar, cleared his throat, and motioned her closer. He put his lips near Caroline's ear and whispered, "You'll never guess who's drinking alone in his cottage."

Caroline's eyes widened and her lips fell open when the barkeep revealed that a hotel valet had been summoned to Hank Cassidy's cottage this very midnight to bring Hank two bottles of bourbon. The valet said Cassidy was all alone; the duchess was not with him. And, he said Cassidy looked very unhappy.

"Furthermore," he said, "…wait…wait, Mrs. Whit. Where are you going?"

Drink in hand, Hank continued to restlessly pace the darkened cottage. He was drunk and intending to get drunker. His white shirt had dried, but it was wrinkled and open down his dark chest. The shirt's long tails were half in, half out of his rumpled dark trousers. His hair was badly mussed and falling into his eyes. He'd kicked his shoes off an hour ago.

Hank walked out onto the balcony, mindless of the continuing rain.

He was angry.

Angry with himself for being a fool. He had fallen in love with a woman who didn't know the meaning of the word. He had no one to blame but himself. He had known from the start that the frivolous Duchess of Beaumont looked upon having an affair in much the same way as a man. A pleasant diversion. A summertime liaison to be forgotten with the first falling of autumn leaves.

Damn her. Damn himself.

His stomach clenching, teeth gritted, Hank turned his stubbly whiskered face up to the rain and closed his eyes. He saw again the duchess's beautiful face when she'd looked him straight in the eyes and coolly said, "I do not love you, Hank. I'm very sorry."

Hank went back inside. He lifted a tail of his shirt and wiped the rain from his wetly clumped eyelashes. He poured another shot of whiskey and again sat down in the easy chair. He was lifting the glass to his lips when he heard a soft knock on the cottage door.

His heart stopped beating. He lowered the glass

and placed it on the end table. He turned his head to listen. He wasn't sure. Had he really heard a knock or was it his imagination?

It came again.

Hank couldn't breathe. Every muscle in his body tensed so that he couldn't move.

It was her! It was the duchess. She had come to him. She did love him. Loved him just as he loved her!

His heart now pounding, Hank jumped up and rushed across the room. Smiling, he yanked the door open, saying, "Oh, sweetheart, sweetheart, I'm... I..." His smile froze, fled. "What do you want, Caroline?" he asked curtly.

"To keep you company, Hank," Caroline said, quickly stepping forward to throw her arms around him. "You're lonely and so am I. Let me come inside. Let's drink together, have some fun."

Annoyed, Hank peeled her arms from around his waist and set her back. "You're drunk, Caroline."

"You are, too, but I don't care," Caroline said. "We'll be drunk together."

"It's late, Caroline. Time you were in bed."

"Time I was in *your* bed," she said. "The duchess is no longer there. I know she's not. She's left you, admit it. She's left you just like I knew she would. You don't need her, Hank. I can make you forget her."

"Good night, Caroline," Hank said tiredly. He gently pushed her back and closed the door.

Thirty-Eight

At daybreak the summer sun surely rose, but it did not shine through the dense cloud cover. The skies over Saratoga were a leaden gray and a chill wind had risen to drive the falling rain. Great drops forcefully pelted the estate's leaded glass windows while the wind sighed mournfully around the eves of the mansion.

"You sure you wouldn't like to spend a few days with me?" asked Charmaine Beaumont.

Claire and Olivia were packed and ready to leave for the train depot. They were in the wide downstairs foyer, saying goodbye.

"You're very kind, Your Grace," Claire said. "But no, we really must be going."

"Where will you go? What will you do?" asked the concerned duchess.

Claire shrugged her shoulders. "Perhaps we can find employment in New York City. Then in time, home to England I suppose."

"I could use a secretary," said the duchess. She looked from Claire to Olivia, "And a head house-keeper and then if—"

"You're kind, but no, we've taken advantage of your hospitality long enough."

Claire was smiling, determined to present a brave front. But the world was dark and rainy and her heart was heavy. She felt as though the sun would never shine for her again.

The perceptive duchess read her troubled thoughts despite Claire's courageous smile. Charmaine exchanged worried glances with Olivia. Both had tried to convince Claire that it wouldn't matter to Hank that she wasn't the Duchess of Beaumont.

But she had refused to listen.

Now the hour of departure was at hand. The driver brought around the covered carriage. The three women stepped out onto the veranda, Claire and Olivia dressed for travel, the duchess still in her flowing negligee.

The duchess took Claire's hand in both of her own and said, "You'll be making the mistake of your life if you leave without seeing Hank."

"That mistake has already been made, Your Grace," Claire said.

The duchess shook her head, then hugged Claire and Olivia in turn. Each thanked her again for her kindness.

"You're both welcome here anytime you wish to come," the duchess said. Then she laughed when she added, "whether I am in residence or not."

The driver came up onto the veranda and opened a huge black umbrella. Claire and Olivia ducked under it. He held it over their heads and ushered them down the steps to the waiting carriage. When they were settled inside, he returned to the veranda to collect their luggage.

The duchess grabbed his arm and said, "Once you've dropped them off at the depot, come straight back here and wait for me!"

As soon as the carriage rolled away, Charmaine Beaumont turned and hurried back inside to get dressed. She was not one to meddle, but this situation called for intervention.

The duchess was dressed and pacing the rain-spattered veranda when the carriage returned.

"The cottages at the United States Hotel," she said to the driver. "This is an emergency, so lay the whip to the horses."

Taking her at her word, the driver immediately put the matched bays into a fast gallop. The duchess held on for dear life as the covered carriage bumped and swayed and raced down Broadway in the falling rain.

In minutes she reached her destination and was anxiously pounding on Hank's cottage door.

The door swung open and a haggard, hungover Hank blinked in confusion when he saw the duchess's parlor maid standing before him. "What the...?"

"Don't talk, just listen," Charmaine Beaumont said and pushed him back inside.

Claire and Olivia had arrived at the bustling train depot. Directly in front of the station the open square with its splashing fountains and big shade trees was deserted on this rainy morning. But pulling up to the red depot were landaus, phaetons and barouches, all discharging passengers.

Claire and Olivia, parasols raised, hurried inside. Despite the early hour, the little redbrick building with its elaborate iron trimmings and black-walnut interior was crowded with passengers and friends and family who had come to see them off.

At Olivia's insistence, Claire waited while Olivia made her way to the window to purchase their train tickets. Jostled about, bumped by eager travelers, Claire smiled wistfully as she looked around.

Everything was just as it had been on that lovely afternoon when she and Olivia had arrived in Saratoga. The same well-dressed travelers. The same laughing and calling to each other. The same excitement in the air.

But then it had all been ahead of them then.

Now it was all behind them.

"Come," said Olivia, after making her way back through the crowd. "I bought the tickets, they're in my reticule. Let's get on board."

Claire nodded, took Olivia's hand and led the way out the door onto the crowded platform. The wind-driven rain immediately pelted their faces despite their raised umbrellas. They had no choice but to stand in the deluge. There were passengers ahead of them.

While they waited, Olivia smiled mysteriously, reached into her reticule and withdrew a stack of losing pari-mutuel tickets.

She held them up for Claire to see, laughed cheerlessly, and said, "Looks like we finished out of the money this time."

"Oh, didn't we?" Claire replied and managed a smile.

Olivia opened her hand and tossed the losing tickets up. They swirled about in the wind and rain before falling into a rivulet of water coursing along beside the tracks.

Olivia and Claire exchanged looks and stepped up onto the train, collapsing their umbrellas. They moved down the aisle until they found their seats. Dusting raindrops off their shoulders, they sat down. Claire chose the seat by the window. Olivia took the one on the aisle.

Minutes ticked away while other passengers claimed their seats and settled in for the ride down to New York City.

Soon the conductor passed through the cars collecting tickets and the wheels began to turn on the track. The morning train slowly chugged out the station.

Her forehead resting against the rain-streaked train window, eyes swollen from crying, Claire suddenly thought she heard Hank calling her name.

She lifted her head, listened, and immediately scolded herself for being absurd. She sighed wearily, leaned her forehead back against the window and closed her scratchy eyes.

She heard it again.

Claire sat up straight. Eyes round, she turned to Olivia. "Did you hear…?"

"Yes!" Olivia said. "Yes, I did. Open the window. Open the window!"

Her heart racing with hope, Claire anxiously raised the window and poked her head out into the falling rain.

"Hank!" she cried when she saw him running alongside the train.

"Sweetheart!" he shouted. "Wait! Don't go! Don't leave me! I love you!"

"Oh, Hank," she called to him, leaning fully out the window now, frantically reaching out to him.

Unable to catch up and grasp her hand, Hank kept

running faster as the train quickly picked up speed. "I love you, Claire Orwell!" he shouted, long legs taking great strides, arms pumping. "Not the Duchess of Beaumont. You. Only you. Marry me, Claire!"

By now they had attracted everyone's attention. All those on the train and the ones behind at the depot saw a handsome, but haggard man racing frantically after the moving train. His hair was disheveled and wet from the rain and he was badly in need of a shave, dark whiskers covering the lower half of his face. His shirt was open down his rain-slick chest and billowing out behind him as he ran.

The unkempt man was desperately trying to reach the outstretched hand of a pretty, well-dressed young woman who was leaning out of the train window. The rain was peppering her face, saturating her upswept blond hair and spattering the shoulders of her blue cotton traveling suit.

And she was calling his name. "Hank! Hank!"

While people whistled and applauded and rooted for Hank to catch up, Olivia had grabbed her cane and gone hurrying through the cars to find the conductor.

"You must stop this train immediately," she told the startled man, grabbing him by the sleeve. "It's a matter of life and death!"

In minutes the train wheels ground to a screeching halt and an eager Claire drew her head back inside, jumped up from her seat, and rushed down the aisle to the train steps. She squealed as she leaped into the waiting arms of a badly winded Hank.

Happily he swung her around and said, "Honey, I know everything and it doesn't matter. I love you. Nobody else, just you!"

"Oh, Hank, I love you too and I'm so sorry—"

"Listen to me, sweetheart," he interrupted, breathing hard, his chest rising and falling as he struggled to get air into his starving lungs, "you may not be a duchess, but you're a queen to me and you can rule me for the rest of my life."

"Oh, Hank, my love," she murmured and tightened her arms around his neck.

Both were laughing as Hank slowly lowered Claire to her feet beside the tracks. They stood there gazing at each other, so in love they were totally mindless of the wind and the rain.

"Well, what are you waiting for? Kiss her!" someone yelled from the back of the coach and others quickly took up the chant. "Kiss her, kiss her!"

Hank grinned, finally realizing that they were not alone. He didn't care.

Neither did she.

While everyone on the train whistled and applauded, Hank lowered his head and kissed Claire. They kissed and held each other tight. It was a long, sweet caress of a man and a woman who were deeply in love and happy as they've never been before in their lives.

While Hank and Claire kissed, the rain magically stopped. The dark clouds rolled away.

And a radiant summer sun shone down from the bright blue sky.

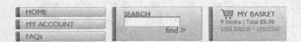